THE MAN UPON THE STAIR

A MYSTERY IN FIN-DE-SIÈCLE PARIS

WITHDRAWN

GARY INBINDER

PEGASUS CRIME

NEW YORK LONDON

In memory of my brother, Barry, artist and teacher

⌒◇⌒

THE MAN UPON THE STAIR

Pegasus Books Ltd.
148 W. 37th Street, 13th Floor
New York, NY 10018

First Pegasus Books cloth edition February 2018

Interior design by Maria Fernandez

This is a work of fiction. Names, characters, places and incidents
either are the product of the author's imagination or are used fictitiously.

ISBN: 978-1-68177-635-4

10 9 8 7 6 5 4 3 2 1

Printed in the United States of America
Distributed by W. W. Norton & Company, Inc.
www.pegasusbooks.us

1

Yesterday upon the stair
I met a man who wasn't there
He wasn't there again today
I wish, I wish he'd go away
                    —Hughes Mearns, *Antigonish*

PARIS—SEPTEMBER 25, 1890
PLACE DE LA ROQUETTE

At four A.M., an unmarked black van drawn by two powerful draft horses rumbled up the avenue toward the gate of the Grande Roquette prison. The District Police Commissary had stationed a cordon of gendarmes around the square to restrain the crowd, which since midnight had burgeoned from dozens to several thousand. The authorities never released the date of execution until hours before the event. However, once the police had assembled and formed the familiar protective lines, the news of an impending decapitation spread far beyond the confines of the Roquette district. The steady light rain and early-morning chill had not deterred a curious crowd from attending the grim ceremony.

The wagon passed through the police barrier and halted next to five rectangular granite stones, which demarcated a level space set aside for the guillotine. Deibler, known publicly by his sobriquet, M. de Paris, stepped down from the driver's perch to the pavement. The executioner and four assistants opened the van, removed its contents, and began the task of assembling the guillotine.

∞

At dawn, Laurent Moreau had less than two hours to live. Deep within the fortresslike prison, three burly warders removed their boots and crept down the somber corridor to Moreau's cell. The imminent appointment with M. de Paris was supposed to come as a surprise, which was considered a humane policy because the condemned could go to bed each evening hopeful that the morning might bring news of a successful appeal.

A warder opened the cell door; his lantern shone a cone of white light onto the face of the sleeping prisoner. Moreau awoke with a start, his eyes wide like a frightened stag's in a hunter's sights. Two guards ran forward to restrain the condemned man. The governor of Roquette entered, followed by Chief Inspector Féraud, Inspector Lefebvre, Examining Magistrate Leblanc, and the District Police Commissary. Now fully awake, Moreau sat on the edge of the bed, pallid and visibly shaking in the warders' grasp.

"Moreau," said the governor in a theatrical baritone, "the day of expiation has arrived. Prepare yourself."

Moreau's lips moved as if in response, but all that came out was an incoherent rasping noise. The officials turned and filed out of the cell. The warders started dressing the prisoner in shirt, trousers, and shoes. When they finished, he would have one hour alone with the priest.

∞

The priest and the warders led Moreau to the prison registry, where the officials, including Inspector Lefebvre, waited patiently. The registry was a gray, stone-floored room; a few flickering gas jets cast shadows on the dingy walls. The prisoner was made to sit on a small wooden stool in the center of the room. There, the warders cut Moreau's hair and ripped away his shirt around the shoulders so there would be no impediment to the blade. The prisoner endured this operation stoically, which impressed Lefebvre. The inspector had seen the toughest criminals shudder at the first touch of cold steel on the backs of their necks.

Moreau caught the eye of the detective who had hunted him down and brought him to justice. Lefebvre gazed back at the prisoner calmly. To the inspector, the condemned man's look was neither angry nor frightened. Rather, the prisoner's stare seemed to ask a question: *Why am I here?* The answer was simple. Moreau had murdered twice and conspired in a bomb plot that could have killed and maimed dozens. Lefebvre's detective work averted the catastrophe.

"Do you want a cigarette, Moreau?" a warder asked.

The prisoner turned his eyes from Lefebvre to the warder and shook his head without speaking.

"Better have a glass of rum, then," the warder said in a kindly voice. "It'll brace you up."

Moreau nodded and half-whispered, "Thank you."

Moreau swallowed his last drink, coughed, and cleared his throat. The governor said, "It's time." The warders pinioned the condemned man and conducted him through the registry door to the prison courtyard; the officials followed. The rain had stopped; the sun shone brightly in a deep blue, cloud-stippled sky. The air smelled fresh and clean.

꧁꧂

At the end of the yard, near the arched gateway, Deibler waited with two assistants. They wore black frock coats and silk top hats, like wedding guests or pallbearers. The assistants took charge of the prisoner; the procession passed through the gate and out into the square.

A roar went up from the crowd. "There he is! Death to Moreau! The murderer! Assassin!"

Moreau, who had until then maintained his composure, halted. He glanced up at the machine and its gleaming blade. The assistants urged him on. If necessary, they would drag him to the bascule, the tilting board that held the condemned under the knife. After a moment, Moreau controlled himself and walked on.

Lefebvre joined a small group of privileged spectators at the foot of the guillotine. He watched the assistants strap the condemned man to the bascule, tilt the board, and guide it forward, carefully positioning the neck in the lunette, a stock-like device that secured the head. With the lunette fastened, Deibler tripped the mechanism. The heavily weighted knife came down with a thud; the severed head dropped into an iron bucket. The assistants unstrapped the truncated corpse and rolled it off the board into a large wicker basket. The crowd cheered. A flight of sparrows rose from the trees and circled the Place de la Roquette.

An elegantly dressed woman, a deputy's wife, turned to Inspector Lefebvre. Her queasy expression reminded Lefebvre of the look on the face of a young detective after his first visit to the dissecting room at the Morgue.

"Well, M. Lefebvre," she said with a slight tremor in her voice, "that was quite . . . efficient, wasn't it?"

Lefebvre smiled politely to put the woman at ease. "Yes, Madame; very efficient."

꧁꧂

Attending Moreau's execution was Paul Féraud's last official act as chief of the Paris Detective Police. With that final duty fulfilled, he relaxed in a leather armchair behind a large, file-cluttered mahogany desk in his office on the Quai des Orfèvres. Across from him sat his protégé, the newly appointed chief, Achille Lefebvre. The detectives silently contemplated each other, each enjoying a Havana cigar. The only sounds were those of a barge chugging up the Seine, the ticking clock on the wall, and the footsteps and murmurings of clerks and detectives in the outer hallway.

They had spoken little during the short cab ride from the prison to headquarters and had said nothing about the execution. Féraud knew Lefebvre's views on capital punishment; the younger detective was skeptical of its deterrent effect and considered legal execution little more than an act of revenge. Nevertheless, he was circumspect about expressing his controversial opinions in public; in such matters, he adhered to his mentor's dictum: "We enforce the laws; we don't make them." The old chief was keenly aware of Lefebvre's attitude when he made the following observation:

"It's always a dreary business, but thankfully it went off without a hitch. Moreau died like a man."

Lefebvre leaned forward and knocked some ash into a brass tray next to the guillotine cigar cutter on the chief's desk. Then he eased back in his chair and smiled wryly. "He didn't lack for guts. When I told Moreau things might go easier for him if he ratted out his pals, he spat in my face and told me to go to hell."

Féraud nodded. "I heard about that. You remained cool in keeping with your role as lead investigator, but Legros knocked the bastard down. Étienne is a good man. He understood your position as his superior and acted for you. You brought him along well."

"Thanks, Chief. With his recent promotion, I expect he'll continue to be of great service to the brigade and me."

"I'm sure he will." Féraud paused a moment; he frowned and spoke gravely. "I've heard that some of Moreau's cronies have sworn revenge."

Lefebvre shook his head and sighed. "I've heard that, too. I won't lose sleep over it. It's always the same with these punks after an execution. Their mouths are bigger than their balls. But I suppose I'll need to take precautions."

Féraud grinned. "Yes, precautions are in order. You don't want to be killed your first week as chief. At any rate, you're thinking and talking like one of us. Keep it up and the old boys will stop calling you the Professor."

Lefebvre had never liked the nickname, but after eight years on the force, he was used to it. Now no one would dare use it to his face, at least no one except for Féraud and the man who gave Lefebvre the moniker, his former partner, Rousseau.

"I suppose I was pretty green when Rousseau gave me that name. And at times I did tend to talk and act like a schoolmaster."

Féraud could not help laughing. "Oh, on occasion you still do, my boy, you still do." He took another puff on his cigar before continuing. "I'm glad you reconciled with Rousseau. He's come up in the world since he left us, and I expect you'll need to work closely with him in future."

Rousseau had left the Sûreté following his botched role in the Ménard case. The veteran detective's fixation on a particular suspect had hampered his judgment and, for a while, led him to work against his partner, Lefebvre.

However, Rousseau had found a position in the newly formed political brigade. There, his wide network of snoops and informers, coupled with his reputation for ruthlessness, made him indispensable in a new era of espionage, intrigue, and terrorism. In that regard, he had worked with Lefebvre in breaking up the assassination plot involving Moreau and several confederates.

"I can work with Rousseau, but I can't always approve of his methods."

Féraud raised an eyebrow. "But you'll do what's necessary in the interest of public safety?"

"Yes, of course. There are exigencies that warrant extrajudicial means, but there remains a line that mustn't be crossed."

Féraud nodded. "Now you're back to talking like the Professor, but that's all right. I know what you mean, and I agree." The old chief took another puff on his cigar and glanced around the office. "I suppose you'll be making changes?"

Achille eyed the messy desk and dusty shelves stacked high with relics of cases going back to the last days of the Second Empire. "Not many, Chief, although I might update the filing system."

Féraud shook his head. "You'll change things, all right. I've seen your office. It's as neat and sterile as a modern operating room. And what's to be done with that typewriter contraption? The clerks hate it, and none of the detectives will touch the damned thing."

"I'm giving it to Étienne. I taught him how to use it, and he'll set a good example. As for the others, their reports had better be legible or I'll make them take typing lessons."

"Ha! And they said I was a hard taskmaster." The old chief scanned the photographs on the opposite wall. His Rogue's Gallery consisted of portraits of the most dangerous criminals captured or killed in battles with the police during his long tenure. There were several photographs of heads posed on slabs in the Morgue. "Will you keep the Rogue's Gallery?"

"What's already there will remain in your honor, but I haven't yet decided whether to continue the practice."

Féraud nodded. "Fair enough." He kept staring at the wall as if reflecting on his more than thirty years with the Sûreté.

Lefebvre detected sadness in the chief's eyes; he said something calculated to cheer up the soon-to-be-retired detective. "There's something I've been meaning to ask you. I know it's an imposition, but I'd like to consult you from time to time. It wouldn't be often and only on the toughest cases or the biggest administrative problems. At least until I get my feet wet."

The tactful suggestion snapped Féraud out of his valedictory mood. "I'd be delighted. You may call on me anytime. For years I've dreamed of my little house in Pontoise—fishing in the river, puttering about in the garden, drinking, playing draughts at the café, and chatting with friends—" He broke off for a moment and sighed. "But now the time's come, and I fear I'll die of boredom. At any rate, when it comes to advice I'm always at your service. And you must come up some Sunday and bring your family. By the way, how are they? I assume they're still at Aix-les-Bains?"

"Thank you for asking. Now that this morning's unpleasant business is over, I'm going to wire Adele to return to Paris. But first, they must stop at Lyon. My uncle Octave lives there; he agreed to accompany my family to the spa. You may remember my uncle, Octave Lefebvre, the retired magistrate?"

"Indeed I do. A fine examining magistrate, and he's a friend of Professor Lacassagne, as I recall."

"Yes, and it was Lacassagne who got me interested in forensic medicine. He's the best; I wish we had him here, in Paris."

Féraud nodded his agreement. "By the way, how is your mother-in-law's rheumatism? Did the waters help her?"

"I believe so, or at least that's what Adele said in her last letter."

The old chief smiled. He reached into his vest pocket, removed a small key, opened a locked desk drawer, and retrieved a bottle and two glasses. "I'd like some prunelle. Will you join me?"

"Thank you, Chief; yes, I will."

Féraud poured two glasses and handed one to Lefebvre. "Let's drink to our future. But remember," he added solemnly, "after today, I'm just plain old Paul Féraud. You're the chief."

2

AIX-LES-BAINS

Madame Berthier rested on a crushed velvet settee in the hotel bedroom she shared with her daughter, Adele. With her voluminous underskirts hiked up over her knees, the old woman soaked her feet in a pan filled with a solution of warm water and healing salts. Her daughter knelt on the carpet, rubbing herbal embrocation on her mother's legs.

Half-exhausted, Adele raised her eyes with an entreating look. "Is it helping, Mama?"

"Oh yes, my dear. You have the hands of an angel. I believe the healing waters and bracing mountain air, coupled with your tender ministrations, have worked wonders."

"I'm so glad to hear it. May I stop now?" she added hopefully.

9

"Yes, you may."

Adele removed the pan and began toweling her mother's feet and legs. Then she helped the old woman with her stockings and shoes. When she had finished attending to her mother, she said, "Mama, since we're leaving this afternoon, would you mind if I went off on my own for an hour or so?"

Mme Berthier frowned. "I hope you're not meeting with that baroness and her parvenu husband?"

Adele shook her head. "No, it has nothing to do with *them*. It's just that all the time we've been here I've been busy with you and Uncle Octave and the children, and it's such a lovely day—"

"I understand, my dear," Mme Berthier broke in. "It's been no vacation for you at all, being separated from your husband because of that unpleasant business in Paris, cooped up with old M. Lefebvre and me, listening to us talk about our aches and pains, and then there are the children. At least you have Suzanne to help you. I believe she's taken the little ones out for some air?"

"Yes, Mama. She took Jeanne and the baby to the park."

"Very well. Old M. Lefebvre has notified the hotel of our departure, and he's arranging for the railway tickets. You want some time to yourself. I understand, especially since you're having such a hard time weaning little Olivier."

Embarrassed by her mother's frank observation, Adele lowered her eyes and answered quietly. "Please, Mama. It's not so difficult. I'm coping."

Mme Berthier raised a critical eyebrow. "Are you, indeed? Well, he's nearly eight months, so you'd better get on with it. He can tolerate pap. Colonel Berthier, may he rest in peace, was very impatient in these matters. I can still hear him: 'What are you waiting for? Do you want it suckling at its first communion?' The colonel could be very blunt. Men don't like their women going around with their breasts dripping milk. It's very unattractive."

"Achille's not like that. He's sensitive and understanding."

The old woman smiled shrewdly. "Your husband is complicated and somewhat enigmatic. He is widely admired, but he's also one of the most feared men in France. He's the sort who keeps things bottled up, unlike your father, who always came straight to the point. At times, you must wonder what Achille's thinking. As for your relationship with *those people*, he would certainly disapprove."

"There is no relationship, Mother," Adele protested. "Achille and I made their acquaintance casually, at Trouville, and we have no intention of pursuing it further. When we arrived here at the hotel, the baroness saw me in the lobby. She approached me and invited me to spend an evening with her and the baron, which I politely declined. That's the end of it, as far as I'm concerned."

Mme Berthier sensed trouble in Adele's voice and the look in her eyes. She did not want to provoke a fight with her daughter. "All right, Adele; I understand. Where will you go?"

"I'd like to walk out to the esplanade to view the lake and the mountains and get a breath of fresh air. I won't be long. By the time I return, Uncle Octave will have made our travel arrangements, Suzanne should be back with the children, and we can finish packing and get ready to leave."

Madame reached for her cane and rose from the settee. She embraced her daughter. "That's fine, my dear. Enjoy yourself; I wish I could join you. And don't worry about me. You see how well I can manage on my own."

⸘

Adele rested in the shade of a plane tree on the esplanade bordering Lake Bourget. A mild breeze came down from the surrounding mountains, rippling the waters, stirring the tree branches, and fluttering furbelows around the hemline of her dark-blue walking suit. The calm, multicolored surface of the Alpine lake reminded her of a turquoise brooch Achille had given her for their last anniversary. She wished he were there beside her to share this moment of natural beauty and tranquility.

Adele fixed her gaze on the Dent du Chat, its massive purple form rising high above the water, the peak half-hidden in a white haze beneath a dazzling blue, almost cloudless sky. A high-pitched cry drew her attention from the mountain to the azure prospect above the lake. Shading her eyes with her hand, she observed a hawk circling the water in search of its prey.

"Good morning, Madame Lefebvre."

Startled, Adele gave a little "Oh!" then turned in the direction of the greeting.

"I'm sorry if I disturbed you, Madame. It's a lovely vantage point, is it not? You have a perfect view of the Cat's Tooth, and the abbey as well."

"Good morning, Madame de Livet. I apologize; my mind was far away. But yes, it is a beautiful view. I didn't want to leave this place without coming here." Adele had planned the sight-seeing excursion, but she had not been completely honest with her mother. The baroness's maidservant had delivered her mistress's cryptic note earlier that morning; Adele had accepted a request for a brief meeting on the esplanade.

The baroness's thin, rouged lips formed an ingratiating smile. Her piercing gray eyes narrowed. "I'm so pleased you agreed to see me. I didn't want you to leave without my offering a sincere apology, both for myself and on behalf of my husband."

Adele frowned. She did not want this rendezvous; it smacked of intrigue. Achille would not have approved, and she had kept it from her mother; that nettled her conscience. On the other hand, to refuse the woman's request would have seemed impolite. The baroness might have considered the refusal an affront and harbored a grudge. Moreover, Adele rationalized that they could have met there by chance. So perhaps there was no harm in it after all. "I don't understand, Madame de Livet. Neither you nor your husband owe me an apology."

"You are very kind to say that, Madame Lefebvre, but we most certainly do. It was an unpardonable liberty to invite you to dinner followed by an evening at the casino without your husband's permission. I told the baron so, but he insisted. I'll be frank, my dear. My husband is a vulgar man. He made his fortune in the South African mines, and it shows. He simply cannot appreciate the niceties. He isn't even French. His name is Schwarz, but he changed it to Le Noir before we were married. Then he took de Livet from my father's estate and became a self-styled baron. So now you understand why I feel the need to apologize."

The baroness's revelation hardly came as a surprise; it simply confirmed Mme Berthier's suspicion. The baron was a parvenu, though a very wealthy and ostensibly well-connected one. However, this information, coupled with an apology, made Adele more sympathetic to Mme de Livet. She was familiar with the plight of young women from noble but impoverished families forced to marry for advantage. She returned the baroness's smile.

"I accept your apology, Madame, though I repeat it's unnecessary. And you may convey my regards to your husband." She glanced around as if expecting the baron to appear suddenly. Adele ought to have cut things short and returned to the hotel, but curiosity got the better of her. "By the way, if you don't mind my asking, where is the baron?"

The baroness raised a gloved hand to her lips and gave a light, little laugh. "Oh, *him*, he's still playing cards at a private party given by a Russian prince who owns a villa hereabouts. As though the baron hadn't had enough play at the baccarat table. By early this morning, I had had enough. I returned to our suite at the hotel, and he went off with the prince and his crowd. I haven't heard from my husband since. I expect I'll receive a message from him presently. These things can go on for days, you know."

Adele regretted asking. She consulted the small gold watch pinned to her jacket. "Oh my, I had no idea of the time. I beg your pardon; my family will worry about me. I must return directly."

"Of course, my dear. Family obligations take precedence over all. *Au revoir.*"

Adele nodded. "Good-bye, Madame de Livet." She turned without another word and walked rapidly up the pathway in the direction of the hotel.

The baroness watched Adele for a moment, then turned her attention to the hawk circling the lake.

⌘

"Mama's back!" Jeanne sprang from her great-uncle's lap and ran to her mother. Adele smiled warmly, lifted the girl, and gave her a hug. "Have you been good while I was gone?"

"Oh yes, very good. Suzanne took us to the park. I met a little boy and girl from Algiers. Their father's an officer, like Papa. We played and had such fun until the baby threw up. Why does he always throw up like that?"

Adele sighed, put Jeanne down, and held her hand. "I hope she wasn't a bother, Uncle Octave?"

"No trouble at all," the old gentleman replied. "You liked my story about a trip to the moon, didn't you, Jeanne?"

"Oh yes, Uncle, very much," the child replied. "Will you tell me another?"

"Of course, my dear, if you like."

Adele gazed affectionately at the retired magistrate. Tall, lean, impeccably dressed, with thinning white hair, a neatly trimmed beard, and weak blue eyes peering through a gold-rimmed pince-nez, he seemed to prefigure her husband as he might appear thirty years hence. "That's very kind of you, Uncle. Are my mother and Suzanne still packing?"

"Yes, they are. That is to say, Suzanne is packing and your mother is supervising."

"I'd better go see if I can help. Would you mind watching Jeanne a little longer?"

"I would be delighted." He smiled, crooked his finger, and beckoned to the child. "Come here, little one, and I'll tell you a story about my first trip to Paris. That was before they extended the railway, and we went most of the way by coach."

"I love riding on the train," Jeanne said. "Look, I'm a choo-choo." She began chugging and tooting in a circle, her little arms imitating a locomotive's pistons.

Adele left the child with Uncle Octave and entered the bedroom where Suzanne had just finished packing for the journey. Mme Berthier cocked an eyebrow at her daughter and gave her a wry greeting:

"Your timing is perfect, my dear. We're done packing."

"I'm sorry, Mother. The walk took a bit longer than I expected." She glanced at the baby sleeping quietly in his portable crib. "Is he all right? Jeanne said he was sick."

"It's nothing to worry about, Madame," Suzanne replied. "He's just getting used to his pap."

Mme Berthier broke in: "Suzanne, now that you're finished here, you may go and see to your own things."

Suzanne said, "Yes, Madame," and left, closing the sliding door behind her.

Mme Berthier eyed her daughter suspiciously before asking, "Did you enjoy your little sightseeing excursion?"

Adele glanced down sheepishly. "Yes, Mother, it was fine, but—"

"But what, my dear?"

"I had a brief encounter with Mme de Livet."

"An *encounter*, you say? Are you quite certain it wasn't a rendezvous?"

"All right, Mother, it was by *appointment*," she replied with a hint of exasperation. "But her purpose was perfectly respectable. She wanted to apologize for inviting me out without Achille's permission. I accepted her apology, and that's an end to it."

Mme Berthier smiled. "I see; she's a woman of delicate sensibilities, no doubt. She accosts you as soon as you set foot in the hotel and, on behalf of her husband, invites you to a private dinner followed by an evening at the baccarat tables. Can you imagine the gossip that would stir up, especially when the Paris newspapers got wind of it? A nice item for the scandalmongers: The wife of the newly appointed chief of detectives has been seen gadding about a fashionable spa in the company of notorious arrivistes."

"For goodness sake, Mother, I refused the invitation and she apologized. I do not intend to pursue the acquaintance. Why must you keep harping on about it?"

"Why, my girl?" Mme Berthier said heatedly. "Because it's as plain as day they want something from Achille, and you're the quickest and surest way to him. People like the de Livets ruined your father's career."

Adele was about to reply when she heard the baby stirring in his crib. She raised a finger to her lips. "Please, Mother," she half-whispered, "you'll wake the baby. I don't dispute what you say, and I'll certainly discuss the matter with Achille."

Mme Berthier nodded and spoke softly. "Very well, Adele." She glanced at her pendant watch. "I think it's time M. Lefebvre notified the front desk to fetch our baggage. The *diligence* to the railway station leaves in a half hour."

3

THE BARON VANISHES

C hief Inspector Lefebvre sat behind the desk in his new office. He took a break from the day's paperwork to enjoy a typical lunch consisting of a croque monsieur and a beer brought in from the local brasserie. His appetite satisfied for the moment, he put down the remains of his sandwich and scanned the surroundings. *I still expect the old chief to walk through the door and ask what I'm doing in his place*, he thought.

His eyes darted from a manila envelope on his desktop to an empty space on the wall and back again. The envelope contained Morgue photographs of Moreau's head posed on a slab.

It had been a week since the execution, and Lefebvre had made a decision concerning the Rogue's Gallery. He would display Moreau's identification portraits taken shortly after the murderer's arrest, but the postmortem photographs would remain in the closed file. This change in procedure would honor Chief Féraud while subtly hinting at the new chief's different views concerning capital punishment and gruesome wall trophies. Lefebvre smiled with satisfaction at his Solomonic judgment; a knock on the door interrupted his musing.

A clerk entered and handed a visiting card to the chief. Lefebvre immediately recognized the name.

"The lady insists upon seeing you, M. Lefebvre. She says it's urgent, and she seems quite agitated."

"Very well," Lefebvre replied. He made a sweeping gesture at his half-eaten lunch. "Get rid of this. Tell the lady I'll see her presently. Then give me a few minutes before you bring her in."

Lefebvre wiped his hands on a handkerchief, put on his frock coat, glanced in a mirror, and brushed a few crumbs from his beard and moustache. He popped a peppermint pastille in his mouth. Then he removed his holstered revolver from the coatrack and placed it in a desk drawer, thinking the sight of the weapon might disturb his visitor. He took his place behind the desk just as the clerk knocked and entered with the lady.

Lefebvre rose, bowed politely, and smiled. "Good day, Mme de Livet. Please tell me how I may be of service?"

"Oh, M. Lefebvre—" She gulped and dabbed at her eyes with a lace handkerchief.

He glared at the clerk and gestured toward the door. The clerk made a hasty exit.

Lefebvre approached the baroness and helped her to a seat. "I trust you'll find this armchair comfortable, Madame. May I get you some refreshment—coffee or tea? Or perhaps something stronger?"

The baroness took a couple of deep breaths before answering. "Have you any liqueur?"

He remembered the bottle in the locked drawer. He and Féraud had consumed most of it, but there might be enough left for the baroness. "I have some prunelle. Will that do?"

"Yes, thank you, Monsieur."

Lefebvre fetched the bottle and brought out what appeared to be the cleaner of the two glasses. He handed the drink to the baroness. She took a sip, licked her lips, then downed the rest and handed him the empty glass.

He returned to his chair, sat, and regarded the baroness with a reassuring smile. "That's better, isn't it? Now please tell me the reason for your visit."

She remained silent for a moment before replying: "An awful thing has occurred, Monsieur. My husband's disappeared."

A lost millionaire. What a way to begin my tenure as chief, he thought. Adele had already told him about her encounter with the baroness at Aix-les-Bains. This did not bode well.

"Please, Mme de Livet, I will need to ask you some questions, and I'll take notes." He grabbed a pencil and writing pad before continuing. "You say your husband is missing. Have you reported this to the police?"

"Yes, Monsieur. I notified the police commissary in Chambéry."

"Can you provide me with the commissary's name?"

"Inspector Forestier."

"And when did you contact M. Forestier?"

"Two days ago, the same day I returned to Paris on the evening train."

"And when and where was the last time you saw your husband?"

"Three days ago at around one in the morning in the casino at Aix-les-Bains."

The morning of the execution, he thought. Not that he could make any connection between the two events, but it helped him establish a reference point for a timeline. "Did you leave the casino together?"

"No; I went to the hotel. My husband went on to a private party at Prince Papkov's villa."

"Was there gambling at the prince's party?"

"Of course, Monsieur, and for very high stakes. That's why my husband went."

"Did your husband carry a large amount of cash or valuables?"

The baroness stared at Lefebvre for a moment before answering: "When he is gaming, he always carries a Gladstone bag filled with thousand-franc notes."

"You said 'filled with' thousand-franc notes. Do you know approximately how many?"

"Several hundred, I should think."

"Did your husband make a large bank withdrawal recently?"

"I believe he did."

"When was that?"

"Last week. Just before we left for Aix-les-Bains."

"And he took the Gladstone bag to the bank?"

"Yes."

"Can you describe the bag?"

"It was ox-hide with brass fittings and was embossed with the de Livet coat of arms. My husband purchased it from J. G. Beard in London."

"I assume the coat of arms is the same as that on your card?"

"Yes, Monsieur."

"Have you had any communication with your husband since you left the casino?"

"Only once, by way of his manservant."

"The manservant's name?"

"Eugene Bonnet."

"Is Bonnet a member of your household staff in Paris?"

"Yes, Monsieur."

"Did he accompany your husband to Prince Papkov's party?"

"Pardon me, M. Lefebvre, I already provided this information to the police in Chambéry."

Lefebvre put down his pencil. He maintained his patient, professional demeanor. "I appreciate that, Madame. However, it's a long way from Savoie to Paris. We can wire M. Forestier for information, but it may take a day or two to obtain a copy of the report. The information you provide me now can save time. Please bear with me. May I continue?"

"I beg your pardon, M. Lefebvre. I'll answer as best I can. You asked about Bonnet. Yes, he accompanied my husband to the prince's villa."

"Thank you, Madame. Did Bonnet carry the bag for the baron?"

"No, my husband never lets anyone touch that bag, including me."

"I see." He paused a moment and glanced at his notes before continuing. "You said Bonnet gave you a message from the baron. Was the communication in writing or by word of mouth, and what did it convey?"

"There was no writing, Monsieur. Bonnet told me the baron had taken the train to Paris. He also said that my husband would contact me by wire immediately upon arrival."

"When did Bonnet tell you that?"

"Last week, the twenty-fifth."

"Did he see his master board the train? Did he say what station and the time of departure?"

The baroness shook her head. "I'm sorry, I don't recall. Oh, M. Lefebvre, I've been so confused and distraught." She choked back a sob and reached for her handkerchief.

Bravo, Mme Bernhardt! he thought. "Very well, Madame. We'll try to get the information from Inspector Forestier. In the meantime, I'm going to have my detectives question Bonnet. I trust you'll make him available for the interview?"

"Yes, of course."

"Thank you, Madame. Did any other servants accompany you and the baron to Aix-les-Bains?"

"Just one, Manuela Otero, my maid."

"Is she a citizen?"

"Yes, Monsieur. Her father is Spanish, her mother French. She was born in Paris."

"We'll need to interview her, too, and the rest of the household staff as well."

"Is that necessary, Monsieur?"

"I'm afraid so. Servants see and hear things they don't share with their employers, unless pressed."

The baroness nodded her understanding but said nothing.

"I believe in addition to your Paris residence you also have a mansion in Saint-Germain-en-Laye?"

"Yes, Monsieur. That is my ancestral home. My husband now holds the title to the property, but my elderly father, the Count de Livet, resides there."

"You said your husband holds the title. Did he purchase the mansion from the count?"

The baroness frowned. "Yes, Monsieur."

"And when, may I ask, did the transfer of ownership occur?"

Her face reddened, and there was a slight tremor in her voice. "Shortly before our marriage."

Lefebvre nodded, made a note, but did not pursue the matter. He continued in a mollifying tone:

"Now, I am afraid I must ask a few more questions of a personal nature. You might find these questions embarrassing, but I request that you answer them fully and frankly. May I proceed?"

The baroness controlled herself. "Yes, Monsieur, please continue."

"How long have you been married to the baron?"

"Two years."

"In that time, has he ever gone off unexpectedly with little or no notice?"

"He has, on occasion, but he always kept in touch. When I didn't receive the expected telegram, I wired our home in Paris. A servant replied that he hadn't seen the baron since we left for Aix-les-Bains."

"When did you wire Paris and receive the reply?"

"I sent the telegram the evening of the twenty-fifth and received a reply the morning of the twenty-sixth."

Lefebvre consulted his notes. "I see. I'll summarize to make sure I have this down correctly. You made your report two days ago, the twenty-sixth. Based on the message you received from Bonnet, if your husband had wired you upon arrival in Paris, you ought to have received the telegram the evening of the twenty-fifth or on the morning of the twenty-sixth at the latest. You wired Paris on the twenty-fifth and received a reply the twenty-sixth. So you knew something was amiss on the twenty-sixth?"

"Yes, Monsieur. I was worried. Did I do right?"

"Yes, Madame. I believe under the circumstances going to the police was appropriate. Did you suspect foul play?"

She seemed flustered by his reference to "foul play." "Why no, I was concerned, but I had no reason to believe . . . I didn't think . . ." She stared at him without completing the sentence.

He noted her reaction and continued. "Well, that's understandable, Madame. You had no reason to believe the worst. Now, have you contacted any of your husband's business associates, friends, or acquaintances to see if they know his whereabouts?"

"No, do you think I should?"

Lefebvre felt like a dentist prodding a sensitive tooth. The baron was a naturalized citizen with close ties to South African mining interests. He knew the baron associated with prominent men of finance, wealthy diamond and gold merchants, as well as a few politicians. In addition, the baron gambled for high stakes among a fashionable sporting crowd that lived on the fringes of society. Such men usually frequented a posh *maison de tolérance* or kept a woman in town, and Lefebvre figured the baron was no exception.

He assumed the baroness wanted to avoid publicity. If she went around asking about her husband, the resulting gossip would spread throughout Parisian society and the matter would soon find its way into the newspapers. On the other hand, once he launched an investigation, it would be impossible to keep the matter quiet.

"For the time being, no. However, I request you provide us with a list of anyone you know who might have information relevant to this matter."

He paused before adding, "Forgive me, Madame, but that would include any relationships the baron might have that are of an intimate nature."

The baroness frowned but did not hesitate to answer. "I understand, M. Lefebvre. I'll provide you with the information you require. Is that all?"

"Yes, Madame, that's all for now. This matter is at the stage of a preliminary investigation. So far, there's no evidence of a crime. Nevertheless, the unexplained disappearance of a prominent citizen is cause for concern. There is also a matter of jurisdiction. The case was opened in Savoie. However, that is a technical issue, and we will certainly cooperate with M. Forestier until the appropriate primary jurisdiction is established. Now, I can send detectives out to question your servants later this afternoon. If necessary, my men will return tomorrow to complete the interviews."

"Thank you, Monsieur. I'll let the servants know." She paused a moment before adding: "I suppose this will get into the newspapers?"

"I'm afraid so, but let's be optimistic. Perhaps the baron will reappear shortly with a perfectly reasonable explanation. Unless you have more questions, there's just one thing I need from you before you leave. Do you have a recent photograph of your husband?"

The baroness reached into her handbag and retrieved a *carte de visite*. She handed the portrait to Lefebvre. "Will this do?"

"Thank you; this will do splendidly. We will also need a detailed physical description, but I won't detain you further. We can get that from other sources." He rose from his chair and walked over to the baroness. "I bid you good day, Madame."

Madame de Livet smiled wanly and took his extended hand. Lefebvre escorted her to her carriage. He watched the vehicle pull away from the curb, sighed, and lit a cigarette. Then he walked up the quay in the direction of the Pont Saint-Michel.

He paused near the bridge and took a moment to savor the bright blue sky and crisp, clean autumn air. Across the river, on the left embankment, the leaves on the shade trees were changing color, from green to red and golden hues. A steam whistle announced the approach of a tug hauling a barge; a steady stream of traffic flowed over the bridge from the Île de la Cité to the Boul'Mich. The everyday bustle and familiar sights had a soothing effect until his thoughts reverted to the case of the missing baron. "A well-connected parvenu gambler disappears along with a small fortune in banknotes stuffed into a traveling bag. *Merde alors!*" he muttered.

He tossed his cigarette butt into the Seine. Lefebvre returned to headquarters, climbed the staircase, and headed down the dark, musty corridor in the direction of his old cubbyhole.

❧

Lefebvre glanced around his former office and was pleased to notice few if any changes. "Well, Étienne, how do you like having a little working space all to yourself? I'd say it's an improvement over sharing that crowded, smoke-filled den with the other detectives."

Inspector Legros smiled. "Thank you, Chief; I like it immensely. And as you can see, I'm keeping it neat, clean, and efficient."

Lefebvre nodded approvingly. "How's your workload these days?"

It's a shit storm, Legros thought. "I'm managing all right. Do you have something new for me, Chief?"

"Yes, I'm afraid I do. Have you heard of the Baron Le Noir de Livet?"

"Yes, Chief. People say he's one of the richest men in Paris. He's also well-known at the card tables and the racecourse."

"That's the gentleman. He and a bagful of money have gone missing somewhere near Aix-les-Bains. I've just come from a meeting with the baroness."

"A missing persons' case? Aren't the local authorities handling it?"

"The baroness made a report to Inspector Forestier in Chambéry. Please take this down." He paused for a moment to give Legros time to grab a pad and pencil. "I want you to wire Forestier. Tell him the baroness brought the matter to my attention. We'll cooperate in the investigation and would appreciate any information he has in return.

"It's still his case, as far as I'm concerned, but we should be actively involved. The baron might be in or near Paris. Of course, he could be anywhere now, alive or dead.

"As soon as you've sent the telegram, I want you to pick a good man and go to the de Livets' to interview the servants. Here's the address and the notes I took earlier. Review my notes, make a copy for yourself, and return the originals to me. Begin the questioning with the baron's man, Eugene Bonnet. According to the baroness, he was the last person to see the baron in Aix-les-Bains. To start, ask him some routine questions about his background and employment history. Then ask if he saw the baron board the train. If so, at which station and at what time? Forestier should already have that information, but we can check that later.

"I made reference to a Gladstone bag filled with thousand-franc notes. Did the baron have the bag with him when he boarded the train? Ask Bonnet if he knows whether the baron was a winner or loser at the casino and at Prince Papkov's party. If he won, God only knows how much cash he had stuffed into the bag. Moreover, we need to get as much detail as we can from Bonnet about what went on from the time they left the casino until the baron boarded the train. People, places, actions, anything unusual.

"When you're done with Bonnet, start questioning Manuela Otero, the baroness's maid." Lefebvre noticed Legros furiously scribbling to keep up with his chief's instructions. "Pardon me, Étienne. Perhaps it's better if we work together on this one. I know what I want to ask Bonnet and Otero. You can question the other servants. They remained in Paris, but you know how they talk among themselves. We might get a useful tidbit or two. And we'll check to see if any of them have a record."

Legros almost sighed with relief. "Thank you, Chief. Do you think this was an inside job?"

Lefebvre shook his head. "I don't know. I'll say one thing about cases like this. Our national motto extols equality, but nothing's equal when it comes to missing persons. Some poor bastard goes missing and no one cares much, except for his family and friends. But when a notable disappears, it can turn into a festival of shit. And in this case my wife and I are acquainted with the missing person."

"I see; that complicates things, doesn't it?"

Lefebvre shrugged. "It might." He stroked his beard and pondered the problem for a moment. Then he said, "According to the baroness, the baron made a large withdrawal from the bank before he left for Aix-les-Bains. We need to follow up on that. Among other things, the bank should have a record of the serial numbers. That might be useful. We'll also notify the railway police, if Forestier hasn't done that already. They can pass a description of the baron and his Gladstone bag up and down the line and see if they can locate some witnesses.

"All right, Étienne, go send the telegram. When you're done, meet me in my office and we'll pay a call on the baroness."

⟡

When Lefebvre returned to his office, the clerk said there was a man waiting in the outer hallway.

"Who is he and what does he want?"

"It's Duroc, Monsieur. He says he has a message for you from Inspector Rousseau."

Lefebvre immediately recognized the name. Duroc had left the brigade after he bungled a surveillance assignment in the Ménard case. He had since found a job with Rousseau in the political police.

"Very well," Lefebvre said. "Send him in."

Duroc entered the office, removed his bowler respectfully, and faced his former superior with a sheepish grin. "Good afternoon, M. Lefebvre. Permit me to congratulate you on your recent promotion to chief."

"That's thoughtful of you, Duroc, but I'm sure you're not here to give me your felicitations. What do you want?"

Duroc reached into his coat pocket and removed an envelope, which he handed to Lefebvre.

"I have an urgent message for your eyes only from Inspector Rousseau, and I've been ordered to wait for a reply."

Lefebvre opened the envelope and read the note:

Meet me in the usual place, tomorrow morning at five. Please confirm by reply to the messenger. Rousseau

He folded the letter and stared at Duroc. "Tell your boss I agree."

Duroc bowed politely and left the office. Lefebvre sat silently for a moment before muttering, "I actually *wanted* this job."

4

WHAT BONNET KNEW

Lefebvre and Legros took a fiacre to the baron's mansion on the Avenue Montaigne. They drove up the front entrance driveway and parked under an arched portico. Lefebvre paid the driver and asked him to wait.

The detectives mounted the stairway, and Lefebvre rang the electric doorbell. They could hear footsteps resonating in the marble hallway. The massive oak doors swung open; a tall English footman with long side-whiskers greeted them. Lefebvre handed his card to the footman. The man examined the card before saying, "Please follow me, gentlemen."

As they passed through the hallway, Lefebvre noticed some fine paintings by Bouguereau and Tissot, portrait busts by Nollekens, and several excellent examples of Sèvres. They continued on past white walls decorated with allegorical paintings and statuary niches in the Beaux Arts style; the vast antechamber sparkled with multicolored light filtering through stained-glass windows and lunettes in the high vaulted ceiling.

The footman halted, opened a door, and escorted the detectives into a salon, which Achille assumed was the main reception hall. "Please wait here, gentlemen," the footman said. "Madame will be with you shortly."

The oversize room was like a pharaoh's crypt filled with treasures to be enjoyed in the god-king's afterlife. There were no windows; dozens of Edison's electric bulbs in chandeliers, sconces, and lamps lit the chamber with a warm, golden glow. The eclectic furnishings were many: Persian carpets with their intricately woven floral patterns; salon paintings in gilt frames like those in the hallways; a large marble mantelpiece; Empire vitrines cluttered with expensive bibelots; glittering blue and white Oriental porcelain and Sèvres that might have pleased Emperor Napoleon; Japanese screens with soaring cranes and floating blossoms; Louis Quinze furniture.

Legros's eyes widened. "Whew," he said with a whistle. "It's like a little Versailles, isn't it, Chief?"

Achille nodded, but he said nothing. He wondered if the baroness approved of all this ostentatious clutter. He could not help contrasting this place with Le Boudin's shack in the Zone, filled with the *chiffonier*'s gleanings from the rubbish heaps of Paris.

A few minutes after the footman left, Mme de Livet entered the salon and greeted the detectives. Achille introduced Legros:

"This is Inspector Legros, Madame. He'll be leading our investigation."

The baroness exchanged greetings with Legros. Then she said, "I've notified all my servants. They are ready for you, except for Manuela. The poor girl's quite ill with a fever, which I believe she caught at the spa. I've had the doctor in to see her. I'm afraid you'll have to put off questioning her for a while."

"That's quite all right, Madame," Achille replied. "We can interview her when she's well. Now, I'll begin with Bonnet, and M. Legros will question the other servants."

The baroness took Legros to the kitchen, where the servants would appear, one at a time, for questioning. Achille waited in the salon for Bonnet, who arrived presently.

Achille pointed to a chair in the center of the room and told Bonnet to sit. He paced around the room without speaking to see how the manservant reacted. Bonnet remained calm. Achille got a good first impression of the man. *He's a cool one. Middle thirties, medium build, and very fit. There's a scar on the right cheek, but no other prominent marks. The baron might use him as a bodyguard.*

Achille stopped to the right of Bonnet, which made the man twist his head sideways and look up at the detective. The interrogation began with routine questions that could be cross-checked with Inspector Forestier's report. Bonnet remained composed and answered confidently, providing nothing of significance until they reached the subject of Prince Papkov's party.

"At what time did you and the baron arrive at Prince Papkov's villa?"

"At approximately two in the morning, Monsieur."

"And what did you and the baron do when you got there?"

"After some formal introductions, I accompanied my master, the prince, and two other gentlemen to a salon where they played piquet."

"Do you recall the names of the two gentlemen?"

"One was an Englishman named Sims. The other was a Russian officer. I don't recall his name."

"And with whom did your master play piquet?"

"The baron played with the prince, and M. Sims played with the officer."

"Did your master play with the banknotes in his bag?"

"Yes, Monsieur."

"Was there anyone else present in the salon?"

"Only the prince's manservant, as I recall."

"How long did the gentlemen play?"

"They played until dawn."

"So that would have been about five hours. Did they play continuously?"

"Yes, they did, Monsieur, but with an occasional break for refreshment."

"Did the gentlemen drink?"

"The prince drank a good deal of vodka. My master didn't drink. I'm not sure about the other gentlemen, but I believe they drank champagne."

"Would you say the prince was inebriated?"

"I'd say he was as drunk as a lord, Monsieur."

"I see. Earlier, when I asked about the baron's luck at the casino, you said that your master had won approximately twenty-thousand francs at baccarat; is that correct?"

"Yes, Monsieur."

"And the prince and the other gentlemen had lost at baccarat?"

"That is correct, although the prince had lost the most by far."

"So perhaps this private game was the prince's attempt to get even?"

"Perhaps, Monsieur."

"Did the prince win?"

Bonnet shook his head and smiled wryly. "Oh no, Monsieur. The prince lost a great deal more."

"How much more did he lose?"

Bonnet paused a moment before answering, "About half a million francs."

"Was that all in cash?"

"No, Monsieur. Fifty thousand or so was in banknotes and gold; the remainder was in promissory notes."

"How did the prince react to having lost so much?"

"Not well, Monsieur. In the presence of the other gentlemen, he accused my master of cheating. He called the baron a cardsharp and other names as well."

"Would you say the vodka had an influence on the prince's behavior?"

"I can't be sure, but I'd say it had an effect. The prince was livid."

"How did your master respond to the prince's accusation?"

"He denied the charge vehemently, said he had always played honorably, and demanded payment in full."

"And what did the prince say to that?"

"He said if my master wanted payment he would have to fight for it."

Achille stopped questioning. He circled the room for a moment before returning to face Bonnet squarely. "Did the baron agree to a meeting?"

"Yes, Monsieur, for later that morning."

"Who acted for your master?"

"The Englishman, M. Sims. The Russian officer acted for the prince."

"Where and when did the meeting take place?"

"At nine, in a lakeside clearing, near a dock on the prince's estate."

"Did they use swords or pistols?"

"Pistols, Monsieur."

"Who were the witnesses?"

" M. Sims, the Russian officer, and I."

"And what was the outcome?"

"My master and the prince exchanged fire at twenty paces, without doing injury. Then the seconds intervened and the matter was settled honorably."

"Do you know the terms of the settlement?"

"Yes, Monsieur. The prince retracted his accusation. My master agreed to take half his winnings in cash and gold as payment in full, and he cancelled the promissory notes."

"Did they shake hands?"

"Yes, Monsieur."

"What happened next?"

"My master received payment and placed the winnings in his bag. Then the prince's coachman drove us to the station in Aix-les-Bains."

"Do you recall what time you arrived at the station?"

"At about eleven."

"And you saw your master board the train?"

"Yes, Monsieur. He boarded a first-class carriage at noon on the express for Paris by way of Lyon."

"And he was carrying the Gladstone bag?"

"Of course, Monsieur."

"How much was he carrying?"

"Almost one million francs in banknotes and gold."

"Where did you go after you left the station?"

"I went directly to the hotel to inform the baroness that my master had returned to Paris and would wire her upon his arrival."

"That was the message the baron told you to give to Madame de Livet?"

"Yes, Monsieur."

"Now, Bonnet, have you answered all my questions fully and truthfully?"

Bonnet replied without hesitation. "Yes, Monsieur Lefebvre."

"Is there anything you want to add?"

"No, Monsieur."

"And you reported all this to the police in Chambéry?"

"Yes, Monsieur."

"Very well, that's all for now, Bonnet. However, you are not to leave Paris. We may require you at any time for further questioning."

"Yes, Monsieur. Thank you. May I go now?"

"Yes, you may."

∽∾

On their way back to headquarters, Achille and Legros stopped to discuss the case over a beer. A brisk wind blew up the avenue, rustling leaves and rattling the branches of a great horse chestnut that shaded the pavement in front of the brasserie. They chose a sidewalk table under the tree to avoid the noisy crowd that had gathered inside the bar.

Legros had interviewed two footmen, the cook, two scullery maids, and the coachman. He would return the next day to interrogate the remainder of the household staff. So far, his questioning had gathered nothing of interest. However, the servants had all expressed concern when he mentioned the baroness's maidservant, Otero, who seemed to have been seriously ill since her return from Aix-les-Bains.

"Well, I hope we can question Otero soon," Achille remarked.

Legros took a swig of beer before answering. "Of course, Chief. But the servants say she's very sick. If she doesn't improve overnight, the doctor is going to try a new remedy."

Achille raised an eyebrow at the reference to medication. "Do you know what he's going to give her?"

Legros shook his head. "I asked the servants, but they didn't know."

Achille frowned. "You should have asked the baroness." He noticed the worried expression on Legros's face. "No matter, Étienne. You'll find out tomorrow when you go back to finish your questioning."

"Do you think . . . do you think someone might poison her to keep her mouth shut?"

Lefebvre shook his head. "I don't know, but under the circumstances it seems suspicious that she's too sick to answer our questions. As for poisoning, considering the present state of our medical practice, about half the prescriptions are as likely to kill as to cure."

Legros smiled. "You're right, Chief, but I wouldn't say that to the doctors at the Morgue."

"Oh, heavens no. Of course, the pathologists' 'patients' are mercifully beyond all medical assistance." Achille finished his beer and gestured to the waiter. "Would you care for another drink?"

"Thanks, Chief, yes, I would."

Achille placed the order, the waiter soon returned with two beers, and they continued discussing the case. "Bonnet gave me an inkling of a suspect or two, and one of them is a Russian prince." He proceeded to tell Legros about the argument over cards and the subsequent duel and settlement. "If Bonnet told the truth, Prince Papkov has a volatile temper and is likely to still believe he was cheated, despite the so-called honorable settlement. He could be the sort who thinks he is entitled to recover the money by means outside the law.

"It takes approximately ten hours to travel by train from Aix-les-Bains to Paris. That would be more than enough time for the prince to wire confederates in Paris who could waylay the baron somewhere between the Gare de Lyon and his ultimate destination."

"That's assuming the prince had individuals in Paris ready to act on his orders."

"Good point, Étienne. It's an assumption on my part that we can confirm or refute by further investigation. However, in my experience a man like the prince would tend to have minions stationed in the capital."

"Do you think Inspector Forestier shares your suspicion?"

Achille shrugged. "How would I know?" He thought about the telephone sitting uselessly on his desk. "I'd like to talk to the man. Communicating by telegram is limited and too slow. We ought to have long-distance telephone lines linking police headquarters throughout all the regions and departments in France."

Beer and the convivial brasserie atmosphere had loosened Legros's tongue. "Ah, M. Lefebvre, now you're sounding like Jules Verne. Our telephones hardly work effectively in and around Paris, not to mention regions beyond our jurisdiction."

"It's not so fantastical a proposition, my friend. The Americans have a line running from New York to Philadelphia. That's a distance of 150 kilometers. And they're planning a line from New York to Chicago of approximately 1,200 kilometers, about twice the distance from Paris to Marseille."

Legros smirked and shook his head. "Oh well, the Americans," he said with a hint of disdain for the upstart industrial power.

"Yes, the Americans. What they lack in culture, taste, and intellectual refinement they more than make up for in vision, ingenuity, and persistence. I admire men like Edison, Bell, Carnegie, and Rockefeller. We could use a few of them over here." Achille stopped short, realizing that the beer, which at this brasserie was exceptionally good and strong, was having its effect upon him.

He glanced at his watch. "Time to get back to work. I want you to contact Inspector Hennion of the Railway Squad. Give him the train information I got from Bonnet. Regardless of what they're doing down in Chambéry, the railway police need to start looking for witnesses and gathering information all up and down the line. We also need to check with the hack drivers who may have picked up the baron at the Gare de Lyon. That's assuming, of course, that he made it to Paris.

"I want more information about Prince Papkov and the other two gentlemen at the card party, the Russian officer and the Englishman Sims. I hope Forestier can provide those particulars, but I'm going to start my own inquiry through my sources in Paris. And you'll need to go to records to see if they have anything on the servants. We'll go over the details when we return to headquarters."

"Right, Chief."

Achille paid the waiter. They left the brasserie and walked up the avenue in the direction of the Pont Saint-Michel.

At ten P.M., Achille crossed the Pont Neuf to the right embankment, and from there it was a short walk to his apartment on the Rue Bertin Poirée. Adele greeted him at the front door. She carried an oil lamp to light the hallway. The children, Suzanne, and the cook were asleep; Mme Berthier had retired to her boudoir; Adele had extinguished all the gas jets.

Achille was dog-tired, but he managed a smile. "Good evening, my dear."

"Good evening, Achille. As usual, you missed an excellent meal with your family. I suppose there's a new case that requires your immediate attention?"

He sighed. "Yes, my dear, a new case, and I'd like to discuss it with you since it involves someone you know."

Her eyes widened. "The baroness?"

Why would she think that? Does she know more than she's told me? "Let's go to the sitting room. I'd like a drink."

Shadows flickered on the walls as she led him down the corridor. She opened the door carefully, so as not to disturb the children sleeping nearby. They entered the dark room; Adele set the lamp on a table. "Do you want more light?"

Achille eased back into his favorite armchair, removed his pince-nez, and rubbed his weary eyes. "No thank you, my dear. This is fine."

Adele opened the liquor cabinet and poured a glass of cognac for Achille and a sherry for herself. She handed him the drink and then settled down on a couch opposite him.

Achille took a sip before speaking. "My new case does indeed involve Mme de Livet. She hasn't seen or heard from her husband since he left Aix-les-Bains last week."

Adele sputtered and coughed for a while before clearing her throat.

"Are you all right, my dear?"

She nodded and raised her hand. After a moment she said, "I'm fine. I guessed there was something odd going on with those people, I just couldn't put my finger on it."

"Something odd, you say? Well, perhaps. At any rate, we're both tired, so I'll be brief. You have already told me about your encounters with the baroness in detail, including her inappropriate invitation, your refusal, and her apology. She said the invitation was the baron's idea, but you told me you never saw him while you were in Aix-les-Bains. That's correct, isn't it?"

"Yes, I can't recall seeing him at all."

Achille nodded and scratched his beard for a moment before continuing. "How would the baron have known that you were at the hotel *prior* to the baroness greeting you in the lobby?"

Adele thought for a moment. "I didn't notice him when we arrived, but perhaps he saw me?"

"That's possible. Anyway, it's quite a coincidence that you all happened to be in Aix-les-Bains at the same time and in the same hotel."

"Do you suspect they planned the meeting?"

Achille sipped his cognac and shook his head. "I don't know. It may be of no consequence." He remained silent for a moment before saying, "The baroness was tearful and somewhat distraught when she came to see me, but I have the impression her marriage is not exactly a love match. I'd like your opinion—from a woman's perspective."

"She said he was vulgar, a parvenu. I got the distinct impression that she married him for his money and possibly against her wishes."

Achille nodded his agreement. "There may be even more to it than that. From what she told me I gather the baron bought her father's estate and ancient name; one assumes she was part of the bargain."

Adele shook her head in disapproval of such a mercenary arrangement. "How awful."

Achille finished his cognac. He was so quiet that for a moment Adele thought he had dozed off. Then he asked, "I assume you're familiar with the stories about the Marquise de Brinvilliers and her lover, Sainte-Croix?" Achille brought up the notorious poisoners from the court of Louis XIV, the subjects of a popular novel by Alexandre Dumas, *père*.

"Of course, my dear; everyone knows about them."

"Do you think Madame de Brinvilliers murdered for love or for money?"

"I believe she did it for both."

"Yes, I suppose you're right. Now, again from a woman's perspective, do you suspect Mme de Livet has a lover?"

Adele smiled slyly and replied without hesitation, "I'd be surprised if she didn't."

Achille pulled his watch from his pocket and sighed. "I've a five o'clock appointment with my friend Rousseau."

"Oh no, Achille. What does *he* want?"

He shook his head sadly. "God only knows, my dear."

5

ROUSSEAU'S WAY

A chille arrived at the entrance to the Sainte-Chapelle at five A.M. sharp. He displayed his tricolor badge to the guard on duty. The man snapped to attention and saluted.

"Has Inspector Rousseau arrived?" Achille asked.

"Yes, M. Lefebvre. He's waiting for you inside."

Achille entered the nave that was, at that early hour, lit only by a few sputtering candles. His footsteps echoed throughout the dark vaulted interior. The ancient royal chapel slept peacefully; at dawn, it would awaken with a burst of multicolored radiance, rays of sunshine streaming down through its vast expanse of stained glass.

Halfway up the corridor Achille made out a hulking form half-hidden within the shadows of the dado arcade. Rousseau emerged from the penumbra.

"Good morning, Chief Inspector."

"Good morning, Rousseau. How goes it with you?"

"Not bad, Professor. And with you?"

"I can't complain, my friend, and if I did no one would give a damn."

Rousseau laughed; a deep, descending rumble that filled the chapel like the pedal point tones on an organ. "Aren't you afraid you'll go to hell for swearing in church?"

Achille smiled. "Swearing is the least of my sins. Now I imagine something must be very important to get you out of bed this early. What's the problem?"

Rousseau turned serious. "My men have been tailing Giraud and Breton, a couple of Moreau's pals. They're out for revenge. The *racaille* boast about it all over Montmartre."

Achille shrugged it off. "A couple of punks pissing in the wind. It's always the same after an execution."

"No, Achille, this time it's different. I've been around a lot longer than you have and I've seen it all. I tell you, these guys mean business. And they're armed. Giraud carries a Lefaucheux, and Breton has an Apache revolver."

Achille was familiar with both weapons. The Lefaucheux was the old army pinfire model, obsolete but still serviceable; the Apache revolver was a nasty combination of brass knuckles, knife, and pepperbox pistol, effective only at close range. Had it not been for Rousseau's "these guys mean business" warning, Achille would have remained nonchalant. Under the circumstances, he was not too proud to ask the veteran for advice.

"Thanks, Rousseau. What do you suggest I do?"

"Do you still carry your Chamelot-Delvigne?"

Achille patted a bulge underneath his frock coat. "Always, except when I go to bed."

Rousseau grinned in approval. "That's good. My men will keep shadowing those guys. If they try anything funny, we'll bring them in. And it wouldn't hurt if you didn't go anywhere without a good man to watch your back. You could also detail a couple of detectives to keep an eye on your home." Rousseau paused a moment before adding: "Of course, it would be much simpler to handle the problem *my way*."

Achille knew what Rousseau's *way* entailed. Rousseau's men would pick up Giraud and Breton to bring them in for questioning. The suspects would resist arrest or attempt to escape and be killed in the process. Case closed, no questions asked, and a powerful message delivered on the streets: Don't mess around with Rousseau and Lefebvre.

Achille considered the possibilities before answering. "I appreciate your concern, but I think I'll follow your initial suggestion."

Rousseau nodded. "All right, Professor. I understand. But let me tell you a little story before you make your final decision. Years ago, I had a friend. We grew up on the streets of Belleville, joined the force at the same time, and hung out together. He was a good cop, and like you, he had a wife and kids. Things went well for him. He was up for promotion to sergeant when the war broke out. He did his duty and remained at his post. The Communards lynched him in '71. I saw what they did to him, and when the army retook the Butte, I had my revenge. Now, I have no friends. But I know a few people whose lives might be worth preserving. I put you in that category." Rousseau eyed Achille intensely while waiting for a reply.

Achille knew the story about Rousseau's friend, and he realized that the streetwise detective's longevity seemed proof of Machiavelli's maxim: *It is far safer to be feared than loved if you cannot be both*. But Achille wanted to be loved by honest Parisians of all classes while at the same time being feared by the criminals who threatened the people he was sworn to protect.

Rousseau respected his former partner, but he thought Achille's scrupulousness unrealistic, if not downright foolish.

"You're probably right, but for the time being I think I'll handle this one by the book."

Rousseau shook his head. "I knew you'd say that. At least I tried. Anyway, you'll find this useful." Rousseau reached beneath his coat and removed a couple of envelopes. "Here's what we have on Giraud and Breton, along with their photographs and detailed descriptions."

Achille took the files. "Thanks, my friend. By the way, before you go, I have a new case that might interest you."

"Why should I be interested?"

"Have you heard of the Baron Le Noir de Livet?"

"Of course, but my beat involves subversives and terrorists, not sporting millionaires."

"Well, this sporting millionaire has gone missing, and just before he disappeared he had a serious dustup involving a couple of Russian notables and an Englishman. I thought your Okhrana contact might have something on the Russians and perhaps on the English gentleman, too." Achille referred to the Russian secret agents stationed in Paris who on occasion worked covertly with Rousseau's political brigade.

"Hmm, I see. I could set up a meeting with Orlovsky. I know he wants to maintain good relations with you, and he owes us for saving his ass in the Hanged Man case."

"Thanks, Rousseau; please do. And thanks again for the tip."

"Think nothing of it, Professor. I'm sure you'd do the same for me."

"Of course. By the way, I noticed you're employing Duroc. I hope he's improved his surveillance skills?"

Rousseau frowned. "Don't be too hard on him. He made a mistake, and I gave him a second chance. He's grateful, and loyal to a fault. Loyalty's a rare and precious commodity nowadays, don't you think?"

Achille nodded. "Yes—yes, it is. Good morning, Rousseau."

"*Au revoir*, Professor. And never forget: To survive in this game you need brains, balls, a trusty weapon, and eyes in the back of your head."

<hr />

Achille returned to his office where he studied the files Rousseau had provided. He had thought about having a real breakfast that morning but settled for coffee and a cigarette.

Giraud and Breton were down-and-outers with several arrests each for vagrancy, petty theft, and minor disturbances. They had met Moreau at the Bateau-Lavoir, a ramshackle flophouse on the Rue Ravignan that had been nicknamed for its resemblance to the laundry boats on the Seine. Now radicalized, the pair operated on the fringe of the anarchist movement. Achille pitied them, but they were dangerous and he did not take them lightly. He rang for his clerk.

"Go to the detectives' room and fetch Sergeant Adam."

Adam was the best shadow and toughest cop in the brigade, a younger, leaner version of Rousseau. He knocked on Achille's door and entered.

"Good morning, M. Lefebvre."

"Good morning, Adam. Take a seat. I've a job for you."

Adam sat across from his chief. Achille handed him the files.

"Do you recognize these individuals?"

Adam examined the photographs. "Yes, Chief. Breton and Giraud—a couple of loud-mouthed bums. Moreau's pals. Since the execution, they've been stirring up trouble in Montmartre."

"I just got a tip from Inspector Rousseau. These two are plotting to assassinate me. Have you heard that?"

Adam paused a moment before answering. "There've been rumors, Chief."

"I see. Well, now we have it on good authority. I want you to set up a security plan and pick some men for the detail. I think you're the best man for the job."

"Thank you, Chief. I'll work up a plan and have it on your desk by lunchtime."

"Good. Please coordinate with Rousseau. He already has men shadowing the would-be assassins. Alert our friend Sergeant Rodin. He monitors all the criminals in Montmartre and Pigalle. And I'd like to employ Le Boudin's *chiffoniers*, too. They're my loyal eyes and ears on the street."

"Very well, Chief. Is there anything else?"

"No, Adam; you may go."

The sergeant hesitated. Achille stared at him.

"Why are you still here? Is there something on your mind?"

Adam leaned forward and lowered his voice. "Pardon me, Monsieur. Just give the word and we'll make those two disappear. No trouble, and no one will blame you."

He recalled his conversation with Rousseau. Adam's suggestion offended Achille's fine sense of justice, but he would not condemn one of his most loyal and capable subordinates. Instead, he replied with a mild rebuke. "I know you mean well, Adam, but that's not the way I want to begin my tenure as chief."

Adam looked down at his hands. "I'm sorry, M. Lefebvre. I hope you'll forget—"

Achille broke in: "It's already forgotten. Now, you'd better get started on that plan."

After Adam left, Achille finished his coffee and lit another cigarette. He leaned back in his chair and thought, *Life might be simpler if we did things Rousseau's way. But could we still distinguish right from wrong?*

⌘

The de Livet mansion had a modern kitchen with immaculate white-tiled walls, linoleum flooring, two cast-iron sinks with hot and cold running water, electric and gas lighting, a massive oak icebox, and a spotless coal-burning stove. Light and fresh air streamed in through sash windows and a screened back door that led to the garden.

Shortly before noon, Legros leaned back against a marble countertop, his arms folded and a smile on his face; he gazed fondly at the charming subject of his final interrogation. Mignonette, a seventeen-year-old upstairs maid, sat on a small wooden chair facing Legros.

The young detective's casual, flirtatious approach was not all for his own amusement; the girl had until recently shared a room with Manuela Otero and perhaps had received secrets from the now seriously ill young woman. Moreover, he figured Mignonette was the type who might have caught her master's eye; perhaps the baron had employed her for his pleasure. In that regard, he hoped she would prove careless enough to reveal a confidence that might be useful to the case.

Unfortunately, after more than a half hour of questioning, the girl had provided nothing of consequence. In fact, Mignonette was enjoying herself immensely. The friendly interrogation made for a nice break in her routine, and she welcomed the handsome detective's attention. Rather than giving brief, direct answers to his questions, she digressed, chattering about things she liked to do on her day off, her favorite amusements, her tastes in food, entertainment, and so forth.

Legros was patient, but he figured it was about time to put an end to it. The doctor had been in to see Otero early that morning. Legros wanted to ask the baroness about the maid's condition and any remedies the doctor may have prescribed.

A scream interrupted the interview.

Mignonette stopped babbling and jumped up from her chair. "Oh, M. Legros, that sounds like Madame."

Legros frowned. "Wait here. I'll see what's going on."

He ran out into the hallway, which was in a state of confusion. The baroness stood by the main stairway, sobbing uncontrollably. The servants surrounded their mistress, attempting to calm her and determine the cause of distress.

The circle of domestics parted to admit the detective. Legros spoke firmly. "Please, Madame de Livet, control yourself. Tell me what has happened."

Madame wiped her eyes with a handkerchief and cried, "Oh, how awful. It's Manuela. I think . . . I believe she's dying. God help us, she may already be dead."

Legros glanced around at the servants. "One of you, take me to her immediately. The rest remain with Madame."

The English footman led the detective up four flights of stairs to the maid's tiny dormer room in the servants' quarters. As they mounted the landing, they inhaled a sharp, nauseating stench. The footman retched and covered his mouth with a handkerchief.

Legros entered the airless room first. Manuela Otero was sprawled across the mattress, one limp arm hanging over the bedstead. The sheets were soaked with vomit.

He checked her for signs of life and made note of her rapid decline: shallow respiration, dilated pupils, and faint, irregular pulse. Legros's eyes turned from the dying woman to a brown medicine bottle resting on the edge of a bedside table. He read the label: *Tincture of Aconite.*

Legros spoke urgently. "She's alive—barely. Have you a telephone?"

"Yes, Monsieur. There's one in the sitting room."

"Very well. I'm going to telephone the Hôtel-Dieu to send an ambulance. Then I'll notify police headquarters. I charge you to guard the door to this room. Touch nothing inside and admit no one, including Madame de Livet, without my permission. Do you understand?"

"Yes, Monsieur, I understand."

Legros left the bedroom and ran downstairs.

⁓

Achille considered a telegram that had made its way to his desk. Inspector Forestier would arrive at the Gare de Lyon at four P.M. that afternoon. Apparently, the Chambéry Police Commissary considered the missing baron case important enough to warrant a trip to Paris. Achille was about to notify his clerk of his plans to meet Forestier at the station when the telephone rang.

Achille lifted the receiver and recognized Legros's voice on the line. Legros described Otero's symptoms, referred to the tincture of aconite, and said he had called an ambulance to take the poor woman to the Hôtel-Dieu. He had little hope of her surviving the trip to the hospital.

"Very well, Étienne. Do you have someone guarding Otero's room?"

"Yes, Chief."

"Did you notify the attending physician?"

"Yes; Dr. Levasseur. He'll meet me at the hospital."

"Good. I'm sending a couple of detectives to examine the scene. I'm also going to the laboratory to consult Masson about aconite poisoning. Telephone me as soon as you arrive at the hospital and I'll meet you. However, regardless of what happens, I want to greet Forestier at the station. He's coming up from Chambéry to discuss the case, so you may need to carry on for a while without me."

"Understood, Chief."

Achille hung up, left his office, and stopped at his clerk's desk with orders to notify the stationmaster that Chief Inspector Lefebvre would meet Inspector Forestier's train. He also requested the stationmaster keep the visitor occupied in case M. Lefebvre came a bit late.

He left the clerk and walked down the corridor to the detectives' room. There, he assigned two men to go to the de Livet mansion to secure the scene and gather evidence, and then he proceeded on to the Palais de Justice.

He passed through a long hallway filled with lawyers smoking cigars and cigarettes as they milled around in groups or hid in dark corners to confer with their clients. His destination, the police laboratory, was located at the top of a dimly lit, secluded stairway.

Achille entered through a pair of swinging doors; his eyes scanned the premises, searching for the familiar figure of a gnomish individual in a white lab coat. After a moment, he spotted the chemist seated at the end of a long table laden with bubbling alembics, retorts and other scientific paraphernalia. Masson held a test tube over a flaming Bunsen burner, intently observing a chemical reaction. Achille watched respectfully at a distance, until the chemist completed his test and recorded his findings in a notebook.

Achille walked down to the other end of the laboratory and greeted the chemist. "Good day, Masson. Busy as always, I see."

Masson turned his head, lowered his glasses from his forehead, and smiled. "Ah, Chief Inspector Lefebvre. To what do I owe this honor?"

"I need your expert advice. I may have a witness suffering from aconite poisoning."

The chemist swung his legs around from under the table and came down from his stool. He gazed up at Achille, the top of the chemist's balding head barely reaching the level of the chief inspector's chest. "Aconite, you say? That's interesting. What can you tell me?"

"Not much, I'm afraid. The subject is presently on her way to the Hôtel-Dieu. Legros doesn't expect her to live, but then he's no doctor." Achille referred to the medicine bottle and then gave the symptoms as Legros had described them on the telephone.

"The symptoms could indicate aconite poisoning. As for the amount, five milliliters, or one fluid dram, of the tincture can be fatal."

"But I believe doctors prescribe it in minute quantities in solution, do they not? In this case, the woman was ill with fever and had been seen by a physician."

"Indeed, it is given to patients in a febrile condition. For example, many physicians prescribe it for an acute case of *la grippe*. But of course, that would be in solution; a specified number of drops mixed in water, not the pure tincture."

"How would you determine if aconite poisoning were the proximate cause of illness or death? Is there a test?"

"The tests for the presence of aconite, or more precisely aconitine, the poisonous alkaloid obtained from the plant, are chiefly physiological; one detects a tingling and numbness when a very minute quantity is applied to the tongue or inner surface of the cheek. One can also observe the effects on laboratory animals.

"We can use the Stas-Otto method to extract the alkaloid from vomit, urine, and feces. Postmortem we can find the alkaloid in stomach contents and viscera. Of course," he added with a curious smile, "all I can do is help the doctors determine the cause of death. Whether the poison was ingested as the consequence of criminal intent, negligence, or accident is another matter."

Achille nodded. "Of course, Masson. Have you ever worked on a murder case involving aconite?"

"No, Monsieur Lefebvre. I know of only one recent case, and that was in England. I've also read of cases in India. But here in France, arsenic remains the poison of choice, as it has been since the days of Madame de Brinvilliers, Sainte-Croix, and La Voisin. *La poudre de succession*. However, as I'm sure you know, those incidents of homicidal poisoning have declined somewhat since the introduction of the Marsh test."

Achille glanced at his watch. "I anticipate the subject's arrival at the hospital shortly. I would appreciate your attendance. My clerk can notify you by telephone."

"Thank you, Monsieur; I'd very much like to attend, and of course I'll do what I can to assist in your investigation."

⧼∞⧽

Legros proved prescient; a resident physician pronounced Manuela Otero dead upon arrival at the Hôtel-Dieu. The hospital scheduled an autopsy for later that afternoon; a pathologist would perform the procedure, assisted by Dr. Levasseur. Masson would observe.

The dissecting room was a dismal, vaulted chamber. Light and air entered through large casement windows; two shaded gas lamps situated above the dissecting table provided artificial illumination. A lingering, pervasive odor of putrefaction commingled with the sharp astringency of formaldehyde and carbolic disinfectant.

A half hour prior to the postmortem, Achille and Legros met with Dr. Levasseur in the corridor outside the dissecting room. Levasseur was a tall, elegantly dressed man in his late thirties who confronted Otero's sudden death with professional sangfroid.

Achille was acutely aware of the time. He had ordered a cab to take him to the railway station, and he would leave prior to the autopsy's conclusion. He decided to use the brief hiatus to question the physician.

"Dr. Levasseur, when were you called to attend the deceased?"

"Madame de Livet contacted me three days ago, after she returned from Aix-les-Bains. I saw Mlle Otero that evening."

"What was your diagnosis?"

"I diagnosed a bad case of *la grippe*."

"What treatment did you prescribe?"

"In the initial stages, I ordered the patient to remain in bed where she was to be kept warm and quiet. As for feeding, she was given lukewarm gruel, barley water, and chamomile tea with lemon."

"Do you know who fed her?"

"I believe Madame de Livet gave orders to the cook. You can confirm that with the baroness."

"I see. Did you prescribe any medication?"

"On the first day I gave her a calomel pill as a mild purgative, but she did not tolerate it well. This morning the illness had progressed to the acute stage, so I prescribed tincture of aconite in solution to bring down the fever and ease her chest pains."

"Can you tell me the exact dosage?"

"Yes, Monsieur. I mixed fifteen drops of the tincture in six centiliters of water, and then I gave her five milliliters, or one teaspoonful, of the mixture. She was to have one teaspoonful every ten minutes for the first hour and afterward hourly for the next eight hours."

"When did you give her the first dose?"

"At nine, and I gave her a second dose ten minutes later."

"Who gave the other doses?"

"I left instructions with Madame de Livet. You'll have to ask her. I only gave the first two doses. Then I left. I'm a busy man. I had other calls to make that morning."

Achille noted a hint of irritation in the doctor's voice and manner. "I understand, Doctor. Permit me one more question. When Inspector Legros entered Mlle Otero's bedroom, he noticed a bottle of tincture of aconite on the bedside table. Where did you leave the mixture?"

"It was in an unmarked brown medicine bottle next to the tincture."

Achille glanced at Legros, who frowned and shook his head in response to the doctor's reference to an unmarked bottle. "Thank you, Dr. Levasseur; you've been very helpful. Now I suppose you want to prepare for the autopsy, so I won't detain you. However, we may require your presence for further questioning. I trust you do not have any plans to leave Paris in the near future?"

The doctor's face reddened, but he remained composed. "No immediate plans, Monsieur Lefebvre. I have an active practice that requires my constant attention. Now, if you'll excuse me." The doctor bowed curtly, turned, and entered the dissecting room.

Achille smiled knowingly at Legros. "Touchy fellows, these physicians, especially when there's any implication they bungled the job. At any rate, after you finish up here you'll return to the de Livet mansion. The detectives must search for the other bottle, if they haven't already found it, and you must interview everyone, beginning with Madame. Who gave Otero her medication? Who was in or around the sickroom? How do they account for themselves during the period in question? Can you handle it?"

"Yes, Chief; no problem."

"Good." Achille took his watch from his waistcoat pocket. "Not much time, Étienne. Forestier's train will arrive in little more than one hour."

At that moment, Achille and Legros noticed an orderly wheeling a gurney bearing a corpse covered in a white sheet. Masson and the pathologist followed close behind.

"Here she comes, poor thing. Let's go in now."

6

THE INFORMATIVE M. FORESTIER

The express from Chambéry chugged up the track into the vast iron-and-glass train shed. Passengers, guards, and baggage-toting porters bustled up and down the lengthy concrete island platform. Locomotives shuttled back and forth, belching soot and hissing forth clouds of steam. Whistles shrieked, and signal horns blasted warnings.

Achille and Sergeant Adam passed through a gate that separated the main concourse from the train shed. A brigadier detailed for added protection met them. The three officers made their way through the crowd as the train came to a screeching halt.

Guards hustled to open carriage doors and assist passengers onto the platform. Achille had a good description of Inspector Forestier. He scanned the detraining passengers; after a moment, he spotted a portly man in his fifties carrying a carpetbag. He gestured to the other officers and said, "That's Forestier."

They approached the provincial detective, who glanced around with a bewildered look as he waited on the platform.

Achille walked up to the visitor and greeted him. "Welcome to Paris, Inspector Forestier."

Forestier's brown eyes widened; he looked up furtively. His heavily moustached upper lip twitched. "M. Lefebvre?" he ventured in a voice so hushed it could barely be heard over the voluble throng and chuffing engines.

"Yes, I'm Lefebvre, and these gentlemen are my companions for the day, Sergeant Adam and Brigadier Roche."

Forestier relaxed somewhat. After they had exchanged greetings, Achille made a suggestion.

"You've arrived on a perfect autumn day. Your hotel's a short walk from the station, and there's a first-rate brasserie across the street. After your long journey, I'm sure you'd welcome a sandwich and a glass or two of excellent beer. We may even be able to conclude our business without a trip to headquarters."

Forestier reverted to his furtive manner and tone. "Do you . . . do you think it would be safe, Monsieur?"

Achille smiled reassuringly. "With these gentlemen watching out for us, it's perfectly safe."

Forestier agreed, with some trepidation. The inspector's jitters amused Adam and the brigadier. They left the station and crossed the Boulevard Diderot in the direction of a brasserie situated in the angle where the Rue de Lyon intersected the boulevard. There they found two adjacent sidewalk tables beneath the shade of a bright red awning. Achille and Forestier ordered beer and sandwiches while Adam and Roche kept their heads clear and their eyes sharp, on the watch for Giraud and Breton.

A mild breeze shook the leaves of trees lining the boulevard; shadows of swaying, sunlit branches flickered on the pavement as if projected by a magic lantern. The natural autumn fragrance interfused with the scent of tobacco smoke drifting from the patrons' cigars, cigarettes, and pipes and pungent cooking odors flowing out through the open brasserie doors. A persistent murmur of conversation mixed with the rumble and clatter of horses' hooves and ironshod wheels on paving stones and a multitude of boots and shoes beating up and down the sidewalk.

Charmed by his host's conviviality and satiated with good food and drink, the recently agitated detective drifted into a sea of postprandial tranquility, so much so that he seemed to forget the urgency of his visit. Achille noticed the signs and threw Forestier a line to draw him back to reality.

"This has been pleasant, M. Forestier, but I suppose it's time we discussed the case."

Forestier came to attention, like a sleeping soldier shaken back to consciousness by his sergeant. "Oh yes, of course, M. Lefebvre. I have important papers for you, but before I hand them over I can tell you the results of my investigation." His words implied that he was about to turn sole jurisdiction of the case over to Paris, a hint that was not lost on Achille.

Forestier began with the baroness's report and his subsequent questioning of witnesses. His first reference was to Bonnet. He repeated the manservant's story, including the duel, at which point Achille asked a question.

"Did you ask Prince Papkov about the fight?"

"Yes, M. Lefebvre. The prince mentioned an affaire d'honneur that the gentlemen settled agreeably."

"You didn't pursue it further?"

Forestier shrugged. "Why should I, Monsieur? No one was hurt, and they shook hands."

"The age of chivalry is dead."

"Pardon me, Monsieur Lefebvre?"

"I'm sorry. I quoted an observation made a century ago by a British statesman in regard to our Revolution."

"Oh well, that's the English for you. As the Emperor Napoleon said, they're a nation of shopkeepers."

"It's conceivable the emperor meant it as a compliment to their enterprise, industry, and commercial success."

Forestier smiled. "Surely you're joking, Monsieur?"

Achille nodded. "Perhaps. At any rate, I apologize for the digression. Do you have any information about the seconds? Bonnet mentioned a Russian officer and an Englishman named Sims."

"The Russian officer is Colonel Mukhin. He's a military attaché assigned to the embassy here in Paris."

Achille stared at Forestier in stunned silence while thoughts of Rousseau and his Okhrana contact, M. Orlovsky, and claims of diplomatic immunity raced through his head. After an awkward moment he asked, "Did you interview the colonel?"

"No, Monsieur. The colonel left for Paris on the same train as the baron."

"Bonnet said nothing to me about that."

"Nor to me. I assume he did not know. According to the prince, the colonel had already planned to leave the day of the . . . dispute. He left shortly after the baron and Bonnet, but he did not go to the same station. Instead of going down to Aix-les-Bains, which is within a few kilometers of the prince's villa, the colonel and one of the prince's servants drove up to Annecy in a fast gig."

"How far is Annecy from the prince's villa?"

"About thirty kilometers to the north. It's the next stop on the railway line. He would have boarded the train there. The baron was on the express, which arrived in Annecy at approximately twelve fifty."

"I see. As I recall, Bonnet said he and the baron arrived at the station in Aix-les-Bains at eleven and the baron boarded the train at noon. If the colonel left the prince's villa shortly after the baron and Bonnet, and he traveled in a fast gig, he ought to have had enough time to catch the train at Annecy. Have you confirmed this with witnesses at the railway stations?"

"Yes, Monsieur. I have the names and addresses of witnesses who saw the baron board the train in Aix-les-Bains, and others who identified the colonel at Annecy. Those identifications were based on descriptions I received of both gentlemen from the baroness, the prince, and Bonnet."

"What about Sims? Did you question him?"

"No, Monsieur. According to the prince, M. Sims left for Monte Carlo on the twenty-fifth."

"I see. So he went to Monaco the same day the baron and the colonel took the express to Paris. Have you any information about the Englishman?"

"The prince told me the gentleman resides in London."

"Oh, that's very helpful."

"Excuse me, Monsieur?"

"An idle comment; forgive me, Inspector. Did the prince say where in London?"

Forestier glanced down at his empty beer glass. "Uh, not precisely, Monsieur Lefebvre." Then he looked up with a hopeful smile. "The prince did say that Sims was a retired major in the British Army who had recently returned from India, where he had served in a regiment on the North-West Frontier."

"Well, that's good to know. But didn't you think it odd that Sims would associate with Russian notables? Have you never heard of the Great Game?"

Forestier frowned and shook his head. "The Great Game? No, I don't believe we have that at our casino. Is it like baccarat?"

Achille sighed. "Never mind, Inspector. Did the prince give you a good description of the man?"

"Yes, Monsieur; an excellent description, and it will corroborate what I got from Bonnet."

"Very well. Did you try to locate Sims?"

"Oh yes; I wired the police in Monaco."

"And what did they say?"

Forestier shook his head sadly. "They checked with the railway and all the hotels. They had no record of a recent arrival matching the name or description."

That's hardly surprising, Achille thought. "Did you question Madame de Livet's maidservant, Manuela Otero?"

"Oh . . . I planned to, but by the time I got around to it, they had left for Paris."

Achille replied with a hint of exasperation, "That's a shame, Monsieur. I fear we must do without her testimony. The woman is dead."

"How awful. Do you know the cause?"

"No, I do not. An autopsy is under way. We should know more later today."

Forestier frowned. "Good heavens, what a mess."

"Yes, indeed. Now, Inspector, is there anything else?"

"No, Monsieur Lefebvre. You'll find it all in the report I brought with me."

"May I have the documents?"

Forestier leaned forward over the table. His eyes darted around suspiciously, and his voice lowered. "You mean here and now?"

"Yes, Inspector; if you please."

Forestier reached for his carpetbag, removed a file, and handed it to Achille. "Here it is, Monsieur. I believe you'll find it in order. I discussed the matter with our *juge d'instruction*. Since the baron went missing on the train to Paris, we have concluded our preliminary investigation; the matter is now out of our jurisdiction. Therefore, we leave it in your capable hands."

That's right, get it off your desk, he thought. "Thank you, M. Forestier."

The inspector smiled with relief. "Oh, you're very welcome, M. Lefebvre. And please be assured we'll continue to cooperate with your investigation to the best of our ability."

To the best of your ability, I'm sure. Achille returned Forestier's smile. Then he gestured to the officers at the adjacent table. Adam and Roche came over.

Achille addressed Roche. "Brigadier, please escort Inspector Forestier to his hotel. Then you may return to your regular duties. Sergeant Adam and I are going back to headquarters."

Roche walked up the boulevard with Forestier; Adam hailed a cab. On the way to the Quai des Orfèvres Achille asked, "Give me your frank opinion, Adam; what did you think of M. Forestier?"

Adam hesitated before saying, "Forgive me, Chief; I think he's a provincial donkey. The man wouldn't last a week on our beat."

Achille shrugged. "Ah well; we must rely on his preliminary investigation. Let's hope he wrote an intelligible report."

⌒∞⌒

When Achille returned to his office, there were three messages waiting on his desk. The first was from Rousseau:

"Meet O., one in the morning. Cabaret de L'Enfer."

Achille muttered, "Don't these people have families?" The question was rhetorical. M. Orlovsky's "family" consisted of young women who accommodated the Russian's irregular schedule, for a price.

The second was a "call in" from Legros. Unless he received orders to the contrary, he would return to headquarters at six P.M. and have a report on the chief's desk that evening.

The third was by telephone from Fournier, lead crime reporter for *Les Amis de la Vérité*. He was inquiring about the de Livet case.

Achille closed his eyes and rubbed his aching forehead. *"Merde alors!* The press is onto it already." He disliked Fournier, but the publisher, M. Junot, dined with the prefect and remained supportive of the police. Therefore, Achille was obliged to reply, though he would say as little as possible about the case and instruct his men to do the same.

He removed his pince-nez, blinked, and rubbed his eyes. Then he scribbled a note to Adele telling her he was working all night and on into the next morning. He placed the note in an envelope and rang for his clerk, who came at once.

Achille handed the envelope to the clerk. "Have a messenger deliver this to my wife. Once you've done that, get me a large café au lait and a brioche."

"Yes, Monsieur Lefebvre. Anything else?"

"Please tell Adam I want to see him. Then telephone Magistrate Leblanc's office and ask if the *juge* is available this afternoon."

As soon as the clerk left, Achille telephoned the laboratory and asked for Masson.

"Masson here."

"Hello, Masson. This is Lefebvre. What have you got?"

"The doctors agreed that she died of respiratory failure. Whether that was the result of natural causes or aconite poisoning is an open question. I'm running tests; I should have an answer first thing in the morning, unless you need it sooner."

"Thank you, Masson; tomorrow morning will be fine."

Achille hung up. He leaned back in his chair, stared at the ceiling, and listened to the sound of a barge chugging up the Seine. Above the familiar noise of river traffic, he noticed the faint euphony of the police band rehearsing Hérold's "Zampa" overture. "That's good," he murmured. He began humming along and conducting with his pencil until a knock on the door interrupted.

The chief stopped imitating Maestro Colonne, sat upright, and said, "Enter."

Sergeant Adam came in and remained at attention, waiting for orders.

"Adam, are you familiar with the Cabaret de L'Enfer in Pigalle?"

"Yes, Chief, I am."

"Good. I have business there tonight at one o'clock—*police* business. Please detail a detective to accompany me."

"If it's all right with you, Chief, I'd like to go."

Achille stared at the sergeant for a moment. "You've been on duty all day. I don't mind if you send someone else."

"Thank you, Chief, but I'd prefer to do this myself."

Achille smiled. "All right. You can keep an eye on me from the bar, and I don't mind if you brace up with a coffee and cognac, as long as you keep your wits about you."

After Adam left, Achille murmured, "A good man." Then he turned his attention to the beginnings of a timeline and a list of suspects, cross-referencing the baron's disappearance to Otero's suspicious death.

The clerk interrupted with the coffee and brioche. Achille put aside his notes and started enjoying his snack when he remembered he had to telephone Fournier at the newspaper.

The operator put him through to the crime desk; an assistant editor said Fournier was not in the office. *Thank God*, Achille thought. "Please tell M. Fournier that Chief Inspector Lefebvre returned his call. I'm afraid I'll be unavailable for comment for the rest of the day, and tomorrow morning, too. However, I will leave instructions with my clerk, should M. Fournier wish to inquire further."

After hanging up, Achille gave his clerk the following: "If M. Fournier or any other reporters inquire about the de Livet matter, tell them there's an ongoing preliminary investigation and we have no further comment at this time." Achille asked next about M. Leblanc; the clerk said the *juge* was available all that afternoon.

With these matters attended to, Achille returned to his coffee, pastry, and case notes.

Shortly after seven P.M. Achille was still at his desk, reviewing Legros's report. Legros sat across from him, looking on anxiously. Achille glanced from the document to an empty pot and a cup half-filled with cold coffee set on his desktop amid a pile of notes.

"I read somewhere that Balzac killed himself with too much coffee," Achille mumbled.

"Pardon me, Chief. You said something about Balzac?"

Achille shook his head without answering and continued reading. After a moment: "You found the second bottle on the floor under the bed?"

"Yes, Chief."

"Unstoppered and empty?"

"Yes, Chief."

Achille nodded. "How do you think it got there?"

"Based on the position of the body on the bed, I believe Otero, in her distress, lashed out and knocked it off the bedside table."

"But what about the stopper? The fall to the floor wouldn't remove it."

"I asked about that, Chief. You'll see it in my report. The cork was left loose and could have fallen out."

Achille sighed. "A plausible explanation—or so it might seem. All right, Étienne, let's recapitulate." He gathered some notes, including the doctor's prescription, adjusted his pince-nez, and turned up the screw on his desk lamp. "At nine, Doctor Levasseur mixed fifteen drops of aconite in six centiliters of water and gave Otero her first dose of the mixture. He gave her a second dose ten minutes later and then left for another house call. He gave instructions to Mme de Livet; Otero was to have five milliliters, or one teaspoonful, of the solution every ten minutes for the first hour and afterward hourly for the next eight hours.

"According to my calculations, each dosage contained no more than one drop of the tincture, which according to Masson is quite safe. I also asked Masson about the calomel pill the doctor administered the previous day. Again, given in such a small amount it ought to have done no harm." Achille paused a moment before asking, "You said the bottle you found on the floor was empty. Could you tell if any spilled onto the floor?"

"No, Chief, I'm afraid not."

"What about the bottle of tincture? How much was left?"

"Very little. A few milliliters."

"Why do you think the doctor left any of the pure tincture? He had already mixed enough solution for the complete dosage."

Legros was silent for a moment. Then he replied hesitantly, "Perhaps . . . perhaps he left it in case the solution was spilled accidentally and they needed to mix more?"

Achille shook his head. "I suppose that's an explanation—or an excuse. Frankly, if I were a doctor I wouldn't trust a layperson with deadly poison. Can you think of another reason?"

Legros paused ominously before saying, "Negligence?"

"Ah, that's an ugly accusation to level at a distinguished physician, but it might be the truth. Do you recall his irritable manner when I questioned him, insisting on how busy he was? I know the type, Étienne. He's a society doctor who collects big fees from wealthy patients. He probably didn't want to waste much of his precious time on a servant. He gave the poor woman a couple of doses and left in a hurry. Now, what do you make of that?"

"He . . . he forgot all about the bottle of tincture?"

Achille smiled wryly. "That's a good guess. And if he did, he *knows* what he did was wrong. What's more, he thinks *we* know, and that gives us an advantage if at some point we need to put the screws on him. At any rate, make a note of it. Now, you and your detectives made a thorough search of the bedroom, the landing, and the staircase. You found nothing of interest besides the second bottle?"

"No, Chief, assuming you didn't want us to look for fingerprints?"

Achille frowned. "Alas, you assumed correctly. Unless we find something obvious, like bloody prints on a murder weapon, fingerprints won't be of use to us. I'm taking you into my confidence on this matter. We were lucky in the Ménard case. Galton's system is brilliant, but it remains incomplete. Moreover, I've yet to perfect a reliable means of lifting and preserving latent prints at the crime scene, and my present duties leave me no time for experimentation. But there's more to it than that, and this must remain between you and me.

"M. Bertillon's anthropometric system of identification has achieved universal acceptance, which brings great credit to our prefecture. As a result, our chief of records is no longer as receptive to fingerprinting as he once was. As newly appointed chief of detectives, I'd be risking not just my reputation but also the honor of our brigade if I insisted on using such a novel and unproven method. No, Étienne, I'm afraid that fingerprinting, like telephonic communications and motorized transport, are early shoots that won't reach full bloom until the next century."

"I understand, Chief."

"Good. Now let's get back to the timeline and your interviews. You arrived at the de Livet mansion at ten and continued questioning servants. Just before noon, you were in the kitchen conducting your final interview when you heard Mme de Livet scream. According to the prescription, Otero should have received seven doses of solution from nine through ten, followed by another at eleven with the next dose due at noon. Therefore, if her death were the result of aconite poisoning, she would have received the fatal dose between eleven and twelve. Do you agree?"

"Yes, Chief. I used that timeline when I returned this afternoon to question the baroness and the servants. Mme de Livet and the cook were the only members of the household who gave the medicine to Otero. The cook administered the dose at eleven and the baroness was to do the same at noon. According to the baroness, it was when she went up to the servants' quarters to administer the medicine that she discovered Otero in extreme distress."

"I see; just a moment, please." He studied a list of the entire household, including the baroness. In addition to Mme de Livet; her deceased maidservant; and the baron's man, Bonnet, there was a housekeeper, two footmen, an upstairs maid, a downstairs maid, a cook, two scullery maids, a coachman, and a gardener. Only the baroness and Bonnet were not seen between the eleven A.M. dosage and the baroness's alarming scream.

"The baroness said that during the time in question she was either in her boudoir or the baron's study. But none of the servants could corroborate that?"

"That's correct, Chief. Bonnet said he was out on foot, running errands for the baroness."

"But he was back, in the main hallway, when the servants gathered to see what the commotion was about?"

"Yes, Chief. I saw him when I came from the kitchen."

"None of the servants observed him leave the house or return?"

"That's correct. Only the baroness saw him leave to go on his errands. No one saw him return."

"What were his errands?"

"He posted some letters and then went to make a few small household purchases."

"All right. You can have the detectives follow up and make inquiries on Bonnet's route."

"Yes, Chief."

"And no one saw any person or persons going up to, or coming down from, Otero's room?"

"Yes, Chief."

Achille nodded and scratched his beard. "When I last spoke to Masson, he said the onset of symptoms in cases of aconite poisoning is very rapid, a matter of minutes. However, he's yet to determine whether an overdose caused her death. We won't know that until tomorrow morning.

"Based on what we've gathered thus far, Otero might have ingested a fatal dose sometime between eleven and noon; let's narrow it to eleven thirty and noon due to the fast action of the poison. It might have been the result of accident, negligence, suicide, or murder. And if there is any criminal culpability, we haven't sufficient evidence pointing to any particular person or persons. Is that your opinion?"

"Yes, Chief. However, if either the baroness or Bonnet had a motive for murder, they seem to be the only members of the household who had the opportunity."

"That's a big *if*, Étienne."

"I know, Chief. But there is a pretty maid. She shared a room with Otero and they were very close. When I left the mansion with the ambulance, she ran up to me, slipped me a note, and dashed away before I could speak to her. She obviously didn't wish to be seen. She wants to meet me at the Eiffel Tower the day after tomorrow. I think I might get something from her."

Achille smiled. "A 'pretty maid,' you say? Well, I'm sure whatever you *get* will all be in the line of duty."

Legros blushed. "Of course, Chief. It's for the case."

Achille nodded. "Very well, Étienne. At any rate, I've a meeting at one this morning that might prove productive. I'm going to see our Russian friend, M. Orlovsky." Achille briefed Legros on the information he had received from Forestier.

After Achille brought Legros up to date, the young detective said, "The Russian military attaché and the baron were on the same train to Paris? I'll need to follow up on that."

"Indeed you will. Get everything you can from the Railway Squad. First, we need to determine where the baron and colonel detrained. If their destination was Paris, they should have arrived at the Gare de Lyon. I want to know where each of them went from there, and when."

"Yes, Chief. Is there anything else?"

"One more thing. I had a chat with Magistrate Leblanc this afternoon. He needn't be actively involved with the investigation at this stage, but we should keep him apprised of the situation." Achille glanced up at the wall clock. "It's late, Étienne. Go home and get some rest."

"Yes, Chief. Thank you." Legros was about to leave when he added, "Pardon me, Chief. You said you had a meeting at one in the morning. When will you sleep?"

Achille laughed mordantly. "Didn't anyone tell you when you signed on for this job? We of the Sûreté are like Satan. We never sleep."

7

ORLOVSKY'S WORLD

A t one A.M., Achille and Sergeant Adam passed through the demon's mouth doorframe of the Cabaret de L'Enfer. The stage Mephistopheles attendant gave them the customary greeting: "Enter and be damned."

Achille replied, "You have no idea, my friend."

The theatrical devil raised a painted eyebrow. "We're honored by your presence, M. Lefebvre."

Achille smiled wryly and put a finger to his lips. "Thanks, but I'm here incognito."

The doorman leaned forward and lowered his voice. "Of course, Monsieur. But I fear there are no secrets in hell."

A place without secrets hardly seems the proper venue for a spymaster, Achille thought. Orlovsky chose to hold court in the demimonde, a milieu in which he seemed to proclaim his presence with characteristic audacity. However, M. Orlovsky was one of those camouflaged insects that blends into its surroundings and thus remains hidden in plain sight.

Achille and Adam paused at the threshold before plunging into the inferno. Their eyes scanned the grotto-like room with its two rows of tables lining a narrow aisle that led to the bar. Red-painted, high-relief plaster figures of the naked damned and their demon tormentors writhed overhead and along both walls. Colored electric lights created the effect of consuming flames; steam hissing from strategically placed pipes commingled with a yellowish tobacco haze to coalesce in a hellish atmosphere. A diabolical pair of fiddlers serenaded the lost souls with a scratchy rendition of Liszt's "Mephisto Waltz."

At the end of one line of tables, in the dark recesses of the interior near the bar, Orlovsky sat, flanked by his constant companions, Apolline and Aurore. The painted young women wore the scarlet silk dresses and plumed hats of their trade. They smiled and whispered dirty jokes and gossip while toying with the perfumed ringlets that flowed over the back of their master's high starched collar. Orlovsky responded with vague indifference as he puffed on a long cigarette. Suddenly, he pushed one girl aside, reached into his waistcoat pocket, and pulled out his watch. He glanced toward the entrance and immediately recognized the chief inspector.

Achille smiled and nodded at the face that greeted him, a powdered and painted visage adorned with a waxed jet-black Imperial that gave its bearer the appearance of a louche caricature of the late Emperor Napoleon III.

The detectives proceeded up the aisle just as the two young women left their patron's table. The *poules* averted their eyes and stepped aside to make way for the police officers. Achille walked on without betraying any sign of recognition. Apolline was one of his paid informers, and he sometimes wondered what the Russian would do if he learned the truth of her working relationship with the Sûreté.

Achille took a seat across from Orlovsky; Adam continued on to the bar. The detective and the spymaster exchanged greetings. Then Orlovsky said:

"Would you care for a drink? I recommend the Hellfire and Brimstone."

"Yes, thank you. That's just the ticket."

Orlovsky smiled. He caught the attention of a waiter and signaled for two coffees with cognac. After placing the order, he took a moment to scrutinize Adam. "You've brought one of your men with you. He looks very fit. The sort of fellow you'd want on your side in a tight spot."

"Yes, he is."

"I see. Rousseau told me about your problem. Why bother with the *racaille*? Let Rousseau deal with them. Or if you're squeamish, pick them up and hold them till things cool down."

"I'm not squeamish, Monsieur. We haven't enough evidence to arrest them—yet. We're unpopular in certain quarters, more so since the execution. Pretextual arrests would only stir up more trouble on the streets, in the radical press and among the opposition in the Chamber of Deputies. We have no law against loose talk. Paris isn't Moscow or Petersburg. People here think they have rights."

Orlovsky laughed. "They *think* they have rights. That's very amusing, M. Lefebvre."

Lefebvre responded to the sarcastic comment with an icy stare.

The waiter came with the drinks. Achille and Orlovsky broke off their conversation until the man was out of earshot.

Orlovsky took a sip of his coffee and cognac before continuing. "Forgive me, Monsieur. My government and I owe you a debt of gratitude for your brilliant work in the Hanged Man case. Were it not for the clandestine nature of our business, we would have officially recognized your efforts and awarded a high decoration. Now, how may I be of service?"

"I assume Rousseau told you I'm looking for M. Le Noir de Livet?"

"Yes, indeed."

"I believe you know the gentleman—socially."

"Yes—as do you, Monsieur."

"I've come across him once or twice. We're barely acquainted."

Orlovsky raised his dyed and plucked eyebrows. "Is that so? I understand your wife spent some time with Madame de Livet last week in Aix-les-Bains."

"My wife had two brief encounters with the baroness, both of them initiated by Mme de Livet. The baron was not present on either occasion, and he is the subject of my investigation. May I continue?"

"Pardon me. Please do."

"When did you last see M. de Livet?"

"I believe that was about two weeks ago, at Le Chabanais." Le Chabanais was the most famous and fashionable brothel in Paris. The place catered to celebrities both domestic and foreign, including the Prince of Wales, several prominent members of the Jockey Club, and two of Achille's artistic acquaintances, the writer Maupassant and the painter Toulouse-Lautrec.

"Did you speak to him?"

"No, I did not. Gentlemen go there for the ladies, not for one another. At times, recognizing a fellow patron and engaging him in conversation could be bad form, *n'est-ce pas?*"

Achille drank some coffee and cognac. He did not appreciate the Russian's sarcasm. Achille was tired, and he feared it was showing. He decided to avoid Orlovsky's banter and get to the point. "Yes, yes, of course," he replied. "You seem to be informed about matters in Aix-les-Bains. Are you aware of the dispute between Prince Papkov and M. de Livet?"

"Yes."

"Do you know the details?"

"Yes, I do."

"Will you please tell me what you know?"

Orlovsky repeated the same story about the card game, the duel, and the settlement.

"Thank you. Did you know that Colonel Mukhin was observed at Annecy, boarding the same train that M. de Livet had boarded at Aix-les-Bains?"

"I've discussed the incident at Aix-les-Bains with the colonel. He told me he left the prince's villa following the affaire d'honneur. However, the colonel said nothing about traveling on the same train as M. de Livet."

"Did the colonel arrive in Paris at the Gare de Lyon?"

"Yes, he did."

"Did he notice the baron at the terminus?"

"No, he did not. Obviously, they were not in the same compartment on the train, and they may not have been in the same carriage. At any rate, the Gare de Lyon is a big, busy place, and the colonel was not on the lookout for the baron."

"The baron was carrying a large amount of cash in a Gladstone bag. Did you know that?"

"Yes, Monsieur, the colonel told me about the baron's winnings. Apparently, M. de Livet had an extraordinary run of luck at the card tables. Perhaps he was waylaid by a thief?"

"Perhaps." Achille paused for a moment before continuing: "Where did the colonel go from the station?"

"He went directly to our embassy on the Rue de Grenelle."

"Did he hire a cab, or was there a coach waiting for him at the station?"

"There was a coach from the embassy."

"Has he seen the baron at any time since he left the prince's villa?"

"No, Monsieur. He assured me he has not."

Achille smiled and took a moment to savor his drink. He was a devotee of chess, an accomplished fencer, and a master of savate. He decided it was time for a feint to probe Orlovsky's defenses.

"Are the prince and Colonel Mukhin old comrades?"

A network of perplexed wrinkles spread beneath Orlovsky's face powder and rouge. "Pardon me, Monsieur? Are you asking if the gentlemen served together?"

"Please forgive my curiosity. It just seemed likely to me that only men of the same regiment could have managed an affaire d'honneur with such exemplary chivalry and panache."

Orlovsky hesitated a moment before answering, "Yes, they were of the same regiment."

"I knew it," Achille said enthusiastically. "And I'll bet they're the sort of gentlemen who sought out an adventurous post. Could you please tell me where they served?"

"In Central Asia, Monsieur."

"Ah, how exotic. I long to travel there with my wife. Perhaps when I retire. Did you know that Jules Verne wrote about Samarkand in his *Voyages Extraordinaires*?"

Orlovsky frowned. "No, Monsieur, I did not."

Achille continued smiling. "Yes, Samarkand. The name conjures images of the mysterious east: the bazaar, silks and spices, caravans, camels, and fierce tribesmen of the steppe. The muezzin calling the faithful to prayer from the top of an alabaster minaret. I'm wondering, Monsieur; could it be that the prince and the colonel were stationed there?"

Orlovsky stared hard at Achille. The Russians had recently completed an extension of the Trans-Caspian railway to Samarkand, which permitted them to deploy a large number of troops and sufficient matériel near the Afghan border, more than enough to worry the English. "I don't see how this information is relevant to your investigation?"

Achille stopped smiling. "Please permit me, Monsieur, to decide what is, and is not, relevant to my inquiry."

Orlovsky narrowed his eyes. "Yes, Monsieur; their regiment was stationed at Samarkand."

"Thank you. And they returned to Europe recently?"

"Yes, Monsieur; early this year."

The feint had rattled Orlovsky. Now was the time to ask about the Englishman. "There was a man named Sims at the prince's card party. He acted as the baron's second. What do you know about him?"

"He's an English gentleman who can afford to play for high stakes."

"Do you know how the prince and the colonel made the Englishman's acquaintance?"

"They met at the baccarat table in Aix-les-Bains."

"I see. I've been told that Sims is a retired officer who until recently had served in one of Her Majesty's regiments on the North-West Frontier. Did you know that?"

"Yes."

"I'd like to have a chat with M. Sims. Do you know where he is?"

"I'm sorry, Monsieur Lefebvre. I haven't a clue."

You say you haven't a clue, but perhaps you've given me one without knowing it. Achille put his hand to his mouth to stifle a yawn. "Forgive me, M. Orlovsky. I'm tired, and I'm sure you have other plans for this morning. Therefore, I'll detain you no longer. However, before I go, I would like to know if you could arrange for me to interview Prince Papkov and Colonel Mukhin."

Orlovsky sighed. "That would be difficult, Monsieur; diplomatic protocol, you know. But it might be possible; though I'm afraid I'd have to be present at the interviews."

Achille smiled broadly. "I understand, Monsieur. You've been so helpful; perhaps those interviews won't be necessary after all. At any rate, I appreciate your assistance and may call upon you again before this matter's over."

"Please feel free to do so. As I said, I owe you a debt of gratitude, and a gentleman always pays his debts."

"Of course, Monsieur." Achille seemed about to leave when he smacked his forehead, a sign of frustration at his apparent carelessness. "Pardon me; I must be dozy. I almost forgot to ask. Let's assume the baron arrived in Paris; do you have any idea where he might have gone?"

Orlovsky reached into a waistcoat pocket and removed a notebook and silver pencil. He wrote something, tore out the sheet, and handed it to Achille. "The baron keeps a woman in the Marais. You might ask her."

"Thank you. Good morning, M. Orlovsky."

"Good morning, M. Lefebvre."

◦◦◦

The moon hid behind a heavy cloud cover; a light steady rain pattered on the cab roof and streamed down the side windows. The *chiffoniers* and night-soil collectors had finished their hygienic rounds along broad boulevards and avenues and through winding narrow streets and back alleys. Soon, the street cleaners would come out along with an army of lamplighters extinguishing thousands of gaslights.

Sergeant Adam sat silently on the carriage seat next to Achille. The chief inspector seemed lost in thought as he stared into the damp darkness outside the cab window. Achille's mind drifted from the problems of the case to his ghostly, rain-streaked reflection, to the sound of the horse's hoofbeats and the rumble of rubber-tired wooden spoke wheels on the pavement.

"Pardon me, M. Lefebvre. We just crossed the Rue de Rivoli. You'll be home soon."

Achille turned to Adam and smiled. "Thank you, Sergeant."

"If you don't mind my asking, did you get much out of the Russian?"

"Much? I don't know, Adam. I got *something*. But as is often the case, what I got provided me with more questions than answers."

"I'm sorry, Chief." Adam turned and glanced out his window. "This is your street."

The cab pulled up to the curb in front of Achille's apartment building. Adam opened the door, stepped out, and remained on the watch as Achille exited the carriage.

"Thank you, Adam. Go home and get some sleep. I'll see you later, at headquarters."

"It's a tough case, isn't it, Chief?"

"Damned tough, Sergeant. But that's not your problem. Your job is to keep me alive, at least long enough to solve this cursed puzzle. Good morning."

⌘

Adele had left a light burning in the front hallway. Achille removed his shoes, lifted the oil lamp from its place on a small table, and crept up the corridor as noiselessly as possible. He stopped at his study, turned the brass knob slowly, and opened the door with a noticeable creaking. *I must remember to oil those damned hinges*, he thought.

He set the lamp on his desk and turned up the flame. Then he sat in his leather swivel chair, opened a drawer, and rummaged about until he found a clean pad of paper. He picked up a pencil and made the following notes:

What really happened in Aix-les-Bains? Achille underlined "really." He thought about the possible relationships among the Russians, the Englishman, and the missing baron. *Could this have something to do with the Trans-Caspian railway and Afghanistan? Could it involve espionage?* After this, he wrote, *Contact the Deuxième Bureau for information about ex–British officers traveling through France who served on North-West Frontier 1885–90.*

Achille removed his pince-nez, blinked, and rubbed his eyes. He needed a few hours of sleep. But before he left his desk, he compulsively scribbled a few more notes as reminders: *Follow up with Legros and Masson. Need information from the Railway Squad. Follow the lead regarding the woman in the Marais. What about Le Chabanais? The maid who shared a room with Otero—what does she know? Employ Apolline and Delphine?* He had already sent a message to one of his most resourceful agents, the cabaret singer Delphine Lacroix, and he anticipated a response would be waiting on his desk when he returned to the Quai des Orfèvres.

Did he forget something? He shook his head and decided things would seem clearer later that morning. He yawned and stuffed the notes in his coat pocket. Taking the lamp, Achille stepped into the hall. Walking up the shadowy corridor, he took care not to step on Jeanne's scattered toys. When he reached the bedroom doorway he turned the light down low and tried not to make any noise, but the squeaky hinges betrayed him.

As he entered the room, he heard a stirring under the bedclothes.

"Achille?" Adele's voice came out softly as though she had murmured his name in a dream.

He stepped lightly up to the bedside. "Forgive me, my darling. I'm sorry to disturb you."

She stretched and batted her eyes awake. "Goodness, what time is it?"

"About three—or maybe closer to four. I don't know. I'm afraid I lost track of time."

"Are you coming to bed?"

"Yes, my dear; at least for a while. I've a busy day ahead." He sensed her fragrant warmth nearby and inviting; but all he could think of was sleep.

Adele rolled over onto her side with her back to him. "All right, Achille," she mumbled.

As he tiptoed to the wardrobe to change into his nightshirt, he thought he heard her say, "I wish you'd do something about those hinges."

8

THE NETWORK

At the same time M. Lefebvre was meeting with Orlovsky at the Cabaret de L'Enfer, Delphine Lacroix finished playing to a packed house at the Divan Japonais. Delphine exited the stage door into a back alley, opened her umbrella, and walked out onto the steep Rue des Martyrs. She began her ascent in the direction of the Rue des Abbesses. Slanting raindrops glimmered in the radiance of a row of gas lamps pointing the way uphill.

One of the leading exponents of *chanson réaliste*, known affectionately as the *chiffonier*'s daughter, Delphine walked the dark, dangerous streets of the Butte without fear. Her popularity in these quarters provided her some protection, as did her secret association with the Sûreté, but in a tight corner she relied on her own resources and reputation as a fierce street fighter.

She had first learned to defend herself as a child growing up in the poverty-stricken wasteland between the fortifications, known as the Zone. She honed her skills as a teenaged prostitute walking the streets of Montmartre and Pigalle, and later as a Folies Bergère regular, a cancan dancer at the Moulin Rouge, and an artist's model. She was savage in close-quarters combat with a straight razor and hatpin, and Achille had taught her the basics of savate and *canne d'arme*, in which her parasol or umbrella became lethal weapons. She had recently added a Remington double-derringer to her arsenal. Depending on the circumstances, Delphine concealed the tiny pistol in her purse, a muff, or a garter holster, and it extended her deadly reach by several paces.

She turned onto the Rue des Abbesses and walked on through dimly lit squares, past dark shuttered shops, tenements, and seedy hotels. Near the stairway that climbed to the Rue Lepic, she heard what sounded like a baby crying. She stopped, looked to her right, and saw a small kitten perched on top of a *poubelle*. She approached the garbage can; in the dim yellow glow of a gas lamp, she spied a ball of damp gray fur and a pair of wide emerald eyes. She reached out and stroked the back of the creature's head; it replied with a pitiful mew.

Her own Minou had been the victim of an accident, crushed under a cartwheel; she saw this stray kitten as a fortuitous replacement, perhaps even a reincarnation of her dead cat. "Poor little Minette," she whispered. "I bet you'd like a nice saucer of milk and a warm, dry place to sleep." She lifted the kitten gently and sheltered it under her cloak.

Delphine climbed the stairs and turned onto the street in the direction of her apartment. She stopped at the front entrance and was about to ring for the concierge when she heard a familiar voice calling to her from a dim passageway.

"Hey, kid, how goes it?"

Delphine peered into the darkness. "Moïse?"

A small, ragged young man stepped forward to show himself. "It's me, all right. Come closer, where we can talk." Moïse Gunzberg worked for

Le Boudin, Delphine's father, the uncrowned king of the *chiffoniers*. Moïse also doubled as one of M. Lefebvre's most trusted agents.

Delphine walked a few paces in the direction of the passage, stopped, and spoke softly. "What do you want? Make it fast. I'm wet and tired." The kitten mewed as if in agreement.

"Aw, you found a new kitty. How sweet."

Delphine frowned. "Watch it, rat boy. I'm not in the best of moods."

Moïse smiled. "All right, kid; simmer down. M. Lefebvre has a job for you, if you'll take it."

"Do you know what it is?"

"Of course not. You'll have to talk to the chief. If you're interested, he'll meet you this afternoon at two at Lautrec's studio. It's the safest place. As usual, you can tell anyone who gets nosy that you're on a modeling job. M. Lautrec's all right with it."

Delphine nodded her agreement. "Very well. Now I want to go inside."

"Thanks, kid. And no offense meant. I like cats, too."

She smiled, reached out, and tousled his hair. "Okay, kid. *Au revoir.*"

∽

Sergeant Adam detailed six detectives, four primary guards and two alternates, to maintain a twenty-four-hour watch on the chief. According to Adam's plan, two men were always on guard near the apartment building on the Rue Bertin Poirée. When Achille went out, one of the guards would accompany him while the other remained at his post until relieved by the man on the following shift.

That morning, Achille woke about eight after a fitful four hours of sleep. Adele had been up since dawn and was busy with Suzanne and the children; Mme Berthier was out marketing with the cook.

Achille rolled out of bed, pulled out the chamber pot, and relieved himself. Then he stumbled over to the washstand and stared into the mirror with bloodshot eyes. *My God, I look awful*, he thought. He poured cold water from a pitcher into the basin, grabbed a bar of soap, and began scrubbing his hands, beard, and face. Next, he sprinkled tooth powder onto his palm, mixed it with water, and gave his teeth a cursory brushing. Then, he removed his nightshirt and gave himself a quick scouring with a damp sponge followed by a splash of cologne and a vigorous toweling. Finally, he brushed and combed his hair and beard and completed his morning ablution with a fresh change of clothes.

Achille stepped out into the hallway; the sounds of the baby crying, Jeanne whining, and Adele alternately scolding Suzanne and threatening the six-year-old assaulted his ears. He could have escaped without anyone noticing, but he felt it his duty to look in on the family before leaving. He knocked on the nursery door and opened it a crack.

"Well, my love; I'm off to work."

Jeanne took advantage of the interruption to squirm free from her mother's grasp, run to the wardrobe, climb in, and slam the door shut. Adele stared after her daughter for a moment before turning back to glare at her husband. "I don't suppose you'll be home for supper?"

"Sorry, my dear. I . . . I'm afraid I don't know."

"Very well, Achille. Good morning." She turned her attention back to the wardrobe. Adele grabbed a hairbrush from a nearby dresser and began smacking the hard tortoiseshell back of the utensil against her palm. The implications were frightening.

"Good morning, darling," he said. Then he dashed up the hallway, grabbed his hat, overcoat, and holstered revolver from the coatrack, and exited the apartment just as pandemonium erupted in the nursery.

⁂

Detective Bouvier and his relief, Detective Allard, waited for the chief in a passageway observation post across from the apartment building. Achille came out the front entrance and crossed the quiet, narrow street.

"Good morning, Bouvier, Allard. How goes it?"

"Good morning, M. Lefebvre," Bouvier replied. "All's well, so far."

Achille smiled. "That's good to hear. And which bridge shall we take?"

"Let's go by the Pont au Change, Monsieur."

They bid good day to Allard, then walked up the short street in the direction of the quai.

The Pont au Change crossed the Seine on the right bank from the Quai de la Mégisserie to the Palais de Justice on the Île de la Cité. From there, they would proceed to headquarters on the Quai des Orfèvres. Achille often took another route, crossing to the island on the Pont Neuf. Adam wanted to vary the schedule to make it less predictable. He figured that if the two would-be assassins planned an ambush from a hiding place near the bridges, they would have to split up to cover both routes.

With all that was on his mind, Achille could still enjoy a brisk walk along the tree-lined embankment on a crisp, clear autumn morning. When he arrived at headquarters, he thanked Bouvier and released him to other duties. Then he stopped at the clerk's desk, picked up his messages, and ordered his customary breakfast—coffee and a brioche. Achille looked down the hallway and saw Legros talking to Adam. He gestured to the inspector. Legros left the sergeant and walked over to the chief.

"Good morning, Étienne. Is your report finished?"

"Yes, Chief. It's on your desk."

"Good. Give me half an hour, then come down."

Achille entered his office, hung up his hat, overcoat, and revolver, and settled in behind his desk. He had messages from Masson, Legros, and Moïse Gunzberg. He read Masson's first. The chemist detected enough aconite in Otero's vital organs to conclude that the drug was the primary cause of her respiratory failure. Achille scribbled notes: *Question Dr. Levasseur. Get a warrant to search the entire mansion. Shadow the baroness and Bonnet.*

Legros's note simply referred to his completed report. The *chiffonier*'s message confirmed a two P.M. meeting with Delphine at Toulouse-Lautrec's studio in Montmartre. That was risky. Taking along a bodyguard and traveling by cab would be too conspicuous. He decided to go alone and disguised, by tram and on foot. He glanced toward a cabinet where he kept his disguises, including several outfits, makeup, and wigs.

Achille did not like disguises; it had been one of his weak points as a young detective. Years earlier, he had made the novice's mistake of making up like an actor, but he soon learned from masters like Rousseau and Féraud that the best disguises blend with the surroundings and never draw unwanted attention. He would appear as someone who had business in the neighborhood; no one would think of giving him a second look.

He next turned his attention to Legros's report. There was important information from the Railway Squad. They confirmed that the baron and Colonel Mukhin arrived in Paris at the Gare de Lyon, on the same train. They also had witnesses who saw the colonel leave the station in a coach, while the baron left in a cab. Legros was in the process of tracking down the hackney driver. Achille appended a comment: *Must find driver as soon as possible!*

Legros had also received a response from his contact at the Bank of France. He had a list of serial numbers for the notes the baron withdrew prior to leaving for Aix-les-Bains. Moreover, they had an earlier record of the baron withdrawing another large sum. The withdrawals had significantly depleted the account. Finally, Legros had found no criminal record for any of the servants. However, he discovered that Bonnet had been a fighter, training at Julien Leclerc's Salle de Boxe after he had gone into the baron's service. Achille smiled. "Good work, Étienne," he said to himself.

The clerk knocked and entered with the chief's breakfast.

Achille thanked his clerk and added, "Please tell M. Legros I'll see him now."

Achille was sipping coffee, nibbling at his brioche, and pondering the case when Legros knocked and entered the office. The chief put down his coffee and looked up. "Have a seat, Étienne. I've been going over your report. You've done a fine job."

Legros sat across from Achille. "Thank you, Chief. I should have more after my meeting with Mignonette Hubert."

"Oh yes, Otero's friend. You're meeting her at the Eiffel Tower. Isn't there some big event scheduled for tomorrow morning?"

"Indeed there is. A balloonist will attempt to fly his airship from the École Militaire up the Champs-de-Mars, around the tower, and back. Hubert may have thought that we wouldn't be too conspicuous in the crowd, and she'll have a good reason for being there on her day off."

"She's clever if she thinks that. At any rate, she could prove helpful. According to Masson, Otero died of aconite poisoning. However, without more evidence we can't determine whether it was by accident or intent. So this young woman's testimony could be crucial to our case." Achille leaned forward and shuffled through his papers for a moment before continuing. "I'm going to Magistrate Leblanc for a warrant to search the de Livet mansion and the entire surrounding property. We already have the two medicine bottles; with any luck, the detectives might discover something else of interest. And I want a tail placed on Mme de Livet and Bonnet. How are we fixed for detectives?"

"We're running a bit thin, Chief, but we'll manage."

"All right. Pick some good men. We also need to get back to Dr. Levasseur. He won't like it, but that's his problem. I want to make sure he doesn't know more than he's disclosing."

Legros made notes. "Right, Chief. Anything else?"

Achille gave Legros a copy of the name and address of the baron's purported mistress. "I got this from Orlovsky. The baroness hinted that her husband kept a woman in Paris, but she never provided us with a name. You need to get over there and question her. We also need to locate the driver who picked up the baron at the railway station. I have a meeting this afternoon in Montmartre, so I'm afraid I won't be of much help to you later today."

"Are you bringing in your network?"

"Yes. The baron, like M. Orlovsky, is an habitué of the demimonde. Therefore, to learn more about him, I'll employ my demimondaines. They have contacts at the Folies Bergère, the Moulin Rouge, and Le Chabanais, all of which he frequented. I'm also contacting the Deuxième Bureau to see if they have anything on the baron, the Russians, or the elusive M. Sims. Do you remember Captain Duret? He worked with us on the Hanged Man case." Duret was one of Achille's most trusted colleagues in military intelligence.

"Yes, I do. Duret's a good man. Do you suspect espionage is a factor in this case?"

Achille sighed and leaned back in his chair. He thought for a moment before answering. "A jigsaw puzzle isn't so difficult to put together when you have the completed picture as a guide. In our business, we go in blind and must extrapolate our finished mosaic from a jumble of seemingly disparate pieces. At some point, we get a vision of orderliness and completion; we assemble the fragments accordingly. However, we must never reshape the pieces to fit our concept. If we're wrong we must admit our mistake, pull the thing apart, and start over again."

Achille summarized what he had learned from Orlovsky about the prince, the colonel, and Sims and added the information Legros had obtained from the bank concerning the baron's recent withdrawals. "Now the baron has disappeared with a bundle of cash, one of his servants has died under suspicious circumstances, and another may have information relevant to the case. I can't rule out espionage as an important element, but I'm not going to make the mistake of assuming it until I know more. In other words, I won't trim the pieces to fit the puzzle."

"I understand, Chief. What about Bonnet's background as a fighter? Can you make anything of that?"

"It's not surprising that a man like the baron would hire a tough guy for a manservant. Then, why didn't the baron have Bonnet guard him and his moneybag on the train to Paris? M. de Livet could have sent a message to his wife without forgoing his protection. Anyway, I know Julien Leclerc;

85

I trained with his master, Charles Lecour. I'll pay M. Leclerc a visit and see if he can tell me something interesting about Bonnet."

Legros finished taking notes and then asked if there was anything else to put on his list.

"No, Étienne, that's all for now. You may go." As Legros was about to walk out the door, Achille added, "Keep an eye on Mlle Hubert; she may be in danger. And please tell Adam I want to see him before I leave for Montmartre."

After Legros left, Achille finished his coffee and brioche and lit a cigarette. *We often miss the obvious*, he thought. *Is there a forgotten clue in this case?* After taking a few deep drags, he dropped the cigarette in an ashtray, pulled out a notepad, and wrote a column of names: the baron, baroness, Bonnet, Prince Papkov, Colonel Mukhin, and Sims. He bracketed them, and then drew a dotted line to Orlovsky/Okhrana and added a question mark. Below he wrote *Otero* with the symbol of a cross. Then he added, *What does Hubert know?*

Achille returned to his cigarette. He leaned back and stared at the ceiling. For an instant, his mind drifted from the case. *I hope Adele wasn't too hard on little Jeanne.* He shook his head, sighed, and went back to work.

⸙

Achille sat on a slatted wooden bench on the open upper deck of the Rue Caulaincourt tram. The horse-drawn car ran up from the Place de Clichy and over the iron viaduct that crossed the cemetery. He grabbed the brim of his fedora as a gust whipped over the elevated roadway. Wind rustled the reddish-golden-leaved treetops lining each side of the thoroughfare. The breeze carried smoke from dead leaves smoldering in piles gathered around the graves and sarcophagi; the fumes irritated his eyes and nostrils, making them water. He removed a handkerchief from his breast pocket, coughed, and blew his nose.

His disguise consisted of a light brown jacket; dark corduroy trousers; a soft, turned-down collar; and a floppy raspberry silk necktie, all of which, along with his broad-brimmed felt hat, gave him a bohemian look suitable to the neighborhood. There was a print shop near Lautrec's studio; Achille carried a portfolio as though he were an artist going about his business. The few passengers riding on top paid him no attention.

The chief of detectives seemed secure within his cocoon of inconspicuousness, but he never let his guard down on the street. He carried a revolver concealed beneath the casual attire; his eyes scanned fellow passengers and passersby, and he remained alert to any suspicious actions or movements.

On the other side of the bridge, just north of the park-like burial ground, the car came to a squealing halt near the Rue Tourlaque. Achille descended the spiral staircase at the back of the tram and stepped down to the pavement. The driver whistled at his draft horses and shook his reins; the team lifted their great hooves and clomped down on the paving stones. The conductor rang the bell, and the car rolled on up the track.

Achille waited for a cart to rumble by and then crossed the street and continued on to the house at Number 7. He passed through the front door and entered the dimly lit foyer. The concierge, who knew the chief inspector well, greeted him simply as "Monsieur." Achille nodded his acknowledgment and climbed the staircase to the artist's studio.

He knocked on the door at the end of the uppermost landing. A faint voice responded from the back of the studio: "One moment, please." Sounds of a shuffling gait and the tapping of a cane followed the words. Presently the door creaked open; a diminutive bearded man looked up with an amused grin. He scrutinized Achille for an instant before speaking.

"Good afternoon, M. Lefebvre. If you don't mind, please remain on the threshold for a minute. The lighting's perfect; I've had an inspiration."

Achille was accustomed to Toulouse-Lautrec's humor; he played along and waited patiently.

The painter drew back two paces, squinted critically, and tugged at his chin-whiskers before announcing, "Yes, indeed; I've a composition in mind. I'll call it *The Flic's Impression of an Artist*. I could submit it to the next Salon. It might make my fortune."

Achille smiled tolerantly in response to Lautrec's wry critique of the disguise. "Thank you, M. Lautrec. I'm at your service and look forward to the sittings."

Lautrec laughed and gestured for Achille to enter the studio. Achille savored the pleasantly piquant odor of turpentine and linseed oil. A skylight admitted a stream of bright sunshine into the center of the spacious interior, leaving only the obscure corners and recesses in shadow. Finished canvasses covered the walls up to the high ceiling; wooden shelves groaned beneath the weight of plaster casts and miscellaneous paraphernalia. One unfinished canvas, displayed on an easel near a model's dais, caught Achille's eye.

"It appears your design for the new Moulin Rouge poster is almost finished."

Lautrec stopped by a table next to his liquor cabinet, turned around, and glanced toward his painting. "It requires some finishing touches before I take it to the lithographer."

"I see, Monsieur. I suppose Oller and Zidler are itching for it?"

Lautrec shrugged. "Let them itch. They'll get it when it's done." He turned his attention back to the liquor cabinet, opened the door, and retrieved a bottle of cognac and two glasses. "Take a seat and join me for a drink."

"Thank you, Monsieur." Achille sat down at one end of the plain wooden table, removed his hat, and set the portfolio against a table leg. Lautrec poured the drinks, handed one to Achille, and then occupied the opposite chair. After taking a draft of cognac, he leaned forward, eyeing the portfolio with curiosity.

"Tell me, M. Lefebvre, does that folder contain something of interest, or are you just carrying it around for show?"

Achille smiled sheepishly. "Sketching is a hobby of mine, Monsieur. The portfolio contains a sample of my poor efforts."

"May I have a look?"

Achille did not want to show his work to a professional artist, especially one known for his sharply critical tongue. He made up an excuse. "I'd be honored, but I'm afraid Delphine will arrive shortly. We'll need to get on with business."

"Don't bother yourself about Delphine, M. Lefebvre. Since she's become a star she's acquired the irritating habit of being fashionably late." Without waiting for a response, Lautrec grasped the portfolio, placed it on the tabletop, and removed the sketches. He began leafing through the drawings, nodding at some with apparent approval and grimacing at others. Finally, after a few minutes, he replaced the sketches and poured himself another cognac. Then he contemplated Achille with a sly smirk. "I have some advice for you, Chief Inspector."

"Thank you; and what might that be?"

"Stick to detective work."

Achille was about to say something offensive about the art profession—and one artist in particular—when a knock at the door intervened.

"That must be Delphine," Lautrec said. "Would you mind answering the door? My poor legs are feeling a bit wobbly."

"Of course, Monsieur." He got up, walked back to the entrance, and welcomed Delphine with a warm, familiar smile.

At this stage of her career, Delphine Lacroix could afford to order the latest creations from Worth or Doucet. Alternately, she could have patronized one of the chic *grand magasins*, such as Le Bon Marché or Printemps. Instead, she chose to shop "among her people" at the new Dufayel department store on the Rue de Clignancourt, just as she chose to stay in her modest flat on the Rue Lepic. She dressed and lived comfortably without ostentation, retaining a sense of loyalty to her class. Thus, she remained true to her role as an interpreter of *chanson réaliste*.

"You look lovely as always, Mademoiselle."

Delphine lowered her eyes and flushed slightly at the compliment. "Thank you, M. Lefebvre."

Lefebvre escorted the cabaret singer to the table. Lautrec observed them shrewdly. Achille seemed to have few qualms about putting Delphine's life in danger for small compensation, and she reciprocated with an almost unaccountable devotion. She might have loved him. If she did, the artist supposed her secret passion was seriously mistaken. Lautrec had slept with Delphine, but he figured the prudent and virtuous M. Lefebvre would do without that singular pleasure.

Lautrec retrieved another glass from his cabinet. "You'll join us for a drink?"

"Yes, M. Lautrec. Thank you."

Achille seated her courteously before returning to his chair. Lautrec poured the drinks, and Achille offered Delphine a cigarette. They drank, smoked, and chatted for a few minutes before Achille came to the point.

"As you know, I'm searching for M. Le Noir de Livet, who hasn't been seen since last week, when he arrived in Paris on a train from Aix-les-Bains. I believe you both know the gentleman?"

Lautrec answered first. "Yes, I know him. He has piles of cash and likes to spend it on cards, horses, and women, though not necessarily in that order."

"Have you seen him recently?" Achille asked.

"I last saw him at the Moulin Rouge, but that was almost a month ago. We are not friends, you know. We just seem to turn up in the same places, that is to say, the cabarets, brothels, and racetracks. We also have ancient and noble names, though like my deformity I claim mine by right, or more precisely as an accident of birth. The baron got his name the same way he gets other things—he bought it."

Delphine looked down at her drink. "I've known him, Monsieur—on a professional basis."

Her answer was what he had hoped for, but he was sensitive enough not to display his enthusiasm at her revelation. "I see, Mademoiselle. Could you please tell me when was the last time you—saw the gentleman?"

She took a puff on her cigarette and exhaled a plume of smoke before replying. "It's been more than a month, M. Lefebvre. He had a woman he visited regularly, at Le Chabanais. Not long ago, he paid her debts to the house and set her up in a pied-à-terre in the Marais."

"Do you know the woman's name?"

"Valentine Behrs; but her real name is Valentina Berezina."

Orlovsky had given Achille a name, but he had not disclosed the woman's nationality. "Is she Russian?"

"Yes, Monsieur; she's an émigré."

"I know her," Lautrec broke in. "I've enjoyed her companionship, on occasion, as has your friend, M. Orlovsky."

A pattern was developing; a picture formed in Achille's mind's eye. He hoped it would not prove to be false and misleading. "Was that at Le Chabanais, M. Lautrec?"

"Yes, it was. I haven't seen her since she left the establishment."

Achille put his next question to Delphine. "You said you haven't seen the baron in more than a month. Do you know if Apolline has been in his proximity more recently?"

Lautrec smiled and muttered, "In his *proximity*. How droll."

Delphine ignored the artist. "Yes, M. Lefebvre. There were parties at the house in the Marais. The baron and M. Orlovsky like to gamble, and Apolline, Aurore, and Valentine were there to serve and entertain the gentlemen. I was invited on occasion, but I didn't go."

Lautrec shook his head and laughed softly. "To *serve* and *entertain*, I'm sure."

Achille glared at the painter. "Please, M. Lautrec. This is serious business."

Lautrec made a mock bow. "Pardon me, Monsieur." Then he eyed the cognac. "Excuse me a moment. I think it's time to open another bottle."

Achille moved closer to Delphine and lowered his voice. "Mademoiselle, I have an assignment for you and Apolline. It's dangerous, but if you accept I'll compensate you both at the usual rate, with a bonus for good results."

Delphine nodded. "I accept, M. Lefebvre. I cannot vouch for Apolline, but I'm sure I can persuade her."

Lautrec returned with an uncorked bottle. "Is this a private conversation? Do you wish me to leave?"

"Forgive me, M. Lautrec," Achille said. "I appreciate your time and the use of your studio, but I'm about to provide Mlle Lacroix with confidential information that it's better for you not to know. It may seem an unpardonable liberty—"

Lautrec interrupted with a wave of his hand. "I understand, Chief Inspector." He pointed toward a sheltered nook on the other side of the studio. "I'll take my big ears and little bottle over there. Please feel free to get on with your cloak-and-dagger stuff."

Achille rose to his feet and bowed politely. "Thank you very much, M. Lautrec."

The artist turned and hobbled away to his dark corner. "Think nothing of it, M. Lefebvre," he mumbled over his shoulder.

Achille waited until the artist was out of earshot before continuing. "You mentioned parties at the house in the Marais. Do you know if others, besides the baron and Orlovsky, were in attendance?"

"Yes, Apolline mentioned other gentlemen, but I don't recall their names."

"Do the names Prince Papkov, Colonel Mukhin, or M. Sims sound familiar?"

"No, Monsieur. I'd have to ask Apolline."

"What about the baron's manservant, Bonnet?"

She thought a moment before answering. "I do remember Bonnet; that is, I've seen him on occasion in the baron's company."

"Good. Now I want you to remember these names. Don't write them down. Do you think you can repeat them for me?"

"Yes, Monsieur: Prince Papkov; Colonel Mukhin; M. Sims; and Bonnet."

"Very good. You know how to proceed. I suspect some collusion among these individuals leading up to a recent meeting in Aix-les-Bains. Anything of particular interest that Apolline can recall from their conversations might be helpful in solving the case."

"What about letters, notes, or other writings?"

Achille frowned; he hesitated a moment before saying, "She'll have to use her judgment and exercise extreme caution. Orlovsky's a dangerous man. I'd rather she missed something than risk exposure."

"I understand. How are we to communicate?"

"You and Apolline can arrange meetings and a method of communication between yourselves. She must avoid any direct contact with me. Do you have the book of poems I gave you?"

"Of course, Monsieur."

Achille reached into a jacket pocket. "Follow our normal procedure. Here's a new poem and an updated encryption key. If you have an encoded message, place four white chrysanthemums on Virginie Ménard's grave. Then leave your message under the bench on the pathway that runs under the viaduct. You remember which one?"

"Yes, Monsieur."

"Moïse will check the grave and the bench each morning. If I have a message for you, he'll deliver it directly at a time and place of his choosing."

Delphine nodded her understanding.

"Thank you, Delphine. Now, if either you or Apolline at any time fear for your safety, you must go directly to Sergeant Rodin. He'll take care of you. Do you understand?"

"Don't worry, M. Lefebvre. We won't let you down."

Achille looked at her gloved hands on the tabletop; they were resting closer to his than he had realized, almost at the point of touching.

If he were to crack this case, he needed her help and Apolline's, too. Yet he could never overcome a sense of shame for putting their lives at risk for a small reward. After a moment, he looked up and said, "I can't express how much I appreciate your assistance. You do so much and ask for so little in return. But please be assured, Mademoiselle, that you are performing an important service for France."

She placed a hand on his, tilted her head to one side, and smiled enigmatically. "Is it *only* for France that I do this, M. Lefebvre?"

Achille cleared his throat nervously and withdrew his hand. "Of course, Mlle Lacroix. You are a good citizen. It's all in the line of duty." He reached into his waistcoat pocket and took out his watch. "Now that we've concluded our business, we ought not to impose on M. Lautrec's hospitality." He got up from his chair, bowed stiffly, and offered an arm to escort her to the door.

∞

Before returning to headquarters, Achille stopped at the *salle de boxe* on the Rue de Richelieu. He had a twofold purpose for the visit. First, he wanted to question Leclerc about his former pupil, Bonnet. Second, and perhaps more important, Achille wanted to test himself with a match.

Upon entering the hall, he noticed the familiar sharp odor of tobacco smoke and sweat and the resounding thump of fists and feet on punching bags and practice dummies. The maître observed the activity critically from his vantage point on a dais in the center of the hall.

In the tradition of the *salle d'armes*, the high oak walls and surrounding gallery displayed arms from the Age of Chivalry, crossed swords, shields, and daggers. In addition, there were rich tapestries and salon paintings depicting jousting and the hunt as practiced in the days of François I. However, despite the trappings of the romantic past, the maître taught the most modern and scientific methods of self-defense.

Achille approached the dais. Leclerc turned to greet him.

"Good afternoon, Monsieur. How may I help you?"

Achille smiled broadly and came closer. "You don't recognize me, Maître?"

Leclerc walked over to Achille and inspected him with a skeptical squint. "Is that you, M. Lefebvre?"

Achille laughed and held out his hand. "Fooled you, didn't I, Maître?"

Leclerc smiled and shook the chief inspector's hand. "Indeed you did, Monsieur. In that outfit, and with the portfolio under your arm, I took you for one of those fellows who peddle their daubery to tourists in the Place du Tertre. My congratulations on a clever disguise."

"Thank you, Maître. Now to the purpose of my visit. If you don't mind, I'd like to ask you a few questions about Eugene Bonnet. I believe he's a former pupil of yours?"

Leclerc frowned as though he had smelled something putrid. "Yes, I remember Bonnet. What do you want to know about him?"

Achille glanced around. A few men had stopped practicing and were staring at them. "If you please, Maître, could we go somewhere less conspicuous?"

Leclerc glared at the handful of loiterers. "I hope you gentlemen aren't exhausted from your exertions?" The students bowed respectfully and went back to work. Leclerc turned to Achille. "Very well, Monsieur; please follow me."

Leclerc led Achille to a dark alcove beneath the gallery. "I believe this is private enough, M. Lefebvre. You asked about Bonnet. He studied with me for a few weeks. That was about one year ago. His master, Baron de Livet, paid his tuition."

"Can you tell me anything about the man: his associations, his fighting style, his character?"

Leclerc shook his head. "I teach the art of self-defense to gentlemen, Monsieur. Bonnet's 'fighting style,' such as it is, might do in a brawl, but not in the ring or on the field of honor. In short, he's a dirty fighter with no interest in the art and science of boxing. I don't want that element in my hall, and I said as much to the baron."

"I understand, Monsieur. Is there nothing more you can tell me about him? Perhaps he made some friendships among the other pupils?"

"I'm afraid you've wasted your time, Monsieur. I know nothing more about Bonnet. As for my pupils, they avoided the fellow, and who could blame them?"

Achille shrugged. "Well, Maître, if there's nothing more—"

"Excuse me, Monsieur," Leclerc broke in. "Is Bonnet in trouble with the law?"

"Not yet, Monsieur, but between you and me, he could be." Achille seemed dejected and on the point of leaving when Leclerc made a suggestion.

"Don't let your visit be for nothing, M. Lefebvre. You honor us with your presence. I can offer you a match with one of my most promising pupils."

Achille perked up immediately. "Thank you, Maître; I was hoping you'd say that. But it will have to be a brief set-to. I fear I'm pressed for time."

"How about going one round on points, or the first knockdown wins?"

"That would be splendid; thank you."

In his youth, Achille had fought a duel with the épée. In retrospect, the cause of the quarrel—a perceived insult to a woman of dubious reputation—seemed trivial; however, the fight itself was significant. He had met the challenge by fighting an older, more experienced adversary. Achille had performed admirably. He wounded his opponent with a skillful thrust to the chest. Thankfully, the wound was minor. They shook hands, the man recovered, and Achille's reputation rose among his peers.

Since the time of his duel, he lived with the ambivalence of a man whose rational mind rejected the affaire d'honneur at the same time his romantic heart embraced it.

Achille had ventured onto the streets without a bodyguard, over the protests of Sergeant Adam. In doing so, he was testing himself and his would-be assassins, almost daring them to come out of hiding and do their worst. He believed he knew their weapons and probable method of attack. He had kept fit by rowing on the Seine and training in savate and *canne d'arme*. Achille had one deficiency—his nearsightedness—but he compensated with a long reach in arms and legs, agility, timing, and a quick and devious mind. He was also an expert with his double-action Chamelot-Delvigne, and he practiced assiduously to the point where he was deadly accurate at twenty paces.

Leclerc led Achille to the ring where two young men sparred while another observed. In the short time it took to walk from the alcove to the center of the hall, Achille noted each boxer's style, reach, and tendencies to attack and defend. As the maître approached with his guest, the men stopped sparring, the observer turned around, and others ceased their exercises and began to gather near the ring.

The maître called the hall to attention. "Gentlemen, we have an honored guest: M. Achille Lefebvre, Chief of the Sûreté." A polite round of applause followed Leclerc's announcement. "M. Lefebvre has kindly agreed to participate in an exhibition of *boxe française*. The match will be decided after one round on points or upon the first clean knockdown. M. Leroy will represent the hall, Messieurs Roux and Lecocq will act as seconds, and I will judge and keep time."

Achille had already identified Leroy as the more dangerous of the sparring partners, with a long reach comparable to his own. He had also noticed the young man's tendency to go for high kicks, especially the spectacular *fouetté haut*.

Achille removed his jacket, shirt, and pince-nez and handed them to his second, M. Lecocq. Then Achille put on a pair of lightly padded leather gloves, and Lecocq laced them securely.

Achille and Leroy met at the center of the ring, touched gloves, and took their stance: left foot slightly to the front, weight evenly distributed between left and right, on the balls of the feet. They raised their forearms to defend their bodies and their hands to protect their heads, which were angled down a little to cover their chins. They waited for the maître's signal.

Leclerc set his stopwatch; he raised his hand and then dropped it, calling, "Begin!"

Leroy began dancing and weaving while Achille remained relatively still in a defensive posture while adjusting to his opponent's movements. Leroy darted in with low and medium *chassé frontal* kicks in combination. These were feints to see how Achille would react. Achille maintained his cautious stance. He guessed the feints were a setup for the *fouetté haut*, his adversary's attempt at an early knockout, and he was not about to be surprised and caught off guard.

The anticipated high *fouetté*, aimed directly at Achille's head, followed the feints like thunder after lightning. Achille blocked and dodged the kick skillfully. He countered with a deft, precisely measured front leg *coup pied bas* that caught Leroy on the shin and nearly brought him down. Sensing victory, Achille instantly slipped in against his unprotected opponent and threw a stinging left jab to Leroy's ear, followed by a hard right cross to the chin that knocked the young man on his back.

A gasp echoed throughout the hall. Leroy's second ran to his stunned companion. Roux knelt and whispered to Leroy, who sat up with his second's assistance, shook his head, and mumbled incoherently. Roux turned toward Leclerc.

"Your judgment, Maître?"

"It was a clean knockdown. I award the match to M. Lefebvre."

Achille walked over to his adversary, who rose slowly to greet him. He extended a gloved hand. "A fine set-to, M. Leroy."

Leroy wiped a bloody lip on his arm and smiled. He put out his hand, and the fighters touched gloves. "Thank you, M. Lefebvre. I look forward to a rematch."

Achille bowed. "I would be honored, Monsieur."

Achille returned to his corner to a burst of applause and cheers. As Lecocq unlaced Achille's gloves, the young man said:

"That was splendid, M. Lefebvre. I hope someday to be worthy of a match with you."

"Thank you, Monsieur. I look forward to it with pleasure."

As the maître escorted him to the front entrance, Achille considered how this meeting would add to his reputation. He hoped that it would discourage some individuals from taking him on, but he also realized that it might have the opposite effect. The man who defeated the formidable chief of detectives would gain great credit on the street.

When they reached the door, Leclerc turned to Achille and held out his hand. "You took down my best pupil in less than a minute, M. Lefebvre. An impressive performance. You obviously did not agree to the match just for the exercise."

Achille smiled and shook the maître's hand. "You are perceptive as always, M. Leclerc. If I had played for points, I'm sure the young man would have won. His high *fouetté* is a thing of beauty, but it's not much good on the street."

"I understand, Chief Inspector. Perhaps you are thinking of Bonnet?"

Achille nodded. "Yes, Maître; Bonnet—and others."

"In a fair fight, Bonnet could not touch you. Then, as you well know, fairness counts for little on the street. If there were such an encounter, I'm sure you would do what was necessary to prevail. As for the others you mentioned, are you thinking of anyone in particular?"

"I'm considering two individuals. Neither of them has a reputation as a fighter, but I've heard they carry arms. One is said to have an old Lefaucheux; the other, an Apache revolver."

"I assume you carry your Chamelot-Delvigne?"

"Always, Maître."

"Well then, you'd better be prepared to use it. But in very close quarters, I believe you could handle two of that sort without your revolver."

"Thank you, Maître. I'm curious: What do you think would be my chances with three or even four? Many years ago my former partner Rousseau got the best of four thugs while armed only with his truncheon."

Leclerc shook his head. "Ah, but that was Rousseau. People say he's not human."

Achille laughed softly. "Yes, Maître; that *is* what people say. Thank you for your courtesy and good advice. Good afternoon."

"Good afternoon, M. Lefebvre. And if I hear anything about Bonnet, I'll certainly let you know."

⸎

Legros took a cab to Valentine Behrs's pied-à-terre on the Rue de Turenne. So far, he considered this day one of mixed success. On the positive side, he had located the cabdriver who picked up the baron at the railway station; however, he had not yet interviewed the man. He had questioned Dr. Levasseur without gaining much information. The doctor admitted no wrong for having left a small quantity of tincture of aconite on the bedside table; he had left precise instructions as to the dosage, and it was not his fault if Mme de Livet or others in her household had not followed his orders to the letter. In other words, he blamed the baroness and seemed confident that the medical community would back him in that regard.

Legros had served a warrant on the baroness and left a sergeant and two detectives to search the premises. He was prepared for a hostile reception and was surprised by Mme de Livet's calm acquiescence and cooperative manner. He tried to avoid Mignonette so as not to betray their collaboration, but the few times their eyes met, he detected signs of anxiety on her normally cheerful face.

The cab came to a halt in front of a seventeenth-century, mansard-roofed three-story townhouse built of cream-colored stone. This was a genteel quarter, not far from the Place des Vosges. As he walked to the front entrance and rang for the concierge, Legros wondered what the neighbors thought about the kept woman in their midst; he and his detectives would certainly make inquiries.

He waited patiently until a man who looked as though he had entered the world at the same time as the ancient residence emerged from a doorway and limped to the front gate with the assistance of a cane. The grandfather raised his rheumy eyes and stared at Legros.

"May I assist you, Monsieur?" the old man asked.

Legros pulled out his tricolor badge. "I'm Inspector Étienne Legros of the Sûreté. I'm here to see Valentine Behrs. Is the lady in?"

The man put on his spectacles and studied the detective's credentials for a moment before answering. "I'm sorry, Monsieur. Mme Behrs is gone."

"Gone? What do you mean by 'gone'?"

The concierge unlocked the gate. "If you please, Inspector. Come with me and I'll explain." Legros followed the man down a short garden pathway to a cramped ground-floor kitchen that smelled of bacon grease and coffee. The old man gestured to a small chair next to an unpainted wooden table. "Please take a seat, Monsieur. I was just enjoying a little snack. Would you care for some refreshment?"

Legros sat, but he politely declined the coffee. The man sat across from him, blew at the steaming cup, and took a sip. "It's really quite good, Monsieur. You sure you won't have some?"

"No, thank you," Legros replied impatiently. "Now, you say Mme Behrs is gone. Can you tell me when you last saw her?"

The concierge stroked his white whiskers. "Let me see. That was last week."

"Can you please be more precise?"

The old man thought a moment. "Do you see that calendar on the wall? Over there, near the oven. That's it. I believe I marked the date. Would you please be kind enough to bring it here? I'd do it myself, but I'm afraid my rheumatism's acting up."

Legros sighed and went to fetch the calendar. *This fellow ought to be in a home for the aged*, he thought. He returned and placed the calendar on the table in front of the concierge.

The old man peered through his glasses and scanned the dates until he found what he was looking for. "There it is, Monsieur." He pointed with a gnarled finger to a circled date. "She left the twenty-fifth, and I haven't seen her since."

Legros took out his notepad and pencil. The twenty-fifth was the same day the baron arrived in Paris on the train from Aix-les-Bains. "Do you remember what time she left?"

"It was in the evening, Monsieur. Quite late as I recall, though I couldn't give you the exact time."

"Was anyone with her?"

"Oh yes, Monsieur; there were two gentlemen."

"Can you give me their names and descriptions?"

"One was M. Noiret. He's the gentleman who . . . who pays the rent." He then gave a description that matched the baron, and Legros noted that Noiret was a variation of Le Noir. The use of a pseudonym when renting a pied-à-terre for one's mistress was a common practice. "The other gentleman I had never seen before, and there was something odd about him."

"Oh, and what was so odd?"

"His face was all bandaged, as though he had been in an accident or had recent surgery."

"Do you recall if the gentlemen were carrying any luggage?"

The concierge thought for a minute. "I believe M. Noiret had a bag—I think it's the type that's called a Gladstone bag. I know he had it with him when he arrived, but I can't recall if he still had it when they left."

"Did the gentlemen arrive together?"

"Yes, Monsieur; they came in a cab."

Legros made a note to check with the cabdriver who picked up the baron at the Gare de Lyon. "Did they leave in the same cab?"

"No, Monsieur; they left in a coach, with Mme Behrs. It came about two hours after they arrived."

"You said they didn't come with luggage, except for M. Noiret's Gladstone bag. Did they take anything with them?"

"Just a couple of suitcases, as I recall. I assume they were Madame's bags, and I thought that was strange."

"Why did you think it strange?"

"Mme Behrs is a fashionable lady, Monsieur. Such women never travel without at least one portmanteau."

"I see. Can you please describe the coach, the horses, and the driver?"

The old man shook his head and sighed. "Alas, Monsieur, I remember nothing about the driver and the horses. It was very dark when they left. But the coach was a closed landau, and I recall it had a coat of arms painted on the door. The bright colors stood out in the lamplight."

"Can you describe the coat of arms?"

The concierge smiled. "I fear my eyes and memory are not as sharp as they once were. No, Monsieur, I cannot say. But I distinctly remember a coat of arms on the carriage door."

"Did Mme Behrs say where she was going and when she would return?"

"She said she was going to visit friends in the country for a few days, but she did not say where. She said she would return before the end of the month. Now the rent is due. I'm afraid if they don't pay soon, we'll have to enter the apartment and remove her belongings. We don't like to do that; it looks bad, you know."

Legros followed with a series of questions about the comings and goings at the apartment: visitors, parties, activities, unusual incidents, and so forth. After several minutes of questioning, he said, "I would like to search the apartment, if you please." He hoped the concierge would cooperate. Legros did not want to wait for a warrant.

The old man hesitated before answering, "I suppose that would be all right, Monsieur."

The concierge led Legros down an arched corridor and up a short stone stairway. He stopped in front of a large oak door and fumbled with a key ring chained to his belt. The old fellow tried a key and failed. "No, that's not it. It's hard to see in this light," he muttered. After two more unsuccessful attempts, the lock clicked and the carved oak-paneled door swung open. "Eureka!" he cried, as though he had discovered buried treasure.

Upon entering, Legros smelled the mustiness of a sitting room that had not been aired for several days. He particularly noted the lingering odor of tobacco smoke. He walked to the center of the chamber and scanned the surroundings. He noticed some muddy footprints on the carpet, which he examined closely. He also noticed a coffee table set with a half-emptied decanter and three glasses on a silver platter. Next to the platter, there was a porcelain tray containing two half-smoked cigars and a cigarette butt stained with lip rouge. After several minutes' inspection he remarked, "This is a well-appointed room. Do the furnishings belong to Mme Behrs?"

"Oh no, Inspector. It's hired for the term of the lease. I have a complete inventory in my quarters."

"Very well. I'll take that with me and have it copied. You'll get a receipt, and the inventory will be returned to you."

The concierge sighed. "Yes, Monsieur."

Legros noticed something in the fireplace. He walked over, knelt by the hearth, and picked through the ashes. "Someone burned papers recently."

"Pardon, Monsieur?"

Legros brushed off his hands, got up, and eyed the concierge sternly. "I said they burned papers before they left."

"Oh, they burned papers, did they?" The old man shook his head and frowned as though he shared the detective's concern, though in fact he had no idea what the burning might signify.

Legros turned his attention to a velvet *portière* drawn back to disclose the entrance to another room. "Is that Madame's boudoir?"

"Yes, Inspector."

As he entered the room, Legros noticed that the bed was made and there were toiletries on the washstand. He examined the wardrobe, chest of drawers, and a trunk in which he found expensive dresses, hats, shoes, lingerie, and some costume jewelry. He recalled something the concierge had said: *Mme Behrs is a fashionable lady, Monsieur. Such women never travel without at least one portmanteau.*

Legros said, "It's hard to believe a woman would leave so much if she didn't intend to return."

The concierge nodded. "Yes, Monsieur. Perhaps . . . perhaps the landlord might claim some of it in lieu of the unpaid rent?"

"I'm afraid that must wait. My case takes precedence." Legros continued making a thorough inspection of the room. When he peered under the bed, he saw a dark object that looked like a bag or case. He reached in, pulled it out, and showed it to the concierge. "Is this M. Noiret's Gladstone bag?"

The concierge came closer and examined the bag. "Yes, Inspector; I believe it is."

Legros placed the bag on the bed, unfastened the brass latch, and opened it. The case was empty. *Did they transfer the money to the suitcases?* he wondered.

He closed the latch, turned around, and said, "I'm taking this as evidence." Legros left the boudoir carrying the Gladstone bag and returned to the sitting room; the old man followed. When they reached the door, Legros stopped and made a severe pronouncement: "This apartment is sealed pending the outcome of the investigation. No one is to enter except on police business. Everything in the apartment is to be left as it is. Moreover, all the movables will be impounded until further notice. A detective will serve a warrant to that effect within the next twenty-four hours.

"In addition, I charge you to report any suspicious activity related to this case, including but not limited to the names and particulars of anyone inquiring about Mme Behrs, M. Noiret, and the yet-unidentified individual. Do you understand?"

The old man looked down and sighed deeply. "Yes, Inspector; I understand." His face wrinkled in a bitter frown. "I knew that woman would be trouble," he muttered.

Legros smiled. "You *knew* she would be trouble, my friend? That's interesting. Let's return to your kitchen and discuss Mme Behrs and her associates over a cup of your excellent coffee."

9

A TANGLED WEB

At five A.M., Achille sat at his desk, sipping coffee and nibbling a brioche while harmonizing his notes with Legros's reports. Legros sat silently, trying to anticipate his chief's questions while at the same time formulating intelligent responses to each hypothetical.

Achille finished chewing the last piece of his pastry and washed it down with café au lait. He pulled out a handkerchief and wiped away a few crumbs from his moustache and beard before commenting on his protégé's work. "You had a productive day. M. Aubert, the concierge, could make a good witness or at least prove to be a mine of valuable information."

"I hope so, Chief; although at times he seems senile."

"Don't underestimate your elders, Étienne. Sometimes the old folks are much sharper than they let on. At any rate, what you can't get from Aubert you might pick up elsewhere. Your detectives need to question everyone in the neighborhood. We should at least get some leads." Lefebvre consulted his notes before continuing: "Aubert corroborates the information you received from the cabdriver. After the driver picked up the baron at the station, he drove to a hotel on the Rue Castex, where his passenger met a man with a bandaged face.

"He then drove the two a short distance to the apartment on the Rue de Turenne. Of course, we'll need to identify that mysterious individual. You can begin by contacting the Hotel Squad. They can check the registration slips and assist you with questioning the front desk, the porters, the maids, and the bellmen."

Legros made a note. "Very well, Chief. What do you make of the device on the carriage door?"

"It might be one of the baron's coaches. You can look into that. On the other hand—" Achille broke off mid-sentence. He leaned back, closed his eyes, and focused on the problem, a habit he had acquired from Chief Féraud. After a moment, he turned his attention back to Legros. "I'm meeting with Captain Duret this morning, and my network is on the case, too.

"I have a theory, but I don't want you to be distracted by it. If you recall, Orlovsky said Colonel Mukhin was met at the station by an embassy coach. It's possible the device Aubert saw was the Russian double-headed eagle. You should provide Aubert with pictures of the de Livet coat of arms, the Russian national emblem, and a few others to see if he can make a positive identification."

"Right, Chief."

Achille nodded and returned to the report. "Burned papers, cigar and cigarette butts, muddy footprints, glass and decanter," he muttered. He frowned and shook his head. "I don't know if any of that will be helpful, but we should preserve it all as is, just in case. As for Mme Behrs's expensive clothing and personal articles, about all that signifies is that she left in a hurry and traveled light. Whether she intended to return is a matter of conjecture. The empty Gladstone bag and the two suitcases are intriguing. What do you think?"

Legros considered the possibilities before saying, "They transferred the money from one container to the others."

"Why would they do that?"

"We had a good description of the Gladstone bag; it's quite distinctive. Aubert couldn't tell me anything about the suitcases beyond the generic description."

"I agree; that's our best guess." He returned to the report before continuing. "Dr. Levasseur remains obstinate. That's hardly surprising. We have nothing on him. His negligence *might* have contributed to Otero's death, but without incriminating evidence, that's of no consequence to our case.

"It seems the baroness has been quite cooperative, but I'm not surprised. After all, she reported her husband missing within a reasonable period. We must be cautious with our assumptions. So far, the detectives searching the mansion have turned up no evidence against the baroness, Bonnet, or anyone else. Otero's death could have been an accident, totally unrelated to the baron's disappearance. I hope that we'll know more after your interview with Mignonette Hubert. At any rate, it looks like you'll have a good day for an airship exhibition."

"Yes; it should be clear and mild. A perfect autumn afternoon."

Achille reached for a piece of notepaper and took a pen from its inkwell. "If Mlle Hubert does have important information, I fear she may be in danger." He handed the letter to Legros. "Use your judgment, Étienne. This note is for my wife. If you think it necessary, take Mlle Hubert to my apartment. She can stay with us for a while."

"I understand, Chief. What should I say to the baroness?"

"Tell her the truth. Of course, don't let on where you've taken the young woman. Just say she has been placed in protective custody in a location you're not at liberty to disclose. If the baroness, Bonnet, or anyone else makes a move based on that information, it might lead to something important."

Legros folded the letter and placed it in his jacket pocket. "Speaking of Bonnet, did you learn anything more about him from M. Leclerc?"

Achille shrugged. "The maître confirmed my suspicions in one regard. Bonnet is a thug. But that doesn't necessarily mean he's guilty of anything, at least not in this case."

"It's certainly a tangled web, isn't it, Chief?"

"Yes, it is; and I hope we untangle it soon."

⌖

Achille and Sergeant Adam waited on a bench located along one of the wide pathways radiating from the central basin in the Tuileries Gardens. Captain Duret would arrive shortly.

A mild breeze rustled the branches of neatly trimmed trees and hedges of many varieties; red, brown and gold leaves floated for an instant before reaching their final resting place on the walkways and broad expanses of clipped, green lawns.

From his vantage point, Achille could see the top of the Eiffel Tower rising above trees, roofs, and spires, its reddish-brown painted ironwork glistening in a bright azure sky. "We might be able to see the airship from here, if it flies high enough, that is."

"Yes, Chief; if they succeed. It's not *La France* this time, is it?"

"No, it's some rich sportsman flying a machine built with his own funds. Apparently, the army has better things to do with its money than spend it on aeronautic experiments."

"That's understandable, Monsieur. They had some success with *La France*, but those things aren't practical, at least not for military purposes."

"Not yet, they aren't; but I believe they will be someday. Imagine this, Adam. Airships patrolling our city, spotting crimes as they occur and signaling to motorized squads on the ground. At night, we could use electric searchlights to scan the dark alleys and side streets. We'd catch the criminals before they knew what had hit them."

Adam smiled. "That's a fantastic idea, Chief. Inspector Legros told me how much you admire Jules Verne."

109

"Ah yes, Jules Verne. But everything he writes has a basis in scientific fact. Twenty years from now, his stories won't seem so fanciful. Nowadays, if I put my futuristic ideas in a proposal to the prefect, he would have me locked up with the lunatics in the Salpêtrière."

Achille took out his watch. "Duret should be here any minute; he's very punctual." He glanced up the pathway toward the Louvre, the direction from which he expected the captain to arrive. The statue of a marble female nude caught his eye. The classical beauty reminded him of Adele. He had neglected her of late, and he missed her. As he gazed at the statue, a sense of sadness came over him, as though the springtime of his marriage had passed into autumn. He shook his head and sighed.

"Are you all right, M. Lefebvre?"

Achille snapped out of it immediately. "Sorry, Adam; it's nothing. My mind wandered for a moment, that's all."

Adam turned his attention to the passersby. "Look there, Chief. That's Captain Duret, isn't it?"

Achille looked up the walkway and spotted a tall man dressed in impeccably tailored civilian clothes, marching in their direction as though he were on parade. "That's Duret, all right. You'd better take a walk, but don't go too far."

"Of course, Chief. I'll be on the watch." Adam got up and walked toward the captain. They passed each other. Duret glanced at the sergeant and continued on to the bench.

Achille rose to greet the officer. "Good morning, Captain Duret."

"Good morning, M. Lefebvre. I assume the gentleman who was with you is one of your detectives?"

"Yes, that's Sergeant Adam, one of my most trusted men. He's here for added security."

"I understand, Monsieur."

Achille and Duret sat and exchanged a few pleasantries before tending to business.

The captain said, "I understand you're looking for the Baron de Livet. I trust we can work together in this matter, as we did in the Hanged Man case. We've taken an interest in the gentleman and his activities and are presently searching for him, too."

Achille was hardly astounded by this revelation, but he thought it prudent to feign surprise. "Is that so? If I may inquire, why isn't the baron on the list?" Following the passage of the 1886 Espionage Law, the former minister of war, General Boulanger, had created two lists for purposes of national security and surveillance: *Carnet A*, which included all foreigners of military age living in France, and *Carnet B*, aimed at French or foreign nationals suspected of espionage. The police cooperated with Military Intelligence in the enforcement of the law that required the arrest and internment of suspected individuals in time of war or a general mobilization.

Duret removed his bowler and mopped his forehead with a handkerchief. "Unseasonably warm, isn't it, M. Lefebvre?"

Achille smiled at the officer's evasive response. "Indeed it is, Captain. Now would you be so kind as to answer my question?"

The captain replaced his hat and fumbled with his handkerchief as though playing for time while deciding on an appropriate answer. Finally he said, "It's complicated, Monsieur; very complicated. Let me put it to you this way: We've kept the baron off the list because we . . . we've taken a special interest in him."

"Please, Captain. If we are to help each other, we must be frank. After all, we're playing on the same team. Did you try to recruit the baron as an agent?"

Duret winced but he replied directly. "That's the gist of it, Monsieur."

"I see. And could you please tell me why?"

"As you may already know, the baron is a recently naturalized citizen, a South African of German extraction. He made a fortune in the diamond and gold mines, but more important, he played a prominent role in negotiating a major deal between a French consortium and M. Cecil Rhodes. The interests of M. Rhodes, and the British government, do not necessarily coincide with our own. The British recently entered into an accommodation over disputed territories with both our government and the Germans.

"However, such agreements are temporary at best. This is especially so in relation to the further colonization and development of Africa, where the competition among the powers is most dynamic. The baron is well-placed to provide us with valuable intelligence concerning our competitors' intentions."

Achille nodded. "I understand, Captain. But how do the Russians fit into this picture? As far as I know, they have no great ambitions in Africa."

"Our country and Russia have already entered into an economic agreement, and we are close to a military alliance. Our Russian friends have their own . . . disagreements with the British in the East."

"By the 'East' do you mean in the vicinity of the Afghan border?"

Duret stared at Achille for a moment before saying, "Please tell me what you suspect, M. Lefebvre."

Achille smiled and shook his head. "First, I'll tell you what I *know*." Achille summarized the information he and Legros had obtained from their investigation. He followed with a series of questions.

"What do you know about Valentine Behrs, aka Valentina Berezina?"

"She works for us—and M. Orlovsky."

"So she's a double agent?"

"Yes, Monsieur. It's complicated, as I said. We assigned her to the baron, and she provided information to both the Russians and us. Of course, our department vetted everything she gave to Orlovsky. If anything she received from the baron might be used against our interests, the Okhrana did not get it. We lost track of her last week when she failed to report as usual."

"I see. And I suppose you have an agent in the embassy monitoring Colonel Mukhin?"

"Yes, Monsieur."

"Do you know if the Russians have anything to do with the baron's disappearance?"

"No, we don't. We were hoping you could help us in that regard."

"Do you have any information about M. Sims?"

"Nothing more than you've already discovered, Monsieur."

"What about the man with the bandaged face?"

The captain shook his head. "You know as much as we do."

We could know more when the Hotel Squad gets back to Étienne, he thought. "Very well. We're investigating, and I'll let you know what we find out."

"Thank you, Monsieur. By the way, have you employed your own secret network in the investigation?"

"Yes, I have, and I'm very much concerned for their safety."

"Of course, Monsieur. But we must exercise the utmost caution when dealing with the Russians. We want to maintain our cordial and cooperative relationship. And we need to be careful about what gets out to the press."

Achille thought of Fournier; he and the other reporters could not be held off much longer.

"I'm quite aware of that, Captain. Now, as to what I suspect. I *suspect* what happened in Aix-les-Bains had nothing to do with a game of cards." Achille consulted his watch and gazed up in the direction of the Eiffel Tower. "The airship should be ascending about this time."

Captain Duret turned and looked in the same direction. "Oh yes, the airship. I wish them luck. France ought to lead the world in aeronautics."

"Yes, Captain; indeed, we should."

∞

Several thousand men, women, and children gathered on the Champs-de-Mars to witness the aeronautical event. The long, verdant parade ground and surrounding parkland had been a choice spot for ascensions ever since the advent of ballooning during the last days of the *ancien régime*.

The spectators anticipated a demonstration of controlled, powered flight that would equal or exceed Krebs and Renard's 1884 breakthrough aerial adventure in *La France*. The army officers had piloted their airship a round-trip distance of eight kilometers in twenty-three minutes. Today's route began at the École Militaire, continued past the Eiffel Tower, across the river to the Palais du Trocadéro, and back; twice around the circuit would surpass the record eight-kilometer mark.

The airship, which measured approximately twenty meters in length, had been transported to the field in two vans. There, it was assembled and the cigar-shaped balloon filled with almost six-hundred cubic meters of hydrogen gas. The gondola was an open bamboo framework, upon which was mounted a battery-powered electric motor that produced eight horse-power. The lightweight engine drove a four-bladed tractor propeller, and there was a rudder and elevator to assist in steering the craft. The gondola displayed a tricolor flag on its stern.

A few police officers were there to hold back observers at the launching site. Reporters and photographers assembled to record the event. Dressed smartly in English tweeds and sporting a long silk scarf, the aeronaut posed for photographs and answered the reporters' questions.

After he finished with the journalists, the aeronaut checked the wind speed and direction, barometric pressure and temperature; conditions appeared optimal for flight. He consulted with a mechanic who had built and tested the engine and spoke to the men who were responsible for filling the balloon with gas. Feeling confident in the success of his venture, the aeronaut climbed into the gondola to cheers and a round of applause. He smiled and waved at the onlookers. Then he signaled his crew to release the mooring lines.

The ship rose quickly; the aeronaut leveled off and started the motor. The propeller turned, the blades beat the air, and the craft moved forward and gained speed. Far below, the crowds gathered on the Champs-de-Mars gazed upward and gasped and shouted in awe; many among them waved tiny tricolor flags. A band struck up Saint-Saëns's "Marche Militaire Française"; the swaggering melody echoed throughout the vast field as the machine floated gracefully overhead, its passing shadow aimed directly at the tower.

Inspector Legros waited for Mignonette at their designated rendez-vous, among a crowd congregating near the arch at the tower's base. While all eyes fixed on the approaching airship, Étienne scanned the area in search of the young woman. After a moment, he spotted an attractive girl wearing a blue frock and a straw bonnet. She was standing among a group of spectators sheltered beneath the shade of a tall chestnut tree. The young woman glanced around, as if she were searching for someone. Then their eyes met; she waved and began walking toward Legros.

Étienne smiled at Mignonette and gestured for her to join him. Then he heard a murmuring that rolled through the crowd, gathering momentum like a breaker surging ashore. The sound of the band faded and died. Looking up into the sky, he noticed that the airship, which was about four hundred meters from the tower, seemed to be losing altitude precipitately. The aeronaut tugged frantically at a line dangling from the balloon. A man standing next to Legros said, "He's in trouble." A moment later someone shouted, "He's coming down!" Another screamed, "It's going to crash!"

Less than two hundred meters from where Legros was standing, the aeronaut cut the motor. The out-of-control airship pitched and drifted with the wind toward a tall stand of chestnut trees. Spectators scrambled out of the way of the plummeting craft. Mignonette disappeared among the scattering throng.

The loud groan and sharp crack of bending and snapping wood resounded over the field as the gondola snagged in the treetops. The deflated gasbag flopped over the branches; the aeronaut dropped a mooring rope and shinnied down to safety. A few policemen ran to him, having already given up hope of controlling the crowd.

Hundreds had fled the Champs-de-Mars. The remainder, now seem-ingly out of danger, swarmed to the crash site to examine the wreckage. The police formed a cordon to ward off the milling curiosity seekers. Legros spotted Mignonette standing by herself in the middle of the field. He ran to her.

"Are you all right, Mademoiselle?" He could see she was trembling.

Mignonette stared at him without speaking.

Legros offered his arm. "Please come with me. I have a fiacre."

She nodded and accompanied him. Legros escorted her to the Avenue de la Bourdonnais where his cab waited by the curb. He opened the door, helped her into the fiacre, and gave the driver instructions.

Legros sat beside her, reached into his pocket, and took out a silver flask. "Would you care for some brandy, Mademoiselle? It'll do you good."

She held out a shaking hand and stuttered, "Thank . . . thank you, Monsieur." She took a long draft, wiped her lips, and returned the flask.

Legros waited patiently for the young woman to calm down. When she appeared more composed, he asked, "Do you feel like talking to me now?"

She took a deep breath and turned to him. "Forgive me, Monsieur. So many things have happened lately, and now this. It's too much. I'm afraid; I can't help thinking about Manuela. But yes, I'll talk to you. I fear that Bonnet may have had something to do with her death."

"What makes you think that?"

"First, you must understand the relationship between Madame and Bonnet. They're lovers. All the servants know, and Monsieur doesn't seem to care. According to Manuela, the baron encouraged the affair. I suppose he figured it would keep Madame occupied and distract her from his own liaisons.

"Before they left for Aix-les-Bains, Manuela overheard an argument between Madame and Monsieur. The baron had paid Bonnet a good deal of money for some service he was to perform, and Madame demanded to know why."

"Did Manuela say what that service was?"

"No, she didn't, but it must have been very important. She said the baron paid Bonnet five thousand francs."

"Did she know—did she say what he did with the money?"

"Yes, Monsieur. She saw him hide the five thousand francs."

"Where did he conceal it?"

"There's a loose floorboard under his bed. That's his hiding place."

"How did she see him? I assume he closed the door."

Mignonette looked down at her hands. "She . . . she peeked through the keyhole. Manuela suspected Bonnet was up to no good. She believed he'd give her something to keep her mouth shut, but she was afraid to ask."

"I see. Did the baron pay Bonnet in gold or banknotes?"

"Manuela said banknotes, Monsieur."

I hope he hasn't moved the swag, Legros thought. "Pardon me, Mademoiselle. Was Manuela in bed with *la grippe* when she returned from Aix-les-Bains?"

"Not at first, Monsieur. She had a bad cold, that's all. She didn't get really sick until later, when Madame had the doctor in to see her."

"Is there anything else?"

"No, Monsieur. That's all I know. But I believe . . . I'm almost sure Bonnet sneaked into her room and gave her too much medicine. He must have found out that she spied on him."

Legros thought a moment before pursuing: "Only Madame and the cook were supposed to administer the drug, and if what you've told me is true, Manuela feared Bonnet. I doubt she would have taken the medicine from him without a struggle."

Mignonette shook her head. "I don't know, Monsieur. Manuela snored. Perhaps she was asleep and he poured some into her open mouth?"

She would have gagged and thrashed violently, he thought. Legros smiled and touched her hand reassuringly. "That's enough for now, Mademoiselle. I'm taking you to a safe place. For the time being, you'll remain under police protection. You needn't worry about Bonnet."

Her eyes widened, and her voice quavered. "What . . . what about my position, M. Legros? What will Madame say?"

"This is police business, Mademoiselle. I'll explain everything to Madame de Livet. Her husband is missing, and one of her servants is dead. She should want to get to the truth."

"Pardon me, Monsieur. Do you mean even if the truth sends her lover to prison?"

A good question, he thought. "Please calm yourself, Mademoiselle. Do you trust me?"

"Yes, Monsieur," she said quietly.

"Good," he replied. "I'll see to it no one harms you."

⁂

Legros rang the Lefebvres' doorbell. Suzanne answered. She opened the door and smiled at the inspector. Her pleasant expression changed when she saw Mignonette Hubert standing behind the detective. Suzanne's cool greeting matched her censorious frown. "Good day, M. Legros. How may I help you?"

"Good day, Suzanne. I have an important message from M. Lefebvre. Is Madame in?"

"Yes, Monsieur. Please wait a moment." She turned and left them in the hallway. Had Legros been alone, she would have invited him in to the sitting room.

Adele came to the door. Her anxious expression reflected her bewilderment after Suzanne told her Inspector Legros had arrived on "urgent police business" with "some woman."

"Good day, Étienne; Mademoiselle. You have a message from M. Lefebvre?"

"Yes, Madame." He removed the letter from his jacket pocket and handed it to Adele.

After reading the note quickly, she said, "I understand, Étienne." Then she greeted Mignonette with a sympathetic smile and gentle voice: "Well, Mademoiselle Hubert, it seems you are to be our guest."

Mignonette curtsied nervously and brushed away a tear. "I'm so sorry, Madame Lefebvre."

Adele reached out, took the young woman's hand, and guided her across the threshold. "Nonsense, Mademoiselle. You are welcome. My mother and I were about to take tea. Will you join us?"

Mignonette wiped her eyes with a handkerchief and nodded. "Thank you, Madame; I'm in your debt."

She smiled at Legros. "You're invited, too, Étienne."

"Thank you, Madame, but I'm afraid I must return to duty."

"I understand. Will you dine with us at eight? Cook is making an excellent cassoulet."

Legros flushed with embarrassment and cleared his throat before answering. "That's very kind of you, Madame, but that would depend on the chief. I . . . I'll mention it to him this afternoon."

"I see. Please tell Monsieur Lefebvre that I expect you both for dinner."

Legros tipped his hat politely. "I'll try to persuade him, Madame Lefebvre. Good day." Then he looked at Mignonette. "Please don't worry, Mademoiselle. You're safe. *Au revoir.*"

The young woman smiled faintly. "Thank you, Monsieur. *Au revoir.*"

As he exited the foyer door, Legros spotted Detective Allard watching from his observation post on the other side of the Rue Bertin Poirée. Legros signaled to the detective to remain where he was. Then he crossed the street and walked over to his subordinate's station. "Is everything all right, Allard?"

"Yes, M. Legros; all's quiet. Who's the young woman, if I may ask?"

"She's an important witness. She'll be staying with the Lefebvres for a while. Please inform your relief. I'll speak to Sergeant Adam when I return to headquarters."

"Very well, Inspector. Good day."

"Good day, Allard."

⌯∞⌯

When Legros arrived at the de Livet mansion, Sergeant Marechal met him in the foyer.

"How goes it, Marechal?"

The seasoned detective frowned and shook his head. "Not very well, M. Legros. We've turned up nothing, and Madame's growing more impatient by the hour."

"Where is Madame de Livet?"

"Sulking in her boudoir, I suppose."

"Where's Bonnet?"

"Out running errands for his mistress, as usual."

"You have someone shadowing him?"

"Of course, Inspector. I put one of my best men on his tail."

"That's good. Have you searched his room yet?"

"Not yet, Monsieur. It's one of the last on our list, and we're just about done."

"Excellent; we'll do it now."

The veteran smiled slyly and lowered his voice. "You've got something, Inspector?"

Legros nodded. "Perhaps. Come on; let's do this quickly."

Legros followed the sergeant up three flights to Bonnet's little room in the servants' quarters. They entered. Legros said, "Watch the door, Marechal. I'd prefer no one saw us."

The sergeant remained on the threshold while Legros dashed to the bed, crouched, and felt around the floorboards. After a moment he muttered, "Got it." Legros removed a loosened board and pulled out a glass jar stuffed with hundred-franc notes. He put the banknotes in his pocket, closed the jar, and returned it to its hiding place.

The sergeant said, "The way is clear, Inspector."

Legros and Marechal left the room. Legros stopped on the landing and whispered, "How much longer do you need to complete the search?"

"An hour at most, Inspector."

"All right. Say nothing to anyone about what I found. I'm going to speak to the baroness to let her know we'll be out of here soon."

"That'll make the old girl happy."

"I suppose so, but I've other news for her that she won't like as much."

They proceeded downstairs. Legros stopped at the first-floor landing and knocked on Madame de Livet's door.

"Yes, who is it?" she asked impatiently.

"Inspector Legros, Madame. May I enter?"

"The door's unlocked," she replied.

Legros approached the baroness, who was reclining on a settee, a fashion magazine in one hand and a cigarette in the other. He noticed a glass and a half emptied sherry decanter set on a small round table next to the settee.

Legros removed his hat and bowed. "I regret disturbing you, Madame."

"How nice of you to say that, with your detectives poking their noses into every corner of my home."

Legros ignored her sarcasm. She was irritated, and what he had to say could irritate her more. "I've good news for you, Madame. Our search is nearly completed; my detectives should be finished in no more than an hour."

Madame put down her cigarette and magazine, sat up, and smoothed her skirts with a rustle of silk. Her sour expression changed to a hopeful smile. "Thank goodness, Monsieur. Did they find anything of interest?"

Legros shook his head sadly. "Alas, I regret to say they did not. I apologize for putting you to all this trouble."

"No need for apologies, Inspector. I fear I was somewhat abrupt just now. Regardless of the inconvenience, I will do everything I can to assist your investigation. After all, my husband is still missing and poor Manuela's dead."

"Thank you, Madame. You have been most helpful. Unfortunately, I must mention something that might further inconvenience you. I regret to inform you that Mlle Hubert won't be returning to your household this afternoon. She'll be residing elsewhere for a while."

"Mignonette not returning? Why not?"

"The poor girl's had an awful shock, Madame. She and Mlle Otero were very close, as you know, and now Mlle Hubert feels threatened."

The baroness's normally smooth face wrinkled in a worried frown. "Why does she feel that way? Who in my household would hurt her?"

Legros smiled as if to shrug off the matter. "Madame, that's exactly what I said when she came to me. The child thinks Bonnet might do her an injury."

"Bonnet? What nonsense. She must be imagining things."

"I'm glad to hear you say that, Madame. So you think there's no reason for her to fear?"

She thought a moment before replying, "Not to my knowledge, Inspector."

A carefully worded response, he thought. "Very well, Madame; but perhaps we should indulge her until this matter is settled."

The baroness's eyes narrowed, and she replied coldly, "Is M. Lefebvre aware of this?"

"Of course, Madame. I'm acting under the chief inspector's orders."

"I see. And where will Mignonette be staying until this issue is resolved?"

"Alas, Madame, I'm not at liberty to say."

She stared at him for a moment before saying, "Is that all, M. Legros?"

He bowed. "Yes, Madame de Livet. I'll leave you in peace. Good afternoon."

"Good afternoon, Inspector."

After Legros left, the baroness paced the room for a minute or two. Then she stopped at the round table, poured another drink, and lit a cigarette. She sat on the couch, leaned back on the bolster, and stared at the ceiling. She remained there, smoking, drinking, and flipping through magazines, until the detectives left the mansion.

∞

Achille and Legros met late in the afternoon. An hour before sunset, the shades were drawn in the chief's office; gas jets filled the room with a warm, golden glow. M. Lefebvre was in a good mood. Placing his elbows on the desktop, he leaned forward and smiled at his assistant.

"That was clever, Étienne; very clever. You're certain no one saw you take the banknotes?"

"I'm positive, Chief. Marechal kept watch at the door."

"I'd give five thousand francs to see the look on Bonnet's face when he discovers his little fortune's gone missing."

"It'll stir things up, all right. And I doubt he'll report the 'theft' to the police."

Achille laughed. "I'd give *ten thousand* francs if he tried. You checked the serial numbers against the list you got from the bank?"

"Absolutely, Chief. The baron paid Bonnet from the notes he withdrew before they went to Aix-les-Bains. That corresponds with the information Mignonette says she got from Otero."

"A picture of this case is forming like a mosaic; it's coming together piece by piece. Tell me, how did Madame react when you told her the news about Mlle Hubert?"

"Surprise followed by anger, culminating in acceptance."

"That's to be expected; she's irritated and troubled, but she hasn't much choice in the matter. The young woman's accusation against Bonnet must have hit a nerve." Achille rubbed his beard meditatively for a moment. "I imagine there will be some interesting conversations between Madame and her paramour. It's too bad we don't have a reliable pair of eyes and ears in the house."

Legros frowned. "Pardon me, Chief. Do you want to send Mignonette back to the mansion? It would be very risky."

"Of course not. But I would not be surprised if someone else on the staff came forward. We'll see. In the meantime, I'm following the cloak-and-dagger leads. I suspect Bonnet was paid to help conceal what really was to happen at Prince Papkov's villa. His story was a fabrication. And money wasn't his only incentive; there's also his liaison with Madame."

"Do you think the Okhrana's mixed up in it?"

"I believe so, and the English may have a hand in it, too. But I don't want to speculate too much. Let's see what we get from Delphine and Apolline. And of course, we need to keep searching for the baron, Mme Behrs, and the fellow with the bandaged face. I hope you can get some leads from the Hotel Squad tomorrow. The neighbors on the Rue de Turenne or old Aubert might come up with something, too."

"Very well, Chief. Do you think we have enough on Bonnet to go to the *juge* for a warrant?"

"You mean bring him in for investigative detention? No, not yet. Let's keep him on the line a bit longer and see how it plays out. Which reminds me: We have the two medicine bottles, a spoon, and a glass in evidence. Is that correct?"

"Yes, Chief; that's what we took from Otero's room."

"Those items might prove useful after all. I have an idea." Achille paused for a moment. He was not ready to share his idea with Legros. He stroked his moustache meditatively before asking, "Is there anything else you wanted to discuss?"

"I was wondering about the aconite. I'm sure Otero wouldn't have taken it from Bonnet willingly. Do you know of any way he could have given it to her while she slept?"

Achille rubbed his chin for a moment and then smiled. "Do you recall how the king was murdered in *Hamlet*?"

Legros replied with a bewildered stare. "Pardon me, Chief?"

Achille shook his head. "Really, Étienne. You're an educated man. You should know your Shakespeare. Hamlet's evil uncle poured deadly poison into his sleeping brother's ear."

"Ah yes, Chief. Now I remember. Do you think that's how Otero was murdered?"

"Perhaps. At any rate, it's a good question. I'll talk to Masson." He glanced at the wall clock. "It's late, Étienne. Your report's finished. Why not go home? There'll be plenty of work waiting for us in the morning."

"I'm sorry; I almost forgot. Mme Lefebvre invited me to dine at eight, and she insisted you come home in time for dinner, too."

"What's on the menu?"

"Madame said a cassoulet."

"Ah, one of my favorites. And I've just the right wine to accompany it: a first-rate Canon-Fronsac. I think we should accept."

"Pardon me, Chief; won't it be awkward? Mlle Hubert will be there, and we must avoid discussing the case."

Achille scratched his beard and pondered the matter for a moment. "You have a point. My wife knows better than to talk about the case, but my mother-in-law is another matter. She tends to rely on conspiracy theories circulated by her confidant, the famous cabbage vendor Mme Gros. She can hold forth on such nonsense ad nauseam. Nevertheless, over the years, I've learned how to handle her. And the young woman's presence should help curb my mother-in-law's loose tongue. At any rate, I suggest we please Mme Lefebvre and ourselves by enjoying good company and an excellent meal."

Achille closed the file and placed it in his desk drawer. On the way out, he turned to Legros and said, "I'm sure Mlle Hubert will welcome the presence of her gallant protector."

Legros smiled shyly and said nothing.

The chief laughed and nudged his assistant playfully. The case seemed to be progressing well; Achille accepted the cassoulet and Canon-Fronsac as a well-deserved reward. But he had more on his mind than a good meal. He anticipated a pleasant evening in bed with Adele followed by several hours' rest, as well.

10

THE DEMIMONDE

A light steady shower sprinkled the Rue Pigalle. Delphine gazed out the rain-streaked cab window. Yellow gaslights highlighted the drizzle and reflected in rippling puddles. She observed a pair of streetwalkers huddling together in the shelter of a rubbish-strewn passageway. *Poor things. Like a couple of stray cats*, she thought. Delphine empathized with these women; between the ages of fourteen and eighteen she had been one of them. Abandoned by their fathers, harassed by the police, and exploited by pimps, such women often turned to their own gender for love and protection.

The cab pulled over to the curb. Delphine stepped down to the pavement, opened her umbrella, and paid the fare. She walked up the block to

Number 75, the unobtrusive entrance of the Hanneton, a brasserie owned, operated by, and catering exclusively to women. Men were not welcomed, with the notable exception of Toulouse-Lautrec, who went there regularly to drink and sketch the proprietress and her clientele.

Mme Armande, the muscular one-eyed manager, stepped out from behind her cashier's cage and greeted Delphine with a bear hug and a kiss. "My dear Mlle Delphine, how good of you to come. We've missed you."

"Thank you, Madame. I'm afraid the demands of my career have kept me away too long."

"Ah yes, your career. We're all so proud of you since you've become a star." Madame lowered her voice and winked with her good eye. "Your little friend is waiting for you, and you've arrived not a moment too soon. She's very popular, you know."

Delphine looked over Madame Armande's beefy shoulder and spotted Apolline seated in a corner on the red banquette. The young woman looked up, smiled, and raised her glass of beer in greeting. Her painted face in gaslight had the appearance of a wanton bisque doll.

Delphine excused herself, walked over, and sat next to Apolline. "How goes it, my dear?"

Apolline shrugged. "It goes, Delphine. Buy me another beer?"

"Of course." Delphine raised her hand and gestured to a waitress, who came immediately.

"Two of the same, please." After the waitress returned to the bar to fill their order, Delphine offered Apolline a cigarette and gave her a light. "I hope you haven't been waiting long?"

Apolline took a puff and exhaled before answering, "Not long, but I had to fend off an old hag who got too friendly. She left in a huff."

"I'm sorry; I got here as soon as I could. Anyway, I guess I'd better come to the point. M. Lefebvre is looking for M. de Livet. I know the baron played cards regularly with M. Orlovsky, perhaps as recently as a week ago. Do you have anything of interest for me to pass along?"

"I might, but I'm afraid it's going to be for a stiff price."

Delphine stared at the young woman. They were friends, but she figured that in this game friendship had its limits. "If what you have is good, M. Lefebvre will pay at the usual rate."

The waitress brought the beers. Apolline waited for her to leave, then took a long drink before replying. "I'm afraid this is a price M. Lefebvre can't pay. M. Orlovsky is waiting with Aurore at the Folies Bergère. He allowed me to meet you here on one condition. I'm to persuade you to join us for a private party at our flat, and you know what that means. But there's more to it. He promised me a pair of pearl earrings if you come, but he said he'd whip me if you don't; he wasn't joking. He's been in an ugly mood all week, and I'm sure it has something to do with the baron and M. Lefebvre's investigation. When he gets that way, he usually takes it out on Aurore's behind. After all, the poor girl seems to like it. But this time—" Her hand trembled as she raised it to wipe a tear from the corner of her eye.

Delphine put her arm around Apolline's shoulder. She leaned over and whispered, "Of course I'll come; I won't let him hurt you."

Apolline took a drag of her cigarette, then fussed with some stray curls on her forehead. "All right, Delphine. What do you want to know?"

Delphine asked questions about the baron, Colonel Mukhin, Prince Papkov, Sims, and Bonnet. Apolline replied:

"I never met the prince or the Englishman, but the baron, the colonel, and Orlovsky mentioned them at a party in an apartment on the Rue de Turenne the evening before the baron and Bonnet went to Aix-les-Bains. I didn't hear details, but I got the impression there was a lucrative deal in the works.

"They drank, laughed like hyenas, and took turns stuffing twenty-franc notes in our garters and down our cleavage. The baron's mistress was there, too. She smoked cigars, guzzled vodka, and played with the men; we had to serve the bitch like the others and call her 'Madame Behrs.' Madame, my ass. She's just a snooty Russian whore from Le Chabanais, where the swells paid thousands to sniff her chamber pot and kiss her dirty feet."

"Was Bonnet there, too?"

"You mean the baron's lackey? He was there all right, the sullen brute. I can tell you a thing or two about him."

"What about Bonnet?"

Apolline smiled slyly. "Well, for one thing, he's Madame de Livet's lover."

"How do you know that?"

"Madame told me so, herself."

"You know Madame de Livet?"

Apolline gave a little laugh. "Oh yes, my dear; I know her *intimately*."

"Where did you meet her?"

"Right here, of course. She dropped in a few weeks ago; her first time, I guess. What an entrance. She sashayed through the door as if she were the Queen of England, with her lackeys and coach waiting at the curb. All eyes were on her, but she came straight to me. I guess the old girl knew what she was looking for."

"Is she . . . one of us?"

"Well, I'd say she's been unlucky with men. Her husband married her for the name and social position, and her father sold her to pay off his debts. As for Bonnet, he's no better than an ape."

Apolline took a swig of beer, then drew close enough to whisper in Delphine's ear. "Now, here's something that ought to interest M. Lefebvre. A couple of evenings before they left for Aix-les-Bains, I sneaked out and met the baroness at a hotel on the Rue des Abbesses. She gave me a gold bracelet and said there would be more as soon as she was 'free.'"

"What did she mean by 'free'?"

"Your guess is as good as mine, but I'll wager she'd like to be rid of both the baron and Bonnet, with enough money to choose her company and do as she pleases. At any rate, I imagine she expected some big change in her life and that it would happen soon."

"I see. Is there anything else you have for me?"

Apolline thought a moment before shaking her head and saying with conviction, "No; that's all." Then her eyes widened as if she suddenly remembered something important. "My God, it's late. We'd better get over to the Folies Bergère or M. Orlovsky will tan my backside for sure."

"All right, dear." Delphine left money on the table for the beers, took Apolline by the hand, and walked to the cashier's cage where they said *au revoir* to Madame. The young women exited to the dark, damp street and headed in the direction of the popular cabaret on the Rue Richer.

∞

Delphine and Apolline passed through the spacious lobby that provided access to the two-tiered, horseshoe-shaped promenade. Several eyes turned toward them in recognition, prompting a round of applause and cheers for a star of the café concerts. Delphine smiled and waved to her admirers; her celebrity distinguished her from the common whores who plied their trade at the Folies Bergère. As for Apolline, she savored the moment as though association with a popular entertainer had elevated her status in the demimonde.

Hundreds of electric bulbs glimmered through a cloud of tobacco smoke, their yellow incandescence dimmed like the lights of an ocean liner steaming in a fog. Through the haze one could make out the red-and-gold-painted, mirror-lined arcade, the artificial garden and spouting, alabaster fountain, the marble-topped bars stocked with bottles of liquor and champagne and bowls of fruit, the women serving drinks to a thirsty crowd, the clientele lounging on chairs and couches as they ogled the perambulating prostitutes.

One inhaled a miasma of countless cigars and cigarettes interfused with the odor of a confined multitude reeking of perfume, cologne, pomade, and sweat. A band blared out a popular tune loud enough to overtop a constant murmuring punctuated by laughter, drunken outbursts, and an occasional scream.

As they approached M. Orlovsky's private box, Delphine and Apolline glimpsed the stage act, a scantily clad young woman swinging from a trapeze high above a gaggle of clowns who gestured suggestively at her deftly exposed anatomy.

The spymaster ignored both the performance and Aurore's desperate attempts to amuse him. His dark eyes darted impatiently, scanning the perimeter. When he spotted Delphine and Apolline, his rouged lips twitched upward, forming a twisted smile. He rose from his chair and prepared to greet his honored guest.

"Good evening, Mlle Lacroix. How kind of you to join us." He bowed formally, then stepped forward to escort Delphine into the loge.

Aurore dashed ahead to embrace her friend and kissed her on the lips. "Thank you, Delphine," she murmured. "We're so happy you could come. Monsieur has ordered the finest champagne, in your honor."

Orlovsky glared at Aurore but said nothing. He smiled and helped Delphine to a chair. "Please be seated, Mademoiselle. I'm at your service. Would you care for something in particular? Whatever delicacies the house can provide are yours for the asking."

"Whatever you're drinking is fine with me, M. Orlovsky."

Orlovsky snapped his fingers and gestured to a waiter. The man came at once.

"The Moët et Chandon 1878, if you please," Orlovsky said. As the waiter rushed off to fetch the wine, Orlovsky reached into his breast pocket and produced a gold cigarette case. "Will you try one of these, Mademoiselle? They're Turkish."

Delphine declined courteously. Knowing his tastes, she suspected the cigarettes contained opium. "No thank you, Monsieur. I prefer my own blend."

"Ah yes, Mademoiselle. I've heard of 'Delphine.' They've become popular with the ladies—and some of the gentlemen, too."

Delphine ignored Orlovsky's sly reference to the "ladies" and "gentlemen" of her former profession. She took a silver case from her purse and retrieved a cigarette. He struck a match and gave her a light. She guided his hand with hers but withdrew quickly as if to avoid contamination, a gesture that was not lost on her host.

The waiter returned with the champagne. He uncorked the bottle expertly, with a pleasing *pop* and no loss of the precious liquid. Next, he poured a small amount in Orlovsky's glass and anxiously awaited the spymaster's judgment.

"An excellent vintage," he announced. "I'm sure Mademoiselle will approve."

The waiter filled Orlovsky's glass, then poured for Delphine and the girls and left the bottle in an ice bucket.

Delphine took a sip and said, "It is quite good. But then, I'm hardly a judge of fine wines."

Orlovsky smirked. "You are too modest, Mlle Lacroix."

"You're mistaken, Monsieur. I'm just being honest. I never pretend to be something I'm not."

"Is that so? You're a superb actress. Your songs can move the toughest audience to tears. I'd say acting is one of your most estimable talents, and verisimilitude—that is to say, pretense coupled with the illusion of reality—is the very essence of acting."

"Pardon me, Monsieur. I'm a simple, uneducated woman; you're far too clever for me."

Orlovsky laughed and refilled her wine flute. "Are you being honest with me? I've heard you enjoy the company of clever men and can give as good as you get."

Apolline and Aurore observed and listened with interest; they waited expectantly for a reply.

Delphine shrugged and took another sip of champagne before answering. "I've known many men, from elegant gentlemen to the Apache, and I believe few if any of them would be considered *clever*."

Apolline put a hand to her mouth to suppress a giggle. Orlovsky scowled and removed her glass. "You've had enough, *my dear*," he muttered.

The young woman folded her hands and lowered her eyes. "Yes, Monsieur," she replied.

Orlovsky turned to Delphine with a wry smile. "My dear Mademoiselle, I've heard on good authority that you are *intimately* acquainted with some very clever men—brilliant, even." He paused a moment to study her expression and give her time to ponder his reference to her intimacy with "very clever" and "brilliant" men. Impressed by her impassive reaction, he said, "But let's not speak of them now. Your glass is almost empty." He poured and signaled the waiter to bring another bottle.

Orlovsky and Delphine drank and made small talk until one A.M. while the two young women watched the acts and remained silent except when their master addressed them. They all left the Folies Bergère in Orlovsky's carriage, which conveyed them the short distance to Apolline and Aurore's Montmartre flat.

∞

Light streamed through half-opened balcony doors; an early-morning breeze ruffled lace curtains. Delphine's eyes flickered open. She awoke to the sounds of Apolline's soft, regular breathing, Aurore's intermittent snorts, the beating of horses' hooves, and the rumbling of cartwheels on the pavement below.

She drew back the sheets on her side of the bed, swung her legs over, and sat up. Blinking her eyelids and shaking her head, she reoriented to the surroundings; her tingling flesh reminded Delphine that she was naked. She sniffed a musky potpourri of perfume, incense, and glowing bare flesh. Her eyes now adjusted to the pale light, she glanced around in search of her clothes. She spotted her dress, underwear, and stockings draped over a corner chair, her shoes on the floor, and her hat, purse, and umbrella sat on top of an adjacent dressing table.

Delphine rose to her feet gingerly, her head still whirling in an alcoholic vortex. *Thank goodness I refused the opium pipe*, she thought. Careful to avoid stumbling on the carpet, she made her way to the chair, where she gathered her garments, sat, and began dressing. As she put on her clothes, memories of early-morning revels returned to her consciousness like a series of slides projected by a magic lantern. She most vividly recalled M. Orlovsky indulging his voyeurism by posing the young women in a tableau vivant reminiscent of Ingres's *The Turkish Bath*. However, high art soon descended into a sex show suitable to the Moorish room at Le Chabanais. True to character, the Russian viewed the performance from behind an Oriental screen, peering through a peephole like a *louche* Sultan spying on his seraglio.

Eager to report her intelligence to M. Lefebvre, she dressed quickly, grabbed her umbrella and purse, and passed through the *portière* separating the bedroom from the sitting room. Upon entering, she saw Orlovsky seated at a corner table. The Russian wore a floral-patterned silk dressing gown casually left open to expose his pallid, hairy flesh. He was enjoying his coffee and brioche while perusing the morning edition of *Les Amis de la Vérité*. Orlovsky put down his newspaper and turned toward Delphine. Exposed to the morning light, his cheeks and jowls exhibited white stubble in contrast to his jet-black dyed hair, moustache, and small beard.

"Good morning, Mademoiselle. Will you join me? I've ordered for two."

"What about Aurore and Apolline?"

The Russian snorted contemptuously. "They're dead to the world; they'll sleep for hours. It's the drug's effect, you know."

Delphine frowned. "Yes, Monsieur; I know all too well."

"I noticed you didn't touch the stuff."

"No, Monsieur; I don't need it."

He grinned knowingly. "You control your appetites. I like that." Orlovsky rose and pointed to the chair opposite him. "Please sit, Mademoiselle. I'd like a word with you. It won't take long, I promise."

She did as he asked, but with some trepidation. Delphine suspected Orlovsky knew that her acceptance of his invitation signified something more than a carnal urge to romp in bed with her girlfriends. She tried to read his intentions in his expressions and manner, but the spymaster's aims remained hidden behind a mask of civility. He filled her coffee cup. She thanked him but declined the pastry.

Orlovsky gazed at her keenly before saying, "I'm reading an article about the case of the missing baron. It seems M. Lefebvre is being very tight-lipped about his investigation, which is leading to all sorts of speculation in the press. By the way, I believe you're acquainted with M. de Livet?"

Delphine sipped her coffee and considered before answering carefully. "I've met him on occasion. But I haven't seen him for some time."

"I know. You refused his invitations to some very amusing parties. May I ask why?"

"A woman may have reasons that she keeps to herself, and it is impolite of a gentleman to question her about them."

Orlovsky smirked. "I'm justly rebuked, Mademoiselle. More coffee?"

"No thank you, Monsieur. I'm in a bit of a hurry, if you don't mind."

"As you please. Before you leave, I have a proposition that should interest you. My associates and I have important business with the baron. His sudden disappearance is distressing, and we'd pay handsomely for information that would aid us in locating him. Have you any idea where he might be?"

"No, Monsieur, I do not. Have you contacted the police?"

"Ah yes, the police. I'm a great admirer of M. Lefebvre and would do anything I could to help his investigation. However, between you and me, my associates and I would like to get to the baron first. Just to settle our business, you understand. Then we would gladly turn him over to the Sûreté. Now, if someone *were* to provide information that led us to Monsieur de Livet, we'd make it worth her while, to the tune of twenty thousand francs."

"That's a great deal of money, Monsieur."

"Yes, it is; and it would all be strictly confidential. No one need know, and no one gets hurt. A nice, neat stroke of business."

"I understand, M. Orlovsky; but as I said, I haven't seen the gentleman in some time and have no idea where his is. Now, if you'll kindly excuse me, I fear I must leave."

"Very well, Mademoiselle. But if by chance you do come across some valuable information, please keep my offer in mind. And if you'll permit, my carriage is at your disposal."

"Thank you, Monsieur. It's a lovely morning; I prefer to walk."

Orlovsky rose from the table and made a slight bow. "As you wish, Mlle Lacroix. *Au revoir.*"

"Good day, M. Orlovsky."

He listened to her footsteps on the stairs and the sound of the front door closing. Orlovsky got up and went to the window. Hiding behind the half-opened shutter, he peered at her through the slats as she walked up the street, turned a corner, and disappeared from view. Then he stepped over to an escritoire; took out pen, ink, and paper; and wrote a brief note. He placed the message in an envelope, addressed it, and rang a small silver bell to summon Aisha, the Moroccan maidservant.

The young woman entered from the adjoining kitchen. "Yes, Monsieur?" she answered.

Orlovsky handed her the envelope. "Deliver this message, and be quick about it."

She took the letter, curtsied, and left the apartment. Orlovsky returned to his coffee, rolls, and newspaper. After a moment, he glanced in the direction of the bedroom and muttered, "Will those lazy bitches sleep all day? I've a good mind to wake them up with my riding crop." He shook his head, lit a cigarette, and continued reading Fournier's article about the missing baron.

∞

Delphine purchased four white chrysanthemums from a street vendor near the cemetery entrance on the Avenue Rachel. The old woman asked, "For the dead, Mademoiselle?"

Delphine nodded. "Yes, Madame; for the dead." Carrying the flowers in one hand and her parasol in the other, she entered the final resting place of both the famous and the obscure.

A brisk wind shook the poplars lining the pathway, scattering leaves over the tightly packed tombs and graves. The crisp, smoky scent of burnt foliage filled the cemetery. She paused for a moment to contemplate the statue of a sad angel, a grieving husband's monument to a young mother who died giving birth. The beautifully carved stone face reminded her of Virginie. She wiped a tear and continued down a narrow path between a row of vaults clustered beneath the Rue Caulaincourt bridge. When she reached her friend's burial place, she knelt for a moment in silent prayer before laying down the chrysanthemums as a signal for Moïse. She rose and scanned her surroundings as a precaution before walking on to the mail drop. From her perspective, she seemed to be the only living person nearby. The place was quiet except for the intermittent rustling of branches and the rumbling of traffic on the viaduct. Nevertheless, she gripped her parasol in her left hand near the handle with her right hand free, a position conducive to defense and attack.

When she reached the bench, she looked around in all directions. Satisfied that she was alone, she sat and deposited her encrypted message in the designated hiding place. She rested for a few minutes, then got up and proceeded toward the exit. She remained alert, her instinct for danger sharpened by years of experience in the Zone and on the dark, twisting streets of Montmartre. As she neared her destination, she sensed a stirring behind a group of tombs. Her thumb flicked a release; her right hand grasped the parasol handle. The two-pronged attack came swiftly but not as quickly as her defense.

In one graceful, fluid movement, she drew a twelve-inch blade, lunged, and slashed at her frontal attacker while at the same time thrusting back with her steel-tipped parasol. Her dagger cut the first assailant's forearm, causing him to drop his knife while the parasol struck the other in the pit of his stomach, making him double over and retch. With one adversary disarmed and the other disabled, she instantly transitioned from defense to attack.

Delphine advanced with her two weapons. Her first attacker gripped his bleeding arm, turned, and fled. She spun around and ran to the other, who had dropped to his knees while hanging his head over a pool of vomit. Grabbing his hair and tugging with her left hand, she put the blade to his throat with her right. "Are you done puking?" she asked.

"Yes . . . yes," the thug stammered. "Have pity, Mademoiselle."

"Pity is for fools. I'm going to count, quickly. If you don't tell me who sent you by the count of three, I'll cut your ugly throat. One, two—"

"Orlovsky sent me. Spare me, please. I'm poor; I have a wife and two little children."

"I'm not interested in your misfortunes. Did he send you to kill me?"

"No, Mademoiselle. We were supposed to frighten you and rough you up a bit. That's all, I swear it."

Delphine smiled. "Do I look frightened?"

The thug stared at her. "No . . . no, you don't."

She let go of the man's hair, withdrew the blade, and stepped back, but not outside her killing zone. "Return to your master. I'm sure he'll be pleased."

He got up slowly, a hand rubbing his sore belly. He stood before her, trembling.

"Why are you still here? Do you want to fuck me?"

"Uh . . . uh . . . thank you very much, but no."

"Well then, go!"

The poor fellow bowed, and then hobbled away as fast as he could. She had just sheathed her dagger when she heard a rattle in the bushes. She turned and spotted something much larger than a hare scurrying behind the vaults. Delphine lifted her skirts and drew the derringer from her garter holster.

"I'm not in the mood for rabbit hunting! Come out, before I lose my temper."

A whiny voice replied, "Spare me, dear Mademoiselle, for the sake of my four wives and twenty bastards. At least there were four wives and twenty bastards, the last time I counted."

"Is that you, Moïse?"

The young *chiffonier* came out from behind a tomb with his hands raised and a broad grin on his scraggly face. "It's me all right. I was back there enjoying the show."

"You little rat. Why didn't you help?"

"May I put down my hands?"

Delphine holstered the pistol. "Yes, you may, but I should have taken a shot at you just for sport."

Moïse dropped his hands and laughed. "If I thought you needed help, I would have given it. But you beat those guys faster than I could move. You fight like a tigress. Why don't you put it in an act? They'd love it at the Folies Bergère."

"This is no joke. Do you have the message?"

Moïse stopped kidding and said, "Yes, Delphine. I'll take it to M. Lefebvre directly."

"Good. I'm afraid Orlovsky's getting wise to our game. Tell M. Lefebvre we can't use the cemetery anymore. And let him know I'm going into the Zone to stay with Papa Le Boudin for a while, at least until things cool down."

"Is it that bad?"

"I'm afraid so. One more thing: Go to Sergeant Rodin and ask him to keep an eye on Apolline. She's on dope, and that makes you careless. Orlovsky might harm her one of these days."

"I understand. Good luck, kid."

Delphine smiled and gave him a playful cuff on the chin. "Same to you, runt."

11

STARTLED SNAKES

Madame de Livet and Bonnet boarded a late-morning train at the Gare de l'Est. A detective shadowed them from the railway station to Joinville-le-Pont in the southeastern suburbs. There, the couple hired a boat and rowed up the Marne toward a nearby *guinguette*. The detective notified the local police and wired a report to Inspector Legros.

Madame handled the tiller; Bonnet pulled at the oars. Light poured down from a deep-blue sky through breaks in low scattered clouds. The boat glided along olive-green waters past muddy banks lined with willows and reddish-golden poplars, their images reflected on the river's smooth surface. The air had a nostalgic country smell; crisp, clean, and earthy, as though the modern, industrialized metropolis had receded in both time and space.

Madame regarded her lover with ambivalence. She admired his brute strength and cunning while detesting his crudity, but she cared more for him than for her cold, indifferent husband. Recently, she had discovered that she preferred Apolline to the men in her life, and that realization led her to conclude that she cared more for women than for men in general. However, that self-revelation only added to her predicament, because whether by fate or by circumstance—she would never admit to having any practicable choice in the matter—she had become hopelessly entangled with the baron and Bonnet.

He rowed around a bend and headed toward a secluded landing. Bonnet, with Madame's assistance, guided the boat in. He grabbed the bowline, climbed up to the dock, and secured the boat to the mooring. Then he reached down and lifted her, as easily as a father might pick up his child. Charmed by her softness, her sweet fragrance, and her enigmatic smile he kissed her deeply; she responded to his warm, rough caress and the strength in his arms.

"I'd love you in hell, Mathilde," he said huskily.

"Would you, indeed? Aren't we there, already?"

Bonnet winced as though she had slapped his face. He turned away from her and started walking up the pier to the stone stairway that led to the *guinguette*'s terrace. After a moment, she followed.

The restaurant perched atop a low bluff overlooking the river. The terrace contained several rough wooden tables and benches set within a circle of lindens. The dying leaves glowed yellowish brown in the pale autumn light. Madame's eyes scanned around the area of the outdoor dance floor, the small tavern, and the restaurant. The place seemed deserted; the only other guests were a couple of oarsmen who sat on the other side of the terrace where they drank wine, smoked pipes, and absorbed themselves in a game of draughts.

"It's very quiet," she remarked.

"Yes, the crowds won't come until later for the music and dancing. That's why we came early. And more important, we needn't worry about the flics."

"And who, may I ask, are the flics?"

"The pigs—the *police*. Lefebvre's snoops are swarming all over Paris, but they avoid certain joints that are known to be bad for their health."

"Ah yes, the police. You seemed particularly concerned about them this morning. Will you let me in on the secret?"

"It's no secret, Mathilde. We're in trouble. They're wise to our game."

She smiled and spoke patronizingly, as if to provoke him. "*Wise to our game?* Will you please speak French?"

"All right, Madame. I'll put it in words you can understand. The five thousand francs the baron paid me is gone. Legros must have taken it the last day they searched the house."

"But Inspector Legros told me they found nothing of interest?"

Bonnet laughed at her apparent ignorance. "He's a crafty one, all right; just like his master, M. Lefebvre." He glanced over his shoulder. "Keep quiet. The proprietor's coming."

The proprietor, a stout, balding man with a long, drooping moustache, came over and greeted Bonnet like an old friend. "Hello, Eugene. Nice day for a row, isn't it?"

Bonnet smiled. "A perfect day, my friend." He placed a hand on Madame's shoulder and made an introduction. "This is my friend Mathilde." He turned to Madame. "Mathilde, meet Jacques Simon, the friendliest tavern keeper on the river."

Madame smiled and gave her best imitation of a coquette. "Pleased to meet you, M. Simon."

"Thanks, dearie," he replied. "But please call me Jacques. We aren't formal here. Now I know how rowing gives you an appetite. It's early, but I could fry some fresh fish, or if you prefer I have a nice rabbit stew."

"Oh, that sounds lovely," she replied. "But I'm not so hungry." She turned to Bonnet. "What do you want—*dearie?*"

Bonnet frowned at her, then said to Simon, "Just bring us red wine, bread, and some good cheese."

As soon as the proprietor left, Madame opened her purse and took out her cigarette case.

"You aren't going to smoke here?"

"That was my intention," she replied. "Do you object?"

"Yes, I do. I don't like it when you smoke in public. It makes you look cheap."

The baroness sighed. "In case you haven't noticed, my dear, this is not the Café Riche." She held the cigarette near her lips and stared. "Well? I'm waiting."

Bonnet took out a box of matches and gave her a light.

Madame carelessly blew a plume of smoke in Bonnet's face. "Now then, what were you saying about five thousand francs and the police?"

"They know something. Manuela must have talked to Mignonette and she tipped off Legros. Now they're holding Mignonette somewhere where we can't get at her. I'm afraid it's only a matter of time before they take me in for questioning."

"What do you suggest we do?"

"I need to get out of France, and soon. I know someone who can smuggle me over the border to Spain—for a price. From there, I can catch a boat to South America. I have friends in Buenos Aires."

"What about me? And where will you get the money?"

"When the time comes, you can join me. The police are after me, not you. I killed Manuela, not that you objected much."

"Your memory's faulty. I advised you to pay her to keep quiet."

He shook his head. "Once you give in to blackmail, it never ends." He glanced around. "Keep quiet; Jacques is coming."

The proprietor served them, made some jokes and small talk, and returned to the restaurant.

"All right," Madame said. "Let's say we change our plans. How will you manage now that your five thousand is gone?"

"I was counting on you for that."

"Me? I haven't any money. The baron's withdrawn every sou from the bank, and all the property is in his name. Why don't you go to him?"

Bonnet laughed bitterly. "I would if I could find him. He should have contacted us by now. Anyway, I can't wait. Why don't you go to your father?"

"The count? You must be joking. All he had is what my husband gave him, and he spent it on himself. I married to get my father out of debt, and he never came close to thanking me for it."

"Well then, you've got plenty of valuables; jewelry, for instance. My friend will take precious gems in lieu of cash."

"Oh, I'm sure he will. How much does he want?"

"Thirty thousand."

"Thirty thousand *francs*?"

"That's right. And I'll need something for myself, say five thousand to make up for what the flics took."

Madame drank some wine and stubbed out her cigarette. She weighed the cost of complying with his demand against the risk of refusing. "Very well," she replied. "When would you leave?"

"As soon as my friend and I can work out a plan to get me to the border. In case you haven't noticed, the flics are watching us day and night."

They said nothing more of consequence, keeping their thoughts to themselves. They finished the wine and ate some of the bread and cheese. Madame left money for the meal; they got up and returned to the stairway that led to the dock.

The rowers at the other table stopped playing draughts. One turned to the other and nodded. He gestured to Jacques Simon, then took out a pad and pencil and jotted down some notes.

Bonnet had been mistaken about this particular *guinguette*. The oarsmen were detectives stationed in Joinville. A detective at the Gare de l'Est alerted his suburban partners by wire as soon as the baroness and

Bonnet bought their ticket. Moreover, "the friendliest tavern keeper on the river" was one of M. Lefebvre's paid informers.

⌘

Achille met Moïse beneath the medieval Conciergerie clock tower on the Quai de l'Horloge. The chief of detectives translated the Latin inscription on the venerable clock for the *chiffonier*'s benefit: "This mechanism that divides the hours in twelve exact parts, instructs us to preserve Justice and defend the laws."

Moïse was duly impressed. "Is that what it says in an ancient language, M. Lefebvre? I would never have known. You certainly have the advantages of a fine education." The *chiffonier* handed Delphine's encrypted note to Achille and gave him a graphic description of the fight in the cemetery.

"Did you teach her those tricks, Monsieur?" the young man asked, his voice filled with admiration for the chief's fighting skills.

"Yes, I taught her French boxing and *canne d'arme*. But Delphine's very tough, as you know. She was an excellent pupil; I didn't have to teach her much."

"Would you teach me, Monsieur?" Moïse asked with a hopeful look in his eyes. "I'm good with a razor and I can kick, but I'm not so good with my hands."

Achille examined the *chiffonier*'s slight, five-foot frame and thin, short arms. "I suppose I could, but I'm quite busy at the moment."

Moïse frowned with disappointment. "I understand, Monsieur."

Achille reached into his pocket and took out two envelopes. He handed them both to Moïse. "This one's for Delphine, the other's for you. I've added bonuses. You've earned it."

The *chiffonier*'s face brightened. "Thank you, Monsieur. I'm sure Delphine will be pleased. Do you have a message for her?"

"Yes, I do. Tell her not to worry for herself or Apolline. I take care of my friends. And please give my regards to Le Boudin."

"Of course, M. Lefebvre. *Au revoir.*" Moïse tipped his battered hat and bowed; then he turned and walked along the quay in the direction of the Pont au Change.

Achille took a moment to enjoy the mild autumn weather and the fresh river breeze. *I've been cooped up in the office too long*, he thought. A couple of rowers heading for the bridge caught his attention. He knew the strength of the currents running under the bridges on both sides of the islands, both upstream and down. On occasion, he had gone out on grim, early-morning patrols searching for bodies that floated beneath the arches and past the quays. The police fished out the corpses and took them to the nearby Morgue on the Quai de l'Archevêché. Achille had become inured to this detail; it was part of his job. But he could not forget some of the dead, particularly the face of a girl of about ten who looked as though she had just gone to sleep. He shook his head, sighed, and lit a cigarette.

He next turned his attention to the Place du Châtelet, on the right bank across from where he stood. This was the site of the ancient Châtelet prison and the old police headquarters. In a bygone era, the place stank from the slaughterhouse effluent that emptied into the Seine from the mouth of the great sewer. The Emperor Napoleon I ordered the demolition of the medieval fortress; at that time, the area swarmed with beggars, cut-throats, and footpads.

In the vicinity, somewhere between the Pont au Change and the Pont Notre-Dame, Hugo's detective Javert had his final confrontation with Jean Valjean. The fugitive had spared the police officer's life, and despite years of tenacious pursuit, Javert let his quarry go. After a lifetime of dedication to strict enforcement of the laws, Javert could not live with the contradiction. In despair, he leaped from the quay to his death in the turbid waters. *A bad way to go*, Achille thought.

He recalled Moreau; his enigmatic stare in the prison registry the morning of the execution. Achille imagined the condemned man's unspoken question: *You preserve justice and defend the laws, M. Lefebvre.*

But what if the law itself is unjust? Will you enforce a bad rule or follow a higher principle?

Thankfully, Achille had not yet faced that predicament, and Moreau was a murderer, not a poor man who stole bread to feed his starving family.

Achille tried to shake off his pensive mood by focusing on something pleasant. He was not far from the flower market. *I'll bring Adele a bouquet this evening to thank her for being so hospitable to Mlle Hubert.* In fact, after just one evening and a morning together, the whole family had taken an interest in the young woman, and she reciprocated by being cheerful and helping with the household chores. Even Suzanne had overcome her initial reticence.

He finished his cigarette and flicked the butt into the river. Then he glanced at his watch. *I've been here too long. Time to get back to the office and decrypt the message.* Achille turned the corner and walked up the Boulevard du Palais. He felt safe this close to the Palais de Justice and police headquarters and therefore had gone out to meet Moïse without an escort. It suddenly occurred to him that Giraud and Breton might have the brains and the guts to take advantage of the situation.

If they don't mind sacrificing their lives to assassinate me, they could attack anywhere, even at the entrance to the Cour du Mai. He considered the possibility for a moment, then shrugged it off and continued on to his office.

⁜

"I'm glad you chose to meet here, Chief. It's too fine a day to remain indoors."

"Thank you, Étienne, but I'm afraid Adam doesn't share your enthusiasm." Achille glanced in the direction of the sergeant, who was pacing around a ring of chestnut trees, on the lookout for assassins.

M. Lefebvre and Legros sat at a table outside a café in the Place Dauphine, not far from the entrance to the Pont Neuf. Achille often passed through the quiet, triangular "square" on his way to and from work.

Located close to the Palais de Justice, lawyers, judges, and police officers deemed it a good place to stop and discuss a case over a glass of wine.

"Adam's doing his job, Chief. You shouldn't take too many chances."

Achille took a sip of wine before answering. "I'm not going to hide in a hole because a couple of thugs want to kill me. Which reminds me: I need to speak to Rousseau. By now, we ought to have enough evidence of an assassination conspiracy to arrest Giraud and Breton. And I need to have a word with my big friend concerning Orlovsky. But that's another matter. What did you find out at the hotel?"

Legros had just returned from the Rue Castex, where he had questioned the hotel staff about the bandaged man. "The individual wasn't registered, Chief; the hall porter was the only one who could recall seeing him. The bandages caught the porter's attention, and of course, they don't like anyone loitering near the entrance. The porter was keeping an eye on the individual and was about to speak to him when the baron's cab arrived. The bandaged man left in the cab and the porter thought little of the incident until I questioned him."

"I see," Achille said. He took out a packet of cigarettes and offered one to Legros. They smoked in silence for a while. Then Achille reached into his coat pocket and retrieved his notes. He studied his jottings before saying, "I just received a wire from Scotland Yard's Special Branch in response to my inquiry about Sims. They have nothing on him, which doesn't surprise me. Moreover, even if they did have something, I'm not sure they'd share it with me."

"I thought you had a good relationship with the London detectives?"

"I did, but things have changed. As you know from our Hanged Man case, our government is cozying up to the Russians. Paris has already replaced Berlin as their banker, and we may be close to a secret Franco-Russian military alliance as well. That relationship is not likely to please our English friends."

"I understand, Chief. And you believe the shifting alliances have something to do with our case?"

"I do, but first I want you to consider a hypothesis. What if Sims and the bandaged man are one and the same?"

Legros took some wine and pondered a minute before answering. "If that's true, then the information we got from Bonnet and Inspector Forestier is wrong."

Achille smiled. "Bonnet is hardly credible. As for M. Forestier, I'm afraid both Bonnet and Prince Papkov duped him. If you recall, the prince told Forestier that Sims left for Monte Carlo on the twenty-fifth, the day before the baroness reported the baron missing. However, no one saw Sims at the station or on the train, and the police in Monaco have no record of M. Sims. But what if he boarded the same train as the baron and Colonel Mukhin and arrived in Paris on the twenty-fifth?"

"With his face bandaged?"

"Yes, with his face bandaged. In my hypothetical, Colonel Mukhin and Sims board the train at Annecy. Upon arrival in Paris, the embassy coach takes them to the Rue Castex. Mukhin leaves Sims at the hotel and returns to the embassy. A short time after that, the baron arrives in a cab and picks up the bandaged man. They then proceed to the apartment on the Rue de Turenne, where they meet Mme Behrs. Later that evening, the baron, Mme Behrs, and Sims leave in the coach old Aubert described, a closed landau with a coat of arms on the door. The coach may have been from the Russian embassy, but we can't prove it. Have you gone back to Aubert to see if he can identify the coat of arms?"

"Not yet; it's next on my list. And I'll check with the Railway Squad and the stationmasters. Someone would have surely noticed a passenger with a bandaged face."

"Of course. If I'm right, then we have another piece to add to our puzzle. Moreover, Delphine has provided some interesting information. There was a big deal in the works before the parties went to Aix-les-Bains, and I believe something went wrong when they returned to Paris. Now the Okhrana is after the baron and they want to get to him before we do. Orlovsky even tried to recruit Delphine to assist in his search.

"The baron is known for brokering lucrative business transactions that have implications of international significance. In this case, I believe he tricked the Russians, with the help of Mme Behrs, Sims, Bonnet, and Mme de Livet. To add a finishing touch, he's left his lackey and his wife in the lurch."

Legros leaned forward and lowered his voice. "Do you have a theory as to the nature of the transaction?"

"Yes, I do; but remember, it's just a theory based on the facts we've gathered thus far and placed within the context of international politics, diplomacy, and intrigue. Our new ally has a vast eastern empire, the riches of which have hardly been tapped. For both economic and strategic reasons, the Russians are pushing their railways eastward, and they're using French capital for this purpose.

"Sims is purportedly a retired English army officer who served on the North-West Frontier. Prince Papkov and Colonel Mukhin served in a regiment that guarded the Trans-Caspian railway terminus at Samarkand. The railway extensions will enable the Russians to mobilize a vast army near the Afghan border, large enough to invade Afghanistan, move south, and overwhelm the Anglo-Indian army holding the line at the Khyber Pass. Military intelligence of the British forces deployed at the frontier, defenses, and new railway construction would be of great value to the Russians."

"Do you think the baron arranged for Sims to sell British military secrets to the Russians?"

Achille stroked his beard thoughtfully. "Perhaps; or it could have been a spectacular confidence trick. Let's hope it was the latter, because the former could precipitate a war."

Legros was speechless. He stared at the chief while trying to cope with the gravity of the situation. After a moment he asked, "Surely an alliance between our government and Russia is intended as a check on German aggression, not as a provocation to the English?"

"Germany is our mutual adversary, but a Franco-Russian alliance does risk conflict with Great Britain at strategic flashpoints where our national interests collide." Achille smiled to put Legros at ease. "Your glass is empty. Would you care for another?"

"Yes . . . yes, Chief. Thank you; I would."

Achille signaled to the waiter and ordered another round. As soon as the waiter returned to the bar, Achille said, "I believe we're close to making an arrest in the Otero matter. You've seen the report from our detectives in Joinville?"

"Yes, I have. The acoustics on the empty terrace at the *guinguette* allowed them to overhear some of the conversation between the baroness and Bonnet. Have you spoken to Magistrate Leblanc?"

"Not yet. I'm going to drop by his office on our way back to headquarters. I have something to add that will interest you. Do you recall my visit to the *salle de boxe*?"

"Yes, Chief, I do. Did you get something more from M. Leclerc?"

"Not from the maître, but from one of my former sparring partners, an old boxer named Pasquet."

"I know Pasquet," Legros said. "He's one of Rousseau's snitches."

"Yes, and he gives me a good tip, now and then. He tends bar at a bistro in Montmartre. The other night he heard some loose talk from a member of a smuggling ring. It appears M. Bonnet's going to bolt for Spain, and we're going to set a nice trap for him and his confederates.

"The gang's been carrying contraband and an occasional fugitive over the Pyrenees for years. I've already wired the police commissary in Pau where the smugglers are on a wanted list. We'll take Bonnet in custody and send his nefarious travel agents to our colleagues in the south.

"Flight is evidence of guilt, and we're going to have Bonnet by the balls. We'll twist them until he squeals. If he believes we have a strong murder case against him, he might tell us all he knows about the baron in an attempt to escape the guillotine.

"As for the baroness, we'll see how she reacts when her lover's in prison for investigative detention. I expect he'll name her as an accomplice, and she might decide to come clean to save her own skin."

The waiter returned with the wine. Achille relaxed and enjoyed the moment. The case was progressing, and he had almost forgotten about Giraud and Breton. He noticed a noisy flight of sparrows circling in the clear sky before settling in the tree branches. *When I go to the flower market this afternoon, I'll buy a canary for Jeanne*, he thought. *And in addition to the bouquet for Adele, I'll bring a flower for all the women, including Mignonette. They'll like that.*

⁓

"I have an urgent message for M. Lefebvre."

Achille's clerk looked up from the pile of papers on his desk. "Good afternoon, M. Duroc. I'm afraid M. Lefebvre has gone for the day."

"When did he leave?"

"About fifteen minutes ago. He and Detective Bouvier are stopping at the flower market—"

"The flower market?" Duroc broke in. "Where's Sergeant Adam?"

"In the detectives' room. He's—"

Duroc turned, ran up the hallway, and burst into the room. He spotted Adam sipping coffee and chatting with one of the detectives. "Come on, Adam!" Duroc shouted. "Giraud and Breton gave us the slip early this morning. We just got a tip that they're lying in wait near the Pont au Change."

Adam grabbed his revolver and followed Duroc. They dashed through hallways and corridors and down two flights of stairs, exiting the building onto the Boulevard du Palais. Dodging traffic, they crossed the street and raced on to the flower market.

Shouting "Make way for the police!" they pushed past vendors and customers shopping at stalls filled with multicolored, fresh-cut blossoms. Halfway across the market Duroc cried, "Look there, Adam. It's the chief and Bouvier. They're headed for the bridge."

⁓

M. Lefebvre and Detective Bouvier walked toward the entrance to the Pont au Change on the Quai de la Corse. The chief's arms were filled with a variety of roses. He sniffed the blossoms' fragrance and smiled. "There's nothing like roses, eh, Bouvier? Of course, you must watch out for the thorns."

"Yes, Chief. I'm sure the ladies will be pleased."

"I believe so, but it's a shame about the canary. I forgot they only sell the birds on Sunday. Anyway, I picked out a lovely yellow rose for my little one. That's her mother's favorite. By the way, you must come in for a drink and meet the family."

"That's kind of you, Chief, but Sergeant Adam gave strict orders—"

"Nonsense. Adam's becoming an old mother hen. Why, he's—"

"Monsieur Lefebvre, you're in danger!" Duroc shouted.

Achille stopped, spun around, looked up the quay, and saw Duroc and Adam running toward him. He dropped the flowers on the pavement, reached under his coat, and pulled out his Chamelot-Delvigne. "Cover my back, Bouvier," he cried. There was an exchange of shots behind him, the screams and shouts of bystanders, but Achille remained focused. No more than ten paces in front of him, a man wearing a slouch hat and long gray coat stepped out from behind a stall and aimed a revolver. Achille recognized the Lefaucheux.

They fired simultaneously, Giraud once and Achille twice. The stink of gunpowder mixed with the floral perfume. Achille felt something sharp, like a beesting, on his left cheek above the beard line. He was about to fire a third time when he saw his enemy drop to his knees, clutch his chest, and fall forward facedown on the paving stones.

Duroc halted and stooped to disarm, bind, and guard the wounded assassin while Adam ran on to his chief. "Are you all right, Monsieur Lefebvre?"

Achille wiped a trickle of blood from his cheek. "Yes, it's just a scratch. Where's Bouvier?" He turned around and saw the detective down on one knee, gripping his smoking revolver in one hand as he held the inside of his thigh with the other.

A policeman had arrived on the scene. A small crowd had gathered around Breton, who was lying on his back, kicking and groaning in agony as he grabbed at a gaping hole in his gut.

Achille called out and gestured to the police officer. "Monsieur l'Agent, I'm Lefebvre of the Sûreté. One of my men is wounded. We must get him to the hospital immediately."

The policeman snapped to attention. "Yes, M. Lefebvre. What about the others?"

He scowled at the writhing Breton. "They can die here or in *le bagne*. It makes no difference to me. At any rate, my detective comes first. We can attend to the thugs later. And get these people out of here. This isn't a circus."

"Yes, Monsieur." The officer admonished the curiosity seekers before leaving to flag down a vehicle to carry Bouvier to the Hôtel-Dieu. The laggards dispersed as more police came to secure the area.

Adam knelt at Bouvier's side. The sergeant cut the detective's trouser leg and placed a handkerchief on the wound to stanch the bleeding. "That's better, isn't it?" he said gently. "We'll have you at the hospital in no time."

Achille came over. "Hang on, old man. You'll be all right."

Bouvier looked up and noticed the blood running down his chief's face. "You're wounded, Monsieur," he grunted.

Achille smiled. "It's a fleabite." He reached down and brushed some hair away from the detective's eyes. "Be quiet now."

They heard the rumble of carriage wheels and the clopping of horse hooves. The gendarme had returned with a commandeered fiacre.

"Can you walk on one leg if we support you?" Adam asked Bouvier.

"I think so," the detective replied.

Achille and Adam half-carried Bouvier to the carriage. They lifted the groaning detective into the compartment and tried to make him as comfortable as possible for the short ride to the hospital. The gendarme mounted the running board and took out his truncheon to wave away traffic.

Before they left the flower market, Achille leaned out the carriage door and called and gestured to Duroc and one of the gendarmes. "Get a cart for the *racaille* and take them to the hospital."

"It's the Morgue for them, M. Lefebvre," Duroc replied.

"Very well then, to the Morgue," the chief replied.

The carriage rolled over Achille's scattered roses, made its way up the quay, and turned right onto the Rue de la Cité and then left on the Parvis de Notre-Dame. Achille glanced out the window at the ancient buttressed walls of the cathedral. He turned to Bouvier, took out a handkerchief, and wiped perspiration from the detective's brow. "We're almost there, old man," he whispered.

Bouvier looked up at his chief and tried to smile. "Thank you, M. Lefebvre," he replied.

⚭

Achille waited on a hard wooden bench in a vast vaulted corridor outside the *bloc opératoire*. Light poured in through an apparently endless row of arched windows. The place was quiet except for the echoing footsteps of white-coated doctors, sisters, and attendants pushing gurneys into and out from the operating theaters.

He shifted and squirmed on the uncomfortable seat and glanced at his watch. The sound of a heavy tread made him look up to his right. He immediately recognized the hulking figure of Rousseau.

"Good afternoon, Achille. May I join you?"

"Good afternoon, Rousseau. Please do."

The inspector sat down next to the chief. "My God, these benches are torture on one's buttocks," he muttered. "How long have you been here?"

"Almost an hour. The chief surgeon said he'd come out and see me as soon as they're finished with Bouvier."

"Where did he get it?"

"In the thigh. The surgeons say the bullet missed the bone and major artery. They believe they can avoid amputation. Thank God those Apache pistols aren't too accurate and don't pack much punch at a distance."

Rousseau nodded, then noticed the bandage on Achille's face. "Looks like you took a bullet, too."

"It's nothing, but two centimeters up and a little to the right and I might have lost an eye—or worse."

"You always were lucky, my friend."

"Yes, I'm lucky." He paused a moment before saying, "I wanted to thank Duroc. If he hadn't arrived when he did, things might have been worse."

"I'll give him your thanks. He's always wanted to make up for the Ménard case."

"Yes, I imagined he would. Well, when things calm down he can come to my office and I'll thank him personally."

"That's very kind of you; I'm sure he'll appreciate the gesture."

Achille nodded. "By the way, if you don't mind my asking, how did those two give you the slip?"

Rousseau sighed. "It's an imperfect world. My men were tired from working twelve-hour shifts. The assassins' inactivity lulled them to sleep and they became a little careless. Fortunately, we got a good tip about the ambush. You're usually in the office late; I apologize for not warning you in time."

"Apology accepted. There's something else: Orlovsky sent a couple of his thugs out to rough up Delphine. I won't tolerate that. Do you want to tell him, or should I?"

"I know about the incident. I already spoke to our Russian friend. He was out of line; it won't happen again." Rousseau grinned. "Delphine thrashed the bastards. She's quite a woman, isn't she?"

Achille nodded his agreement without further comment. "We need to discuss the de Livet matter, but not now. Can you meet me at the usual time, tomorrow morning at the Sainte-Chapelle?"

"All right."

They sat quietly for a while, each lost in his thoughts. Achille broke the silence. "I don't feel like going home just now. It's as if I were unclean. Do you ever feel dirty after you've killed a man?"

Rousseau shook his head. "No, but I've killed more than you have, so I'm used to it. Messy but necessary."

"Perhaps, but I would have preferred to let our justice system deal with them." *Am I being hypocritical?* he thought. Achille stared at Rousseau. He noticed the hint of a wry smile on the inspector's granitic face. "I wanted to bring them in, if only to question them. Otherwise, I'll admit they were of little use to society. They won't be missed. At any rate, when it comes to killing criminals I'm catching up to you. I've shot and killed two this year—so far."

"Don't let it bother you, Achille. It's a matter of public health and safety, like sweeping the streets and cleaning out the sewers. Besides, it's easier to forgive your enemies *after* they're dead."

"Have you forgiven anyone, Rousseau?"

The inspector shrugged. "No, not yet. But who knows? Maybe I will, someday."

The chief of surgery exited a nearby operating theater. Achille got up and walked over to the surgeon.

"Pardon me, Doctor. How is Detective Bouvier? Will he pull through?"

The doctor smiled and put a hand on Achille's shoulder. "I believe so, M. Lefebvre. He's young and strong, and the operation went well. The bullet did not penetrate far, and we've cleaned and dressed the wound."

Achille sighed with relief. "Thank God. May I see him?"

"Not now, Monsieur. He's recovering from the anesthetic. Come back tomorrow."

"Yes, I will. Thank you; thank you very much."

Achille said good-bye to the surgeon and returned to the bench, eager to give Rousseau the news. But the inspector had already gone. His heavy footsteps echoed down the corridor.

❦

Achille returned to his office. He noticed detectives milling about, but no one dared approach him without being summoned. He gave orders to his clerk.

"Are Legros and Adam available?"

"Yes, Monsieur Lefebvre."

"Good. I want to see them immediately. Otherwise, I'm not to be disturbed."

"Very well, Monsieur."

Achille entered his office, went to his desk, and took out the bottle of prunelle and a glass. He poured a stiff shot and drank it down. There was a knock on the door.

The chief wiped his lips and moustache, coughed, cleared his throat, and returned the liqueur to its drawer. "Come in."

Legros and Adam entered and approached the desk, where they stopped and remained at attention.

Achille smiled to put them at ease. "Relax, gentlemen. I assure you I'm well, and I have good news: Detective Bouvier's wound is not serious. The chief surgeon is confident our colleague will recover and return to duty." He turned to Legros. "Inspector."

"Yes, Monsieur."

"Assemble the brigade. I'll address them in ten minutes."

Legros left the office. Adam was about to do the same when Achille said:

"I haven't dismissed you, Sergeant."

"I'm sorry, Monsieur."

"That's all right. I wanted to thank you personally. You and your detail have done a commendable service. I now relieve you of that duty."

"But, Chief—"

Achille raised his hand for silence. "Please hear me out. This evening I'll return home as usual, without an escort. The people of Paris must know that I can walk our streets unafraid. However, I have another job for you that's of equal importance and which I'm sure you'll handle admirably.

"I'm going to prepare a statement for the press that will be accompanied by postmortem photographs of the assassins. In addition, I'm going to have the bodies displayed in the refrigeration room on the pretext that they are unidentified. I imagine that will draw quite a crowd to the Morgue.

"I want you to form a special detail to patrol the viewing area. If your men notice any signs of recognition among the viewers, expressions of sympathy and so forth, I want those individuals identified and their names reported to me. Understood?"

"Yes, M. Lefebvre. And thank you for your confidence in me. I won't let you down."

"You've done well, Sergeant. Now go join your men. I'll be with you presently."

As soon as Adam left, Achille dashed off a note to Adele and rang for a messenger. Next, he considered what he would say to the brigade, but with the time constraints, he would have to manage the speech extempore. He began drafting a statement for the press; a knock interrupted.

Legros opened the door a crack and poked in his head. "The men are assembled and waiting for you, Chief."

"Thank you, Étienne; I'm coming." Achille entered a hallway crammed with detectives buzzing with anticipation and speculation as to what M. Lefebvre might say. They fell silent on sight of their chief.

Achille gazed at familiar faces, Féraud's "old boys" interspersed among younger veterans and new recruits. He took a moment to collect his thoughts and clear his throat before speaking.

"Men of the brigade, I've called you together to inform you of the events of this afternoon." *Too damned formal*, he thought. He smiled sheepishly and scratched at his bandage. "This bloody thing itches like the devil."

There was a small burst of nervous laughter.

"All right, men," Achille continued. "As you can see I'm quite well, and your colleague, Detective Bouvier, is on the mend and should soon be fit enough to return to duty. And, thanks to Bouvier, Sergeant Adam, and the timely warning provided by Detective Duroc, the assassins are where they belong—in the Morgue."

There was a round of respectful applause until Inspector Faucher, an old veteran close to retirement, shouted, "What about you, Chief? We know what you did. You stood face-to-face, pistol-to-pistol, with one of them, and shot him down. I say hurrah for M. Lefebvre! Hurrah for our brave chief of detectives!"

The brigade broke out in a roar that resounded through the halls and corridors and reverberated onto the quay. Achille brushed away a tear and tried to speak, but the cheers drowned out his words.

⤬

Achille remained in his office and attended to business, much of it routine, until nine thirty. He worked late on purpose. The extra hours gave him time to compose himself before returning home. Moreover, he did not want to be greeted by anyone except Adele. The children would be long asleep, and the servants and Mignonette should either be sleeping or in their rooms getting ready for bed. His mother-in-law would be awake, but he prayed she would remain ensconced in her boudoir.

He left headquarters and headed home by what he considered the safest route, past the guards at the Palais de Justice, through the Place Dauphine to the Pont Neuf, and across to the Quai de la Mégisserie. In open spaces his focus intensified, his eyes scanning the area for prowlers, his ears alert to the sound of footsteps.

His coat remained open for rapid and easy access to the holstered Chamelot-Delvigne. Before leaving the office, he had ejected the expended cartridge casings and cleaned and reloaded the revolver.

The previous year, Achille had taken Adele and Jeanne to Buffalo Bill's Wild West show at the Universal Exposition. The American marksmanship and quick-draw artistry impressed him, and he had modified his shoulder holster and shooting technique accordingly. He was surprised that Giraud had time to aim and fire. Achille figured the flowers he carried had slowed him down, just by a split second. The image of blood and roses on the pavement had haunted him all afternoon.

He took comfort in the full moon, its light reflected on the dark, rippling Seine, the gas lamps glowing on the bridge and the quay, the radiant Eiffel Tower rising above tall trees, domes and rooftops in the near distance, the running lights on barges chugging under the bridge. Nevertheless, he was especially wary of the clochards who huddled together for shelter on the embankment beneath the arches of the Pont Neuf. In the past, he often stopped to observe the homeless and ponder their plight; that evening he wondered if assassins might be hiding among them.

He walked up the Quai de la Mégisserie past his favorite book stall where he had purchased, among other things, a first edition of Verlaine's *Les Poètes Maudits*. Branches rattled; a sudden cold gust blew up from the river.

His pace slowed; his right hand reached under his coat and grasped the butt end of his revolver. Giraud's ghost emerged from behind the stall, the way he appeared in the flower market. Achille drove away the phantom with a quote from Napoleon I: *The bullet that will kill me is not yet cast.* He picked up his step and walked on.

As he turned the corner of the Rue Bertin Poirée, Achille came upon Gautier, an officer who patrolled the district. The stout, habitually cheerful policeman saluted and greeted Achille: "Good evening, M. Lefebvre. Permit me to congratulate you. Your set-to with the assassins was splendid."

"Thank you, Gautier. I trust all's quiet in the neighborhood?"

"Yes, Monsieur, but everyone hereabouts is talking about the shootout. I spoke to Detective Allard not more than two hours ago. He said you'd relieved him from guard duty but asked me to keep a sharp eye, just in case."

"I very much appreciate that. I'm sure we'll be safe on your watch. Now, I'm afraid it's late and I must get home to my family."

"Of course, Monsieur; I won't detain you any longer."

Achille continued on to his apartment, wondering how Adele had reacted to the gossip about the gunfight. His apprehensions were magnified by Mme Cazenave, the concierge, who waylaid him in the foyer. The old woman speculated as to the assassins' national origins, political leanings, religious affiliations or lack thereof, and sexual proclivities. He listened politely before saying, "Excuse me, Madame; it's late and my family is waiting," which initiated more than a minute of apologies, expressions of sympathy, and praise for his courage and devotion to duty. Finally, with some effort, he escaped her tenacious grasp.

Achille walked up to the first landing, took out his key chain, and unlocked the door. He heard a rustle of silk and soft footsteps and saw a flicker of light at the end of the dark hallway. As the source of the light drew nearer, two female figures emerged from the shadows. He disguised his disappointment behind an amiable mask.

Mme Berthier preceded her daughter; Adele followed respectfully, carrying an oil lamp. As his mother-in-law came forward to greet him, he inhaled a familiar armoire odor of attar of roses and camphor emanating from her old-fashioned bombazine dress.

"Good evening, Achille. I insisted upon the honor of being the first to greet you. We've all heard of your splendid deed; the market was abuzz with it. Mme Gros predicts you'll be awarded the Légion d'Honneur."

"Madame Gros does tend to exaggerate," Achille replied.

"Nonsense, my boy." She adjusted her spectacles and peered up at his bandaged cheek. "But you're wounded. Are you all right?"

"It's a scratch, nothing more."

Mme Berthier smiled and turned to Adele. "You see, my dear. He's just like your father. The colonel almost lost his right arm at Solferino. When he came home I made a fuss about his wounds and he said, 'It's just a scratch,' and would hear no more of it."

"Yes, Mama; I've heard the story many times."

Madame narrowed her eyes. "Are you saying I repeat myself?"

Adele sighed. "No, Mama; please forgive me. I'm sure Achille is tired and would like to get ready for bed."

"Oh of course; of course." She turned back to Achille. "Forgive me, my boy. I'll leave you two alone. Good night, and God bless you."

He smiled and made a slight bow. "Thank you, Madame. Good night."

"Take the lamp, Mother," Adele said. "We'll get another from the sitting room."

They waited silently as Madame shuffled up the corridor and then disappeared into her boudoir.

"I need a drink," Achille whispered.

"Me too," she replied.

They entered the sitting room. "Wait here," Adele said. "You always trip in the dark." She felt her way carefully to a coffee table where she found a matchbox. Adele lit the table lamp and turned up the screw. "All right, my dear; you can come here now. What do you want?"

"Cognac, please." He walked over to his favorite armchair, sat, and eased back in its warm, familiar embrace.

Adele returned with the drinks. She handed Achille the cognac before saying, "I'll take off your shoes and get the footstool."

"Bless you, my dear; you're an angel."

He sipped cognac as she removed his boots, fetched the stool, and lifted his feet. She massaged his toes and soles until he sighed with pleasure.

"Are you comfortable?" she asked.

"Yes, thank you; very comfortable," he replied.

"Good." She brought a chair and sat opposite him. "Now, please tell me what happened this afternoon, and don't leave anything out."

Achille put down his glass, sat up, and stared at her through his pince-nez. He tried to read the thoughts hidden behind her enigmatic smile but could not. He decided to be as forthright as possible.

"I'll tell you what I can, my love, but some things must remain unsaid. Do you understand?"

"I'm not sure I do, but please continue."

Achille narrated the assassination plot and its outcome, while downplaying the danger and omitting the names of the assassins. He said the "unidentified" individuals could have been friends of Moreau; their motive was revenge. He did not disclose his veiled reason for putting the bodies on public display.

When he finished she asked, "Why didn't you tell me you had detectives watching our home?"

"I did it in an excess of caution, my dear; I didn't want you to worry needlessly."

"You might have been killed. You say it's nothing but a scratch, but the bullet came very close to your eye. You were lucky."

Achille smiled. "Rousseau said something similar, but you're both wrong. Luck had little if anything to do with it."

"Please explain."

"There's a difference between relying on luck and taking calculated risks. Bouvier and I have superior weapons and training. The assassins didn't have a chance. They were lucky to hit us."

"How did you *know* they carried inferior weapons and lacked your skills?"

Achille realized he had said too much. He shrugged it off. "I know the *type*, my dear. How about another drink?"

She got up and started toward the liquor cabinet. As she came by his chair, Achille reached out, took her wrist gently, and pulled her onto his lap. "I'm sorry to have worried you so," he said. "But please trust my judgment."

She gazed at him with moist eyes. "I wish you'd trust *me* with your secrets. You ought to have told me, Achille."

He toyed with a couple of stray ringlets. "You're right, Adele. I apologize. If I seem furtive at times, it's only because I don't want to burden you with the troubles of my office. I need your support, now more than ever. We're making significant progress in the de Livet case."

The news got her attention. She sat up, put her hands on his shoulders, and looked him in the eyes. "Are you about to crack it?"

He smiled slyly. "Perhaps. But for now, I need rest. I've a five o'clock appointment with Rousseau."

"Oh no."

"Oh yes, Madame. Let's go to bed. Shall I carry you?"

Adele laughed softly. "You fool. It's dark in the hallway. You might stumble and land us both in the hospital."

He eased her off his lap, rose from the chair, and swept her up in his arms as effortlessly as he had done on their wedding night. "With the light in your lovely eyes to guide me," he whispered, "I'll never fall."

12

MOVING SHADOWS

The moon hid behind a purplish cloud cover. A steady drizzle burgeoned into a shower as Achille crossed the Pont au Change to the Boulevard du Palais. He opened an umbrella that, like Delphine's, doubled as a weapon for close combat.

On the way to his meeting with Rousseau, Achille considered a tactic the Japanese fighters called Moving the Shadow. When you cannot determine your adversary's intentions, you pretend to initiate an attack to force his hand. *It's time I moved shadows with M. Orlovsky*, he thought. Boots splashing on the pavement, he continued on to the Sainte-Chapelle.

The guard at the entrance recognized the chief of detectives, but Achille still showed his badge as a matter of form.

"Good morning, M. Lefebvre. Inspector Rousseau is waiting inside."

"Thank you, Mathieu. Carry on."

Achille shook out and closed his umbrella before entering the vaulted nave. He spotted Rousseau in his usual place, half-hidden in the shadows under the arcade. He walked toward the inspector, footsteps echoing up the aisle.

"Good morning, Professor. If you don't mind my saying so, you resemble a drowned rat."

"Good morning, Rousseau. Yes, a downpour arrived just as I was crossing the bridge."

"Do you want some brandy to keep out the cold?"

"No thanks; it's too early for me."

"Not for me, my friend." Rousseau pulled out a pocket flask and took a long swig. He wiped his mouth with the back of his hand and said, "That hit the spot."

"Pardon me, Rousseau. Before we get into the case, I'd like to ask you a question."

"Ask away."

"Yesterday at the hospital I was going to give you the good news about Bouvier. Why did you leave so abruptly?"

"I read the news on the surgeon's face. They don't usually smile like that when they tell you the patient's going to croak."

"I see. Over the years, I've noticed you don't like to hang around one place too long. Is that a tactic?"

The inspector grinned. "It's a habit, Professor, formed by more than twenty years on the streets. Keeping on the move is good for your health."

"You've fought off more than one ambush, haven't you?"

"True, but the trick is to avoid getting into situations where you're likely to be jumped and trapped."

"I agree. Not long ago, I asked Maître Leclerc to assess my chances against two assassins like Giraud and Breton. He said my likelihood of prevailing was quite good. Then I asked how he thought I would do against three or four and I mentioned your famous fight with the four Apaches. Can you guess what he said?"

"No, but I believe you're about to tell me."

"'Ah, but that was Rousseau. People say he's not human.'"

Rousseau's laughter rumbled throughout the nave. "It's good to have that reputation; it scares hell out of the *racaille*. On the other hand, there's always some young punk who wants to have a go at you."

"Leclerc was speaking figuratively. He meant you're sui generis."

"Spare me your Latin, Professor. I hope that's not an insult. If it is, I'm afraid I'll have to challenge you and M. Leclerc, too."

"It's far from an insult, Rousseau. It means you're unique—one of a kind. A great compliment."

"Very well, and I suppose I could say the same for you. Now, if we're finished kissing each other's ass, can you please tell me why we are here?"

"First, regarding Giraud and Breton; as far as the public is concerned, they are as yet unidentified. I'm putting them on display at the Morgue, like pieces of cheese to draw the mice out of the woodwork and into my trap."

"Good thinking, Professor. I assume if you identify any persons of interest you'll share the information with me?"

"Of course, but I'm not going to keep them on the slabs too long. Someone might get wise, and that would be embarrassing."

"All right, Achille. Anything else?"

"Yes. I understand the Okhrana wants to get its hands on the baron before I do. Do you know why?"

Rousseau raised an inquiring eyebrow. "You've developed a theory of the case?"

"You're answering my question with a question."

Rousseau stared at Achille for a while before responding. "Orlovsky's scared, and so is Colonel Mukhin. The baron must have outsmarted our Russian friends. Naturally, they like working in Paris. If they've been duped and it gets back to their masters in St. Petersburg, Orlovsky and

Mukhin could be reassigned somewhere less pleasant, like a Siberian penal colony. That's all I know."

"All right; that's their problem. I need to send a strong message to the Russians, and I want to do it in person. They can play their cloak-and-dagger games as long as they don't cross the line and commit a serious crime in my jurisdiction. If they screw up on my watch, I'll arrest them."

"They'll claim diplomatic immunity. Have you discussed this with M. Leblanc and the prefect?"

"No, not yet. I want to see Orlovsky first, but not in Montmartre. The three of us can meet at the brasserie on the Rue de Harlay in daylight."

"Across from the Palais de Justice, eh? That'll make him squirm. All right, I'll arrange it. What about the Deuxième Bureau?"

"I'll keep them informed. One of their agents, a Russian émigré, might be working with the baron. I don't know. At any rate, as long as this matter doesn't involve trading in our military secrets they don't need to take a more active role.

"Here's my chief concern: If the Okhrana gets to the baron before I do, they're to turn him over to me unharmed. The same goes for his confederates. It's my case, Rousseau. I want the meeting here to make a point. I might even take M. Orlovsky on a tour of the Conciergerie, the Dépôt, and holding cells. He could find it educational."

The inspector smirked at his former partner. "You're still angry about the incident with Delphine, aren't you?"

"That's my affair."

Rousseau shrugged. "Of course, Achille." He glanced around the dark nave and scrutinized the sunless windows. "Do you think we're closer to God in this place than we are on the street?"

Achille was surprised. In all the years he had known Rousseau, he had never heard the detective mention God. He recalled what he had learned about aesthetics, the relationship between the divine and the beautiful. The Saint-Chapelle represented the ancient and medieval concepts of beauty: integrity, harmony, and clarity. Achille appreciated these things, just as he appreciated the beauty of nature when he rowed on the rivers around Paris. Moreover, he considered himself fortunate to have a lovely and loving wife and children who could pull him away from the dark underworld where he fought with demons, an environment portrayed in a new aesthetic by artists like his friend Toulouse-Lautrec. *Scenes from hell in gaslight*, he thought. Nevertheless, he was attracted to that world just as he was drawn to Lautrec's art.

"I'm waiting, Professor." Rousseau broke in on Achille's musing.

"I didn't know you were interested in theology," Achille replied drily.

"I'm not. I'm just asking a question. After all, you're the professor. I thought you had all the answers."

Achille shook his head. "I have many questions, my friend, and few answers." He looked up at the vast expanse of stained glass, asleep in predawn darkness, lulled by a dull patter of raindrops. "You should return when the chapel is filled with sunlight and shimmering beauty. That might answer your question."

"It *might* answer my question? Perhaps, or perhaps not. At any rate, this day will be gray and gloomy, and as you've noticed, I don't like to hang around one place for too long. I'll see you this afternoon, at the brasserie near the Place Dauphine. I'm certain Orlovsky will accept your kind invitation. Duroc will bring a message to confirm the time."

"Good. That will give me a chance to thank Duroc personally for his warning. But make our meeting with Orlovsky for the late afternoon. Legros is out finding facts that could be of significance to our investigation, not to mention quite interesting to the Russians."

"Very well, Professor. *Au revoir.*"

"*Au revoir*, Rousseau."

◈

Legros sat in the concierge's kitchen at Mme Behrs's apartment house on the Rue de Turenne. Outside, a cold steady rain came down, streaming along gutters, flowing through drainpipes, and gathering in puddles on the pavement.

M. Aubert carried a freshly brewed pot of coffee to the table. "It's nice to be in a warm, cozy place on a day like this, isn't it, Inspector Legros?"

"Indeed it is, M. Aubert, and especially when one can enjoy an excellent cup of coffee in good company."

The old man smiled. "That's exactly what I was thinking, M. Legros." He set down the coffee service and poured for his guest before taking his seat at the table.

Legros had ingratiated himself with the concierge. He concluded that the old man was lonely and would be more forthcoming in response to the inspector's congenial approach. Unfortunately, this tactic had so far produced nothing but gossip and speculation as to the goings-on in Mme Behrs's apartment, which proved nothing except for the prurience of the old man's imagination. Legros hoped that the photographs in his briefcase would yield something of value to the investigation.

Aubert blew into the steaming cup and took a couple of sips. "Ah, that's perfection," he remarked. "Is it to your liking, M. Legros?"

Legros tasted the coffee. "Thank you, M. Aubert. It's just the way I like it."

"Are you sure you wouldn't care for a lump of sugar?"

"No, thank you, Monsieur. It's fine as it is."

The old man shrugged. "As you please, Inspector." He opened the sugar bowl, dropped a lump in his cup, stirred, and took another sip. After a moment, he put down his coffee and asked, "Have you more information concerning Mme Behrs's whereabouts?"

"No, Monsieur, but I've brought something that I hope will help in that regard."

The statement piqued Aubert's curiosity. "Oh, and what might that be?"

"With your permission, Monsieur." Legros lifted his briefcase and placed it on the table. "I've brought a group of photographs for your inspection."

"Photographs? What sort of photographs?" Aubert's eyes lit up as though he anticipated pictures of Mme Behrs in compromising situations.

"They are photographs of coats of arms. I was hoping you might be able to identify the insignia you saw on the coach door. If I may?"

Aubert could not conceal his disappointment. "Very well, M. Legros. I'll have a look at them."

Legros opened the briefcase, took out the photographs, and arranged them on the tabletop. "Now, Monsieur, will you please examine each one carefully. Take your time; there's no rush."

Aubert adjusted his spectacles and started viewing the pictures. He went down the first row, frowned, and shook his head. When he reached the middle of the second row, he stopped and picked up a photograph for scrutiny. He studied the picture for a full minute before saying, "Yes, M. Legros. This is it; I'm certain."

Legros looked at the emblem Aubert had identified. "Are you sure this is it? Would you like to reconsider the others?"

"No, Monsieur. This is the insignia I saw on the coach door."

"Could you swear to that in court?"

Aubert hesitated a moment before declaring, "Yes, Inspector. If necessary, I would swear to it."

"Thank you, M. Aubert. Thank you very much." Legros snatched the photograph from Aubert's hand, marked it with a pencil, and made a notation on a chart. Then he packed everything in his briefcase, put on his hat and overcoat, and grabbed his umbrella, which he had left to dry in a corner near the oven. "You've been very helpful, Monsieur. I apologize, but I must leave at once. Thank you again for your assistance and your hospitality." With that, he dashed out into the rain, slamming the door behind him.

Legros seemed to have vanished like a ghost. Aubert stared at the doorway. Then he turned his attention to the inspector's cup. "He hardly touched it," the old man muttered. Aubert sighed, shook his head, and returned to his coffee and fantasies of Mme Behrs.

Mme Renard, the cook, and Honoré, the gardener, sat at a kitchen table in the de Livet mansion. The sound of raindrops clattering in the gutters and beating against the windowpanes mixed with the lugubrious tones emanating from a grand piano in the music room.

"I wish she'd stop, Mme Renard," Honoré muttered. "Or at least play something cheerful. That music gives me the creeps."

"I think it's the only thing Madame plays well, poor thing," Mme Renard replied.

The two oldest servants had come together for tea and a Tarot reading. Mme Renard had a reputation for clairvoyance and a knack for descrying the esoteric cards. With Manuela dead, the baron still missing, and Mignonette in police custody, the household staff was naturally anxious. Moreover, Madame had become increasingly moody and withdrawn and Bonnet more irritable and menacing. There was backstairs grumbling and talk of giving notice, but good positions were hard to find in Paris, especially when a servant came from a house tainted with scandal.

The most superstitious servants had resorted to fortune-telling to determine the household's future. Mme Renard continued interpreting the cards she had placed on the tabletop, each row representing the past, present, and future, until she turned over the Hanged Man. She paused in her reading and took a sip of tea.

The gardener's face wrinkled in a worried frown. "I don't like that card, Madame. We used to call it 'The Traitor.' In the old days, they'd hang villains upside down."

She put down her teacup and smiled. "It's not necessarily bad, Honoré. The card signifies suspense, a state of inaction and contemplation. The fortunes of the house of de Livet are at a crossroads and could go forward in any number of directions. The next card will be revealing."

A lightning flash lit the kitchen followed by a thunderclap that rattled the windows.

"*Sacristi!* That reminded me of the Prussian guns in '71."

Mme Renard gazed through the rain-streaked windows at a gray-green sky. *Is it a sign?* Her eyes widened in anticipation, and she hesitated before turning over the next card—Death.

Honoré crossed himself. "God help us, Mme Renard. Surely that can't be good?"

She swept up the cards and shuffled them back into the deck. The fortune-teller stared at the gardener for a moment before saying, "How about some rum for our tea?"

&

Bonnet knocked at the music room door. "It's me, Mathilde. I'm coming in."

The music stopped. Bonnet entered and closed the door behind him. Madame sat in the shadows, her face turned away from him, her eyes on the keyboard. The electricity was off, and she had not lit the lamps or the candles. As Bonnet approached, he smelled the heavy odor of tobacco smoke mingled with Madame's musky perfume. An ashtray filled with lip rouge–smeared cigarette butts rested on the piano next to an almost-empty brandy decanter and a glass.

Bonnet tried to place his hand on her shoulder, but she shrank from him, like a nervous cat.

He sighed. "I'm so sorry, Mathilde. I came to thank you again for the diamonds. It's arranged for early tomorrow morning. I can't tell you when; it's best you don't know."

"I see," she said without looking at him. "I'll miss the diamonds. They meant a great deal to me."

"I'll try to make it up to you. When I get settled in Buenos Aires I'll send for you—if you'll have me."

Madame sniffed and shook her head. She wiped away tears and said, "Please go."

Bonnet stood silently for a moment before turning and leaving the room.

After he left, Madame looked up and gazed out the French windows that opened onto a terrace. Through the rain, she could make out the form of an overflowing alabaster fountain. *Why waste tears on a worthless man?* she thought. She reached for the decanter and poured another glass. The cognac burned her throat and she coughed.

After a while, she put down her drink and continued playing Chopin's "Raindrop Prelude." She recalled reading about Chopin and George Sand's romantic interlude on Majorca. It had rained heavily on the island, and the prelude's repeating A-flat reminded her of raindrops. Moreover, the dirgelike section seemed to portend the composer's premature death. "Romantic nonsense," she muttered.

Mme Renard was right; the bittersweet prelude was the only piece Mathilde de Livet played well.

c⌀ɔ

Le Boudin, ex-Legionnaire and uncrowned king of the *chiffonniers*, established his domain between the two lines of fortifications surrounding Paris, in the strip of wasteland called the Zone. To enter his "kingdom" you exited the capital through the Porte de Clignancourt, passed by the glacis and weed-clogged ditch of the Thiers wall, and continued toward the town of Saint-Ouen.

Le Boudin built his compound on a low mound near the road, a place once occupied by Prussian artillery during the Siege of 1870–71. From this vantage point, the ragpicker king contemplated the walls of Paris and the flea market where he and his people peddled their wares.

Over the years, the market had transformed from a dangerous den of thieves into a legitimate business catering to shoppers looking for a duty-free bargain. Le Boudin employed a host of *pêcheurs de lune*, all licensed to pick through the city's rubbish from which they gathered a rich harvest of rags and scrap metal.

Le Boudin was a nondiscriminatory employer; all were welcome as long as they obeyed his rules, a simple code that M. Lefebvre would have recognized as the *jus naturale*, or natural law. If you lived and worked by the code, you had food, shelter, and a share in the profits. There was even provision for the aged and infirm. In that regard, Le Boudin's domain might have resembled a commune more than a kingdom, except that the king's word was final and his share of the profits the greatest by far. As for the *jus civile* of Paris and Saint-Ouen, Le Boudin figured that if he and his people lived according to his code, they would not conflict with the laws of France. In fact, he had formed a cooperative relationship with the authorities, most particularly with the newly appointed chief of detectives.

Le Boudin and Delphine sheltered from the storm in his storehouse, a treasury of the choicest gleanings from the streets and back alleys of the twenty arrondissements. They sat at a rough-hewn table, enjoying a meal of bread, cheese, and coffee laced with rum. An occasional drop from the leaky roof splattered the unpainted pine tabletop and the surrounding floorboards.

Delphine looked up and said, "Why don't you get that fixed, Papa?"

Le Boudin glanced upward and scratched his beard with his hook, a replacement for the hand he had lost fighting in Mexico. "I'll get around to it—one of these days," he mumbled through a half-full mouth. Then he finished chewing and washed it down with fortified coffee.

Moïse knocked and entered. He shook himself off like a wet dog before coming to the table.

"Hello, boss; Delphine. It's pissing down like an old drunk on a bridge. Do you mind if I join you? I've news from M. Lefebvre."

"Pull up a chair, kid," Le Boudin replied.

"How is M. Lefebvre?" Delphine asked anxiously.

Moïse smiled. "The chief's all right. Mind if I have some coffee before giving you the details?"

Le Boudin reached over to a nearby shelf and grabbed a mug. He looked into the cup and sniffed before handing it to Moïse. "You can use this. I don't think the cat peed in it—at least, not recently."

The young *chiffonier* grinned. "Thanks, boss." He poured some coffee, took a swallow, and gasped. "Whew, that's strong. Did you spike it with that roach poison you call rum?"

Le Boudin glared at his employee. "Are you complaining?"

Moïse shook his head. "No, boss. It's great. Just the way I like it."

"Would you please stop clowning and give us the news?" Delphine asked.

Moïse winked at Le Boudin. "All right, I won't keep you in suspense. M. Lefebvre is fine. He'll just have a little scar on his cheek. One of his detectives is in hospital, but he's on the mend. As for the assassins, they've moved from the Bateau-Lavoir to the Morgue. Knowing both places as I do, I'd say that's an improvement."

"Did he have a message for me?" Delphine asked impatiently.

Moïse sipped his coffee before saying, "Keep your panties on, kid. I'm coming to it."

"I'm warning you, runt," Delphine said.

Moïse smiled and shook his head. "Feisty, isn't she, boss?"

"Yes," Le Boudin growled. "But she's right. Get on with it."

"Very well, boss. M. Lefebvre sends you both greetings. Delphine's not to worry. She can go home any time she wants. Sergeant Rodin arrested the thugs who ganged up on her, and they squealed on the Russian. M. Lefebvre's putting the screws on. But if you ask me, Delphine doesn't need the police. You should have seen her fight. She's awfully tough—for a girl."

Delphine frowned. "Tough enough to kick your scrawny ass."

Moïse raised his hands in mock supplication. "Peace, big sister. I'm not looking for trouble."

"Good," Le Boudin said with a grunt. He turned to Delphine. "Well, my girl, it looks like you can go back to Montmartre, and I won't have to keep feeding you and your cat."

Delphine smiled. "Thanks, Papa Le Boudin." She looked at the raindrops plopping on the table and the floor. "I guess I'll go when the rain lets up."

"Me too," Moïse said.

Le Boudin glared at the *chiffonier*. After a tense moment, he said, "All right, runt. I guess you'd better eat. Have some bread and cheese."

Moïse grinned, grabbed some food, and stuffed it into his hungry mouth. "Thanks, boss," he mumbled between bites.

⌘

"Are they taking good care of you, Bouvier?" Achille asked.

"Very good, M. Lefebvre. I'm going home tomorrow."

"I'm glad to hear it, Detective. We can use you at headquarters. Sergeant Adam will assign you to a desk job until you're fit to go back on the street."

"Thank you, Chief. And thanks again for visiting my wife. You didn't have to do it, but it meant a great deal to her."

"Think nothing of it. I'm writing up a commendation. You've earned it."

They were in the surgical ward. Achille sat in a small chair occupying the cramped, curtained-off bedside space. The chief had stopped to visit his detective before returning to the office to meet with Legros. A sister pulled back the curtain. Achille got up and removed his hat.

The middle-aged nun smiled at the chief of detectives. "Good afternoon, M. Lefebvre."

"Good afternoon, Sister. How is the patient?"

The sister glanced at Bouvier and looked back at Achille. "He's coming along splendidly, Monsieur. M. Bouvier's a perfect patient." She paused a moment. The nuns were supposed to limit their conversations with patients and visitors to subjects directly related to care. However, some of the sisters took a broad interpretation of the rule. She added with a frown, "Not like Inspector Rousseau. That man's a terror. When he was here, he complained and leered at the young sisters. I must confess we were relieved when he left."

Achille smiled. "Rousseau's a fine detective, but he can be difficult at times."

"You are charitable, Monsieur. It's one of your many fine qualities."

"Thank you, Sister; you're too kind." He turned back to Bouvier. "I must be off. If you or your family need anything, just let me know."

"Thank you, M. Lefebvre. I look forward to getting back on the job."

Achille nodded, said good afternoon to the sister, and left. The nun waited until Achille was out of earshot before saying:

"He's a great man, M. Bouvier. You are fortunate to work for him."

"I know that, Sister," Bouvier replied.

<hr />

Achille's office glowed with gaslight and oil lamps on the gray afternoon. He glanced from the documents and photographs on his desk to the rain-washed windows and back. Then he looked up at Inspector Legros, who sat opposite him.

"It seems to have let up, Étienne."

"Thank goodness, Chief," Legros replied. "It's been coming down for hours. If it had kept up much longer, the streets would have flooded."

Achille nodded and stared at a photograph. "Aubert identified the embassy coach. It's as I suspected."

"Yes, Chief. And witnesses confirm that the bandaged man boarded the train at Annecy, along with Colonel Mukhin. The embassy coach met them at the station and dropped off the bandaged man in front of the hotel on the Rue Castex."

"Where the baron's cab picked him up and drove on to Mme Behrs's apartment on the Rue de Turenne."

"Yes, Monsieur."

"It seems we're going to be searching for a landau with the Russian double-headed eagle painted on its doors. The insignia would have been conspicuous, unless they had a means of effacing it without drawing attention." Achille sighed and shook his head. He returned the papers and photographs to the file. Then he scratched at his bandage, sipped some coffee from a mug, and made a face. "This stuff's cold," he muttered.

"Do you want me to call the clerk to get a fresh pot?"

He put down the cup. "No, thank you, Étienne. Don't bother." Achille remained silent for a moment. He knew what he wanted to say but hesitated to speak. Then he began with reference to Rousseau's messenger. "Duroc was here an hour ago. I have a meeting with Orlovsky and Rousseau in the Place Dauphine this afternoon at four. I want you there. After all, it's your case and you've done most of the work."

"Thank you, Chief. By the way, rumor has it that you've forgiven Duroc and commended him for his actions in yesterday's attempted assassination."

"That's the rumor, is it? Well, it's just about right. Duroc made a mistake in the Ménard case, and he's paid for it. We shook hands, and I told him if he ever wanted to return to the brigade, I'd have a place for him."

"How did he respond?"

"He thanked me and said he wanted to prove himself in his present job. I told him I admired loyalty and left it at that. Frankly, he's the sort of fellow who'll never make sergeant, never mind inspector. I prefer to bring in men I can promote, but that doesn't mean he can't be of service.

"We're only human, Étienne; we all make mistakes. Nevertheless, it is axiomatic to the point of cliché: the higher we climb, the farther we fall. And history judges our failures, like our achievements, from the perspective of hindsight.

"The Emperor Napoleon I lost five hundred thousand men in Russia, a catastrophe that ultimately cost him the empire. But the outcome might have been different. When it came to war, neither he nor the Russians wanted it, but they hadn't much choice in the matter. The Emperor's continental system and the Russian economy were in conflict. When your back's against the wall, you must yield or fight. In the end, the weather, bad roads, and an angry populace counted for more than generalship.

So you see, in a tight spot even the greatest men can lose control of their destinies.

"Now, I have my own 'Russian problem,' but on a much smaller scale. M. Orlovsky and I will be gaming this afternoon, and you may judge who comes out the winner. The stakes might seem relatively low, but it's all part of a larger game played by the great powers. One false step could lead to disaster."

Legros stared at the chief without speaking.

Achille wondered if he had overstated the situation. He smiled and said, "You should see the look on your face. It isn't as bad as that. Go ahead and call the clerk. We have time to enjoy a fresh pot of coffee."

⁂

Achille and Legros sat in a quiet corner of the brasserie on the Rue de Harlay. The restaurant was located near the entrance to the Place Dauphine, across the street from the Palais de Justice.

The heavy rain had stopped, but it was still overcast with a light drizzle. Rousseau and Orlovsky arrived shortly after four P.M. The Russian seemed distressed in surroundings swarming with police, prosecutors, and judges. When he exited the cab, he hunched over, pulled down his hat brim, and glanced around distrustfully before entering the restaurant. Achille observed the furtive behavior with satisfaction. *One should always try to engage an adversary on the ground of one's own choosing*, he thought.

Achille called for service as soon as Rousseau and Orlovsky sat down at the table. They ordered beer and remained silent until the waiter served the drinks. When the waiter returned to the bar, Orlovsky broke the silence with a question:

"May I inquire as to the reason for this meeting, M. Lefebvre?"

Achille put down his beer and stared hard at the Russian before answering. "The *reason*, Monsieur? The reason is justice. You are under arrest."

Achille's unexpected announcement stunned Legros, but he remained outwardly calm; Rousseau smirked knowingly.

Orlovsky was livid; his hands shook. The Russian coughed nervously and cleared his throat before asking, "Will you please name the crime with which I am charged?"

"Of course, Monsieur," Achille replied. "You are charged with soliciting an armed attack on a French citizen."

Orlovsky's eyes widened. He turned to Rousseau. "But I thought . . . you told me . . . ," he sputtered.

Rousseau shrugged and said nothing.

"If you please, M. Orlovsky," Achille said sharply to regain the Russian's attention.

Orlovsky looked back at Achille, his dark eyes burning with anger. "Yes, Monsieur?"

"We have the attackers' signed confessions and witnesses to the assault. In addition, you admitted your crime to Inspector Rousseau. Do you deny the charge?"

"I . . . I demand to see the Russian consul."

"You may communicate with the gentleman from the Dépôt in the Conciergerie, which is but a short walk from here."

Orlovsky controlled himself. He guessed that the threat of arrest was a tactic; Lefebvre might be open to a deal. "May I smoke?" he asked calmly.

"Of course, Monsieur," Achille replied.

The Russian lit a cigarette and took a couple of puffs before asking, "What do you want, M. Lefebvre?"

"The truth, Monsieur. Tell me everything you know about the affair involving Baron de Livet, Prince Papkov, Colonel Mukhin, Mme Behrs, and the Englishman. And please be assured I have a great deal more information now than I had the last time we discussed the subject."

"Will you drop the charges if I cooperate?"

"I'll consider dropping the charges, provided you are forthcoming and remain cooperative. Moreover, I want your pledge that in the future, as long as you're in my jurisdiction, you'll abide by our laws and do nothing contrary to the interests of France."

Orlovsky glanced at Rousseau, who met the Russian's look with a barely perceptible nod. "Very well, M. Lefebvre. Ask your questions. I'll answer truthfully and to the best of my ability."

Achille smiled wryly. "The truth, M. Orlovsky, could have saved us all a great deal of trouble. The last time we met to discuss the de Livet case, you told me a false story about a duel over a gambling debt. I heard the same pack of lies from Bonnet. Obviously that fabrication was a pre-arranged cover-up. Now, Monsieur, tell me who set up the meeting in Aix-les-Bains and to what purpose?"

Orlovsky looked around and leaned forward toward Achille. The brasserie was nearly empty; they could not be overheard. Nevertheless, the Russian hesitated before speaking, and when he did speak, he kept his voice at a level barely above a whisper. "M. Lefebvre, before I pro-ceed, please let me clarify some issues. First, my assignment in Paris is to maintain surveillance and report on Russian nationals who engage in subversive activities harmful to both our countries. In that regard, I work in close cooperation with your colleague Inspector Rousseau and with the full knowledge of your government."

"I'm aware of that, Monsieur," Achille said. "Please continue."

"Thank you, Monsieur. The woman you call Mme Behrs is a Russian. Her name is Valentina Berezina and, until recently, she was one of my most trusted agents. She worked for a time at Le Chabanais, and there she became intimate with M. de Livet. He bought her out of the house and set her up in an apartment in the Marais. I gave you her address, if you recall?"

"Yes, I recall that, Monsieur. No doubt you expected her to tell us another misleading story. However, when Inspector Legros went to inter-view her, she was gone. I assume you've lost track of her?"

"Yes, Monsieur. I've heard nothing from her since she left the Marais. I had assigned Valentina—Mme Behrs—to report on M. de Livet. We had information that he was financing a Russian expatriate arms dealer who sold weapons to revolutionaries in Russia and other countries, including France. Mme Behrs obtained credible evidence that refuted the accusation. Moreover, she said M. de Livet could be useful to us in certain transactions and asked for permission to recruit him for that purpose."

"What do you mean by 'certain transactions'?"

"I'm coming to that, Monsieur. The baron has a wide network of international business contacts, including many who are willing to provide valuable intelligence for a price. Major Sims is such an individual. The major had recently arrived in Paris; Mme Behrs made his acquaintance when the baron brought him to the apartment on the Rue de Turenne. She overheard the baron and Sims discussing British military secrets that would be of great interest to Russia. Sims claimed to have in his possession accurate and up-to-date maps and information relating to Anglo-Indian troop deployments, defenses, and logistics in the vicinity of the Khyber Pass."

"Pardon me, M. Orlovsky. I was unaware that trading in military secrets came within the scope of your assignment in Paris."

"Indeed, it is *not* my responsibility, M. Lefebvre, which is why I brought the matter to the attention of Colonel Mukhin, who in turn informed Prince Papkov. I played a minor role. The whole scheme involving the sale and transfer of documents was worked out among the baron, the prince, the colonel, and Sims, with the assistance of my agent, Mme Behrs."

"And what was the 'whole scheme'?"

"The baron came up with the plan. According to Mme Behrs and the colonel, a meeting was arranged at the prince's villa under the pretext of a card party. Sims brought the maps and documents for the prince's and the colonel's inspection, and the baron brought nine hundred thousand francs in banknotes and gold as a sign of good faith. According to plan, the baron would purchase the documents from Sims in Paris later that evening. He would use currency from his bank that was traceable to him rather than to our government. He was willing to assume the risk of the deal for a commission of ninety thousand francs in gold, which Mme Behrs would pay him on completion of the transaction."

"Pardon me, Monsieur," Achille said. "What about the purported duel?"

"That was also the baron's idea. If word of the duel got out, it was supposed to give people a false impression that the baron had severed ties with his Russian acquaintances. Under the circumstances, we would not be suspected of working together."

"I see. Regarding the transaction, we know the baron bribed Bonnet with five thousand in banknotes. Did you reimburse him for the bribe with gold?"

"Yes, Monsieur."

"We know the baron carried the cash in a Gladstone bag that we found in Mme Behrs's apartment. We also believe that Sims and Colonel Mukhin boarded the Paris express at Annecy. We assume the Englishman bandaged his face prior to boarding the train, to conceal his identity. Is that correct?"

Orlovsky frowned. "Yes, that is correct. Sims wanted the bandages, and Colonel Mukhin agreed. Frankly, if they had consulted me I would have insisted on another disguise. A bandaged face attracts attention."

"I agree, Monsieur. The choice of disguise was poor. On the evening of the twenty-fifth, a witness saw Sims, the baron, and Mme Behrs leave the apartment in an embassy coach. They carried two suitcases, which we believe contained the gold from the embassy."

"How did you know about the coach?"

"A witness identified the double-eagle coat of arms."

The Russian shook his head. "Unbelievable. They didn't cover it?"

"Apparently not. Please address the question of the transaction. What was the original plan?"

"If things had gone as agreed, the baron would have used the cash in his bag to pay Sims, Mme Behrs would have reimbursed the baron and paid his commission with our gold, and Sims would have turned the papers and maps over to Mme Behrs. She would have taken the documents to the embassy, and the gentlemen would have gone their separate ways."

"Who drove the coach?"

"Lieutenant Denisov, Colonel Mukhin's aide-de-camp. Mukhin trusted the man implicitly."

"Where is Lieutenant Denisov?"

"We don't know, Monsieur."

"Was there anyone else in the coach?"

"Not to my knowledge."

Achille paused and took a drink of beer before saying, "Well, M. Orlovsky, it appears that your government is out almost one million francs and you have nothing to show for it."

Orlovsky frowned and stubbed out his cigarette in an ashtray. "Yes, M. Lefebvre."

"Is there anything else you can tell me regarding this matter?"

"No, Monsieur. I swear I've told you everything I know. We've been searching for the parties in question without any success."

"Very well, M. Orlovsky. The last time we met, you said you owed me a debt of gratitude and that a gentleman always pays his debts. Do you remember?"

Orlovsky looked down at his hands. "Yes, Monsieur; I recall saying that."

"It looks like you're going deeper into my debt. I will release you provided you give me your word of honor that you will not leave Paris without my permission. Leaving Paris includes entering your embassy grounds. Moreover, you'll continue to cooperate with the investigation. These conditions remain in force pending the outcome of the case. If you violate the terms of your parole, my detectives will arrest you and take you to the Dépôt like a common criminal. Do you understand?"

The Russian looked up with a faint smile of relief and gratitude. "Thank you, M. Lefebvre; I understand."

"Good. We're going to pursue the theft of your embassy's property. The baron, Sims, Mme Behrs, and Lieutenant Denisov are suspects. We will issue bulletins with reference to the stolen gold and descriptions of the individuals and the embassy coach. We'll say nothing about the documents. You'll inform Prince Papkov and Colonel Mukhin to that effect."

"Yes, Monsieur."

"Regarding the military secrets: The British government would certainly consider the transaction an unfriendly act. We should hope they never learn of it; they already view our 'secret' alliance with alarm. I must report this incident to my superiors, and they will determine how best to deal with it from the diplomatic angle. From my perspective, I think it best to pursue the case as a confidence trick. There will be a stink in the newspapers, but it's better for the public to think the baron and company are thieves than to open up a scandal involving espionage.

"If we recover the stolen property, namely the gold and the coach, we'll impound it until it can be returned to the lawful owner, which in this case appears to be the Russian government. Charging and trying the thieves without revealing the true nature of the scheme will be problematic, but we can deal with that difficulty if or when we catch them. The documents are a matter that will require special handling. Do you agree?"

"Yes, M. Lefebvre. I'll notify my superiors of all you have said."

"Very well. You may go, Monsieur."

The Russian got up from the table. He bowed and said, "Thank you, M. Lefebvre. *Au revoir.*"

"*Au revoir*, M. Orlovsky," Achille replied.

The officers watched silently as Orlovsky left the brasserie. Rousseau spoke first:

"Looks like our Russian friends have pulled us into another bucket of shit."

"You have a knack for understatement, my friend," Achille replied. "I'd say we're in an ocean of ordure. But at least we're all practiced swimmers." He smiled and looked at their empty glasses. "Gentlemen, we've plenty of work ahead of us, but I suggest another round before we go."

13

UNTANGLING KNOTS

A stone wall dating back to the reign of Louis XIV, when the Avenue Montaigne was called the Allée des Veuves, separated the Baron de Livet's property from its neighbor. A section of the wall, partially hidden behind a massive chestnut tree, was the subject of an amusing story. Toward the end of the *ancien régime*, the owner had kept his mistress in the house next door. To evade the eyes of prying neighbors and a jealous wife, the gentleman had loosened some stones near the base, making a breach in the wall through which a man of average height and weight could pass. According to the tale, the lovers enjoyed many midnight trysts without being discovered.

For more than a century, subsequent owners had told the story and maintained the old wall with its loosened stones. The baron was no exception, and he had made a point of passing the tale on to his manservant. "Remember this spot, Bonnet," he had said, as he removed one of the stones to illustrate his point. "If we ever get into a tight corner, here's a clever way out."

About three hours before daybreak, Bonnet reconnoitered the garden through the panes of a cellar window. The drizzle had stopped several hours earlier, but the predawn sky was covered in clouds that dimmed the moon and the stars. He could barely make out the shadowy forms of the wall and the ancient tree, the guideposts of his escape route.

Years earlier, Bonnet had learned some burglar's tricks. He wore a tight-fitting black sweater, sturdy black twill trousers, and rubber-soled shoes; he darkened his face with a mixture of grease and soot. In addition, he wore gloves to protect his hands, since he planned to climb the wall next door and might need to do more climbing before he was in the clear.

Bonnet raised the window and propped it open with a stick. He grasped the brickwork sill, boosted himself up, and slithered out into the damp grass fringing the mansion's foundation.

He remained prone and motionless, listening and searching the area for signs of detectives: a few muffled words or the telltale beam of a lantern. All he heard was the chirring of insects and the croaking of frogs; he saw no light except the pale rays streaming down from a cloud-screened moon. The earthy garden odor was like a whiff of freedom, somewhere far from the urban confines of Paris.

Convinced there was no immediate threat, he scampered across the lawn to the wall. As soon as he reached his objective, he crouched and felt his way along the stones until he came to the chestnut tree. There, at the angle where the old wall running along the property line converged with a modern segment bordering on the back alley, he discovered a loose stone near the base.

He removed the stones and wriggled through the hole. On the other side, Bonnet hunkered down, on the watch for the neighbor's dog, a black Beauceron. He believed they kept the dog chained at night, in an outbuilding closer to the house than the wall. The Beauceron could not reach him, but if aroused, its barking would wake the neighborhood.

Bonnet crept along the wall as quietly as possible, intending to make his climb at the far angle near the entrance to the alley.

He avoided stepping on twigs, crunching leaves, or making any noise that might alert the guard dog. Proceeding slowly and carefully, he reached his goal without incident. The wall confronting him was no taller than the top of his head, and there were protruding stones and a vine to aid his climb.

Prior to scaling the wall, he reached under his shirt and felt the pouch that held Madame de Livet's diamonds to make sure it was securely tucked under his belt. He made the ascent without difficulty until he grasped the crown of the wall with his right hand. A large glass shard penetrated the glove and pierced his palm. The sharp shock of the cut caused Bonnet to flinch and lose his foothold. He fell backward onto the lawn.

Though cushioned by fallen leaves and grass, the sound of Bonnet's fall was still loud enough to wake the dog; its howling and barking roused the household. A light appeared in an upstairs window. Bonnet quickly drew the glass from his palm and climbed again, this time sweeping the top clean before grabbing hold and pulling himself up and over. In his haste, he landed awkwardly, twisting an ankle.

He hobbled up the alley until the light from two lanterns flashed in his eyes, temporarily blinding him.

"Stop in the name of the law!"

"Give up, Bonnet. You're under arrest."

The seasoned boxer lashed out at his unseen opponents; a kick from his good leg caught one of the detectives in the shin. The other dropped his lantern and began a scuffle that might have ended badly for the police had it not been for Sergeant Marechal's timely blow to the back of the fugitive's head. The crack from the sergeant's truncheon stunned Bonnet. He dropped to his knees and fell face forward into the muck.

Marechal knelt, took out a ligature, and bound the semiconscious man's hands. Then he said to one of the detectives, "Hey, Vincent, help me lift this bugger to his feet."

Marechal and Vincent lifted Bonnet and kept him steady. The sergeant searched Bonnet and discovered the pouch containing the diamonds. "Well, my lad," he said to Bonnet with a sly grin, "what have we here? Not talking, eh? Guess you're a bit woozy from that knock on your head. Don't worry. We'll have plenty of time for talk down at headquarters." Then Sergeant Marechal turned to the other detective who was standing aside, rubbing his sore leg. "Are you all right, Allard?"

"I think so, Sergeant, but I'll have one hell of a bruise. I'd like to pay the bastard back, here and now."

Marechal shook his head. "There's been enough rough stuff this morning. We have a nice cell waiting for M. Bonnet back at the Dépôt. Later, when his head clears, he can have a friendly chat with the chief."

The detectives had a good laugh about M. Lefebvre's "friendly chats." They dragged Bonnet to a police van parked nearby on the Rue Montaigne.

⌘

At eight A.M. Achille entered Magistrate Leblanc's office in the Palais de Justice. The examining magistrate greeted his colleague with a warm handshake and a smile. Now nearing the end of his public service, the magistrate had observed the career of the still-youthful chief of detectives with interest. He admired the younger man's tenacious approach to complex cases, his progressive ideas, his compassion, and his commitment to justice. However, Achille's pragmatism and an audacity that at times verged on ruthlessness also made an impression on the seasoned *juge*.

Years earlier, in a conversation with the former chief, M. Leblanc summed up his estimation of Achille's qualities as follows: "Keep an eye on him, Paul. That young fellow is a comer. I like working with him. He's smart, dedicated to the law, full of surprises, and frightening at times. But that makes for a good play, and his unpredictability enhances the performance."

"Good morning, Chief Inspector. I understand your men arrested Bonnet. I assume that's why you are here?"

"Yes, Monsieur *le juge*; to discuss Bonnet in connection with the de Livet case and the Otero poisoning."

"Very well. A most interesting matter. Please be seated. Would you care for some coffee?"

"Thank you, Monsieur; yes, I would."

M. Leblanc rang for his clerk and ordered a fresh pot of coffee. After the coffee was served and the clerk returned to his desk, the magistrate said, "It's a complicated case, M. Lefebvre, and I'll admit you have a much better understanding of it than I do."

"Pardon me, Monsieur *le juge*. I may have been remiss in my duty to keep you informed."

"Nonsense, Chief Inspector. In such cases, I'm pleased to defer to your professional judgment, as I did with M. Féraud during our long association."

Achille smiled at the compliment. "Thank you, M. Leblanc. Now, to bring you up-to-date: Bonnet paid a gang of smugglers to take him across the Spanish border. He was carrying a quantity of diamonds when we took him into custody. My detectives had arrested Bonnet's gang contact around midnight this morning. The smuggler confessed, and he will testify against Bonnet. The examining magistrate in Pau believes these arrests will lead to a prosecution against the entire smuggling ring."

"That's excellent, M. Lefebvre. Please remind me how this relates to the cases of the missing baron and his poisoned servant?"

Achille gave a detailed account of the information he had obtained from Orlovsky. Once the magistrate had a good grasp of the baron's scheme, Achille elaborated on the roles he believed Bonnet and Mme de Livet might have played in the matter, including their culpability in Manuela Otero's death.

"Bonnet lied to the police. He told a story concocted by the baron and his accomplices to cover up the real reason for the meeting in Aix-les-Bains. Furthermore, Inspector Legros discovered five thousand francs in banknotes traceable to M. de Livet, hidden under the floorboards in Bonnet's room. Mlle Hubert, a servant in the de Livet household, tipped us off. According to Hubert, her friend Manuela Otero said the baron gave Bonnet the banknotes for some special service, and we can assume that lying to the police was either all or part of the service he rendered.

"Mlle Hubert believes Bonnet poisoned Mlle Otero, and I've concluded that's the best explanation for the young woman's death. Bonnet had the strongest motive; Mlle Otero knew too much about his dealings with the baron, and he silenced her. Masson's forensic testing following the autopsy confirmed that Otero died as the result of aconite poisoning, and our timeline of events and examination of the household staff indicates that only Bonnet and Mme de Livet could have administered the fatal overdose.

"Bonnet was the baron's bodyguard and confidant. The baron paid him well, and Bonnet could have expected more from his master in future. He's a former boxer with a reputation for foul play both in and out of the ring, the sort who could commit a heinous crime for money. On the other hand, Mme de Livet seems more like a hapless victim of circumstance. I doubt she's a cold-blooded killer."

The magistrate leaned forward and looked directly at Achille. "I imagine Mme de Livet is a far more sympathetic individual than Bonnet. However, I hope you aren't letting sentiment affect your judgment?"

"No, Monsieur *le juge*. Our law presumes that a woman is under her father's control until the time of her marriage, when she becomes subject to her husband's authority. In that regard, the baroness married for advantage according to her father's wishes and acquiesced in her husband's unworthy schemes. Of course, she isn't blameless. A wife's duty to obey her spouse ends when her husband resorts to crime. And I suspect the baron ignored her adultery; he may have encouraged it, since he directed his carnal desires elsewhere.

"Mme de Livet's submissiveness extended to her lover, Bonnet—at least, up to a point. I don't think she was involved in the murder, but I do believe she aided Bonnet after the fact. For example, the jewelry we found in Bonnet's possession may have been stolen, but I would not rule out the possibility that Mme de Livet gave the diamonds to her lover to enable his escape."

M. Leblanc frowned. "It's a sordid affair, M. Lefebvre; scandalous and disgusting."

"Yes, Monsieur; but I'd help the poor woman, if I could. She cannot bear witness against her husband, but she may be compelled to testify against her lover. At any rate, I'm going to speak to her before we question Bonnet. It will be interesting to hear what she has to say about the diamonds. And with your permission, I would like to take the lead in Bonnet's interrogation."

"I grant my permission with pleasure. When will you question him?"

"Tomorrow morning, if that is convenient for you. By the way, I have what the Americans call an ace in the hole, and I may need to play it."

The magistrate's eyes widened with eager anticipation. *So, I'm to witness another of M. Lefebvre's clever tricks*, he thought. "Will you please tell me what you have in mind?"

"Of course, Monsieur *le juge*. I've discovered fingerprints on the two medicine bottles found in Otero's room. If Bonnet's prints match, we'll have him by the short hairs."

The magistrate sighed. "I know you had some success with fingerprints in the Ménard case, but the method is new and unproven. The court is not likely to accept the prints as evidence."

Achille smiled. "*We* know that, Monsieur *le juge*, but our suspect does not."

"Very well, M. Lefebvre. Is there anything else?"

"Yes, M. Leblanc. If you please, I'm requesting arrest warrants for M. de Livet, Mme Behrs, Major Sims, and Lieutenant Denisov. The charge is theft of Russian embassy property; Colonel Mukhin, the military attaché, is the complaining witness."

"I'll issue the warrants this morning. What about the espionage business?"

"I've already notified Captain Duret of the Deuxième Bureau. I'm reporting the matter to the prefect this morning, and I suppose he'll take it up with the minister. If we catch the Russians, Mme Behrs, and Denisov, they can be quietly deported. Unfortunately, de Livet is a naturalized French citizen and Sims is presumably British. I still hope to get more information about Sims from Scotland Yard, but things could get ugly if they discover the baron's plot."

"It's a mess, M. Lefebvre. Perhaps we can keep the cloak-and-dagger business concealed by pursuing the matter as a straightforward case of theft?"

"I agree that would be best, Monsieur *le juge*."

The older man frowned and shook his head sadly. "All our world needs is a stupid incident to provoke yet another senseless war."

"Of course, Monsieur. We must do what we can to prevent it."

⌒◯◯⌒

Achille and Legros studied a map spread out on a table in the chief's office. They focused their attention on the network of railway lines and roads around Paris.

"All right, Étienne; where do you think the baron and his confederates went after they left Mme Behrs's apartment the evening of the twenty-fifth?"

"My best guess is Le Havre, Chief."

"Why Le Havre?" The port was Achille's best guess, too; but he wanted his assistant's opinion.

"I believe they'd want to get out of the country by the quickest route possible. As for their destination, I have no clue, but I assume they'd go somewhere they think is beyond our reach. Just crossing the channel to England would not be far enough. Le Havre is the closest major port with the most ships sailing to faraway places, so that would be my choice."

"Would they have gone by train or taken the coach?"

"I think they would have avoided the railways; too much risk of their being spotted by our detectives, the gendarmes, or the railway personnel. Of course, traveling by road they sacrifice speed. The journey from Paris to Le Havre is about three and a half hours by train and more than thirteen hours by coach."

"Very well; we'll concentrate on the roads and the railway to Le Havre and its vicinity. We have good descriptions of everyone except Sims. The coach should have attracted some attention, whether or not they got rid of the insignia. They might have changed to another carriage, which means they could have abandoned the embassy coach somewhere.

"Check with the local police concerning the hotels, inns, and restaurants along the route; places where they might have stopped to rest or exchange vehicles. And we'll need information about all the ships sailing from Le Havre since the morning of the twenty-sixth. Of course, we must consider and investigate other possibilities, but I agree Le Havre fits the most likely scenario.

"You're in charge of getting out the bulletins to our contacts here and abroad. Monitor the incoming reports and detail a couple of men to assist you. When the press gets hold of this, you can expect a flood of false leads, so be prepared."

"All right, Chief. Has Scotland Yard responded to your inquiry about Sims?"

"No; please follow up with our contact. Our relations might be strained at present, but the Special Branch must deal with Orlovsky, too. In that regard, we're in a similar predicament, having to cooperate with the untrustworthy agent of a not-always-friendly foreign power."

"If you don't mind my asking, Chief, how will we deal with the stolen secrets?"

"I don't know; the decision will be made at a high level. It will probably be covered up, but between you and me, it's likely that the maps and documents are bogus."

"So you think the whole thing was a fraud?"

"Better for us if it was. I'd rather deal with common swindlers than spies."

"Yes, Chief." Legros paused a moment before asking, "Do you want me to question Mme de Livet about the jewelry and her relations with Bonnet?"

"No, Étienne. That's my job." He glanced up at the wall clock and added, "I'll be leaving the office presently. We'll interrogate Bonnet tomorrow morning in M. Leblanc's office. I want you there, unless you turn up something in the search for the baron and company that requires your immediate attention."

"Very well, Chief." Legros wanted to say something about the baroness. He felt sorry for her and believed the chief shared his feelings. However, he prudently decided not to raise the subject unless Achille said something first. Instead, he said, "Pardon me. Could you please tell me if Mlle Hubert is all right?"

Achille smiled. "Don't worry, your young lady has settled in just fine. She's becoming like one of our family."

Legros flushed and stammered, "*My* young lady? Excuse me, Monsieur; she's a witness. I mean to say, she's not . . . I'm not—"

"Forgive me, Étienne," the chief broke in. "I made a little joke at your expense. She *is* doing quite well, and she's asked about you, on occasion. When this is over, I'm going to do my best to get her a new position in a good household. What's more, my wife would like you to dine with us again—once this case is over, that is."

Legros was relieved. In fact, he was concerned about Mignonette and wanted very much to see her again, in an unofficial capacity. "That's very kind of you, Chief. Thank you."

Achille nodded his acknowledgment, shuffled some papers on his desk, and then looked up again at the clock. "All right, Inspector. We've a busy day ahead of us. Let's get on with it."

❈

Achille telephoned the de Livet mansion; he was surprised when Madame answered. They made an appointment to meet at her residence that morning. He could have had her brought in for questioning, but he preferred a gentler approach. When he arrived at the front door and rang the bell, Madame greeted him.

"Good morning, Chief Inspector," she said with feigned cheerfulness. "As you see, I'm reduced to answering the door. *Sic transit gloria mundi.* Please come in."

Her sarcasm reminded Achille of the Mephistophelean doorman's stock greeting at the Cabaret de L'Enfer: "Enter and be damned." However, there was a difference between playacting and personal tragedy. He noticed telltale signs of her decline: a slight slurring of Madame's speech; dark circles under bloodshot eyes; untidiness of dress, as though she had slept in her clothes; the odor of tobacco and liquor on her breath.

She walked unsteadily. At one point, she almost tripped on the runner. She mumbled, "Pardon me, Monsieur," and continued down the corridor. He followed her to the music room.

"I've taken up residence here," she said as she opened the sliding door. She entered the darkened room and went directly to the piano bench, where she sat and stared at the chief inspector. "Please pull up a chair, M. Lefebvre. I'm afraid there's no one left to attend to your needs. The servants are abandoning ship, one by one."

Achille set down his briefcase, grabbed an elegant Louis XV gilt-wood chair, and sat opposite her. He remained stiffly upright on the edge of the seat, as if he feared a clumsy movement might mar the exquisite museum piece.

Madame smiled at his apparent discomfort. "You seem nervous, Monsieur. Would you care for a drink?"

"No, thank you, Madame."

"Well, I'm sure you won't mind if I do." She poured a glass of brandy from an almost-empty decanter. Achille noticed an ashtray overflowing with cigarette butts, balanced precariously on the rim of the closed piano lid.

After she took a sip of her drink, she said, "I've only two servants left: Mme Renard, the cook, and old Honoré, the gardener. I don't know if they stay with me out of loyalty or because they have nowhere else to go. It's sad, don't you think?"

"Yes, Madame; very sad. I'm sorry."

Her eyes narrowed. "Are you indeed *sorry*, M. Lefebvre?"

Achille did not answer. He opened his briefcase and removed a brown paper package. "Madame, we have recovered property that I believe belongs to you." He got up and handed her the package. "Will you please examine the contents?" Instead of returning to his chair, Achille hovered about, waiting for a response.

She fumbled with the wrapper until it opened suddenly, spilling the diamonds onto her lap. She gazed at the jewelry for a while before saying, "These are mine, M. Lefebvre." Then she looked up at him and added, "Are you returning them to me?"

"I regret not, Madame. We found the jewelry when we arrested Bonnet and his smuggler companion earlier this morning. We must keep the diamonds as evidence pending the outcome of the case. I will issue you a receipt." He held out his hands. "If you please, Madame."

She gathered up the gems and returned them to Achille. After a moment, she asked, "What do you want from me, M. Lefebvre?"

"The truth, Madame. As of yet, you are not charged with a crime. Lying to the police is a serious offense, but we can overlook your past misrepresentations if you are now willing to cooperate. Aiding and abetting criminal activity is even more serious, but depending on your frankness in response to my questions and the facts and circumstances of the case, you might avoid prosecution. However, in the matter of Manuela Otero's murder—"

"Murder, did you say?" Madame broke in. "Are you accusing me of killing Manuela?"

Achille noticed the look of horror in her eyes. "Please calm yourself, Madame. So far, I've accused you of nothing except misleading the police, and you might have acted under compulsion." Achille smiled. "I'm not unsympathetic to your situation. Would you care for another drink?"

"Yes, Monsieur, I would."

Achille refilled her glass with the remainder of the cognac. She gulped it down and coughed.

He kept smiling and spoke in a gentle, reassuring tone. "There, that's better, isn't it?"

Madame nodded. "Yes, Monsieur Lefebvre; thank you."

"I was about to say that I did not suspect you of murder or conspiracy to commit murder. However, I do believe you have information that will assist in the investigation and prosecution of the crime. Now, Madame, are you ready to answer my questions fully and truthfully?"

Madame de Livet sighed. "Yes, Monsieur Lefebvre; I'll answer your questions to the best of my ability."

"Thank you, Madame." Achille returned to his chair and assumed a less intimidating posture. "Let's go back to the week before your trip to Aix-les-Bains. The baron withdrew a large sum from his bank, and we know that the money was not to be used for gambling. Moreover, based on information we received from a witness, my detectives searched Bonnet's room and discovered five thousand francs in banknotes traceable to the baron's account. Did you know about that payment prior to leaving for Aix-les-Bains?" Achille stared hard at the baroness while waiting for her answer. If she lied, he was prepared to increase the pressure.

"Yes, Monsieur, I knew about it."

"How did you come by this information?"

"Bonnet told me."

"I see. You and Bonnet are intimate. Have you shared many secrets?"

Madame looked down at her hands and sighed. "Yes, we've shared secrets."

"Did you question your husband about the five thousand francs?"

She looked up with a puzzled frown. "What do you mean by 'question'?"

"It's simple enough, Madame. Did you not have an argument with your husband over his payment to Bonnet?"

The bewildered look gave way to one of indignation. "Did Mignonette tell you that?"

"Please, Madame; I will ask the questions and you will provide the answers."

Madame took a deep breath before answering. "When Eugene . . . Bonnet told me about the five thousand francs, he seemed very smug. His attitude annoyed me. When I asked him why my husband paid him such a large sum, he said, 'Go ask Monsieur.' Later that evening, when we were getting ready for bed, I confronted my husband. I demanded to know why he gave such a large amount of money to his servant. He told me to mind my own business. I persisted, and the argument became heated until he slapped my face and told me to shut up."

Achille had suspected abuse; he hoped the *juge* would consider it in mitigation of her complicity in the baron's and Bonnet's crimes. "Madame, did your husband often mistreat you in that manner?"

She smiled sadly. "Often enough, M. Lefebvre."

"I see. Do you think he might have acted that way because he feared the servants were listening?"

"I don't know; I suppose so."

"In fact, a servant did overhear the argument; your personal maid, Manuela Otero."

Madame's eyes widened in surprise, but she agreed without comment. "Yes, Monsieur."

"But she wasn't killed because she knew about the payment. After all, the baron could have given Bonnet five thousand francs for any number of reasons, legitimate or otherwise. However, Manuela learned why the baron paid Bonnet, and the truth was so damaging that she demanded money to keep quiet about it. And she wasn't the only one in the household who discovered the secret prior to leaving for Aix-les-Bains. You knew about it, too, Madame."

Madame's face flushed; her hands trembled. "I . . . I don't know what you're talking about."

Achille frowned and leaned forward; his voice hardened, and his eyes grew cold and unforgiving. "Do you know a young woman named Apolline Michelet?"

Madame met his challenging gaze with a contemptuous stare. "When you were a child, did you enjoy tearing the wings from butterflies?"

"I collected butterflies, Madame," he replied coolly. "I did not torture them."

"I understand, M. Lefebvre. I'm sure you put them to death humanely before placing them in your collection."

He remained silent for a moment. Then he said, "Madame, I told you I was not unsympathetic. I want to help you, if I can. But you must tell me the truth.

"Shortly before you left Paris you met with Apolline at a hotel in Montmartre; you gave her a gold bracelet. You had plans for the future, after you returned from Aix-les-Bains. I believe you wanted to get away from both the baron and Bonnet, and you made arrangements accordingly. I believe you learned the baron's secret from Manuela, and you tried to use that knowledge to free yourself from both your husband and your lover, Bonnet."

She glanced at the empty brandy glass. "May I smoke, Monsieur?" she asked in a disheartened voice. "My cigarette case is on the piano."

"Of course, Madame," he replied. Achille fetched the case and lit her cigarette. Then he returned to his chair. "Now, Madame, please tell me what happened. Did Manuela come to you with information about the baron's plans for the meeting in Aix-les-Bains?"

She exhaled a plume of smoke before answering. "Yes, Monsieur. She overheard my husband and Bonnet discussing their scheme. She wanted to benefit from this knowledge, but for obvious reasons she was afraid to go directly to either of them. Instead, she came to me. You were right in saying that I wanted to be free. Manuela knew I despised my husband. My feelings for Eugene are more . . . complicated.

"I went to my husband first. I told him I'd play my part in his intrigue in exchange for my freedom and enough money to live on. I'd take care of Manuela out of my own funds. He agreed. I accompanied him to Aix-les-Bains and filed the missing persons' report along with his fabricated story about the card game."

"What about Bonnet and Manuela?"

"After we talked, I thought she agreed to my plan. But I'm afraid greed overcame her fear. She went to Eugene and demanded one thousand francs. He has a temper, you know. He threatened to kill her, and I had to intervene. I told him to pay Manuela and I'd make it up to him. He promised not to harm her.

"Manuela was susceptible to bad colds. She was quite ill when we returned from the spa, and I called in Dr. Levasseur. He diagnosed a case of *la grippe* and prescribed a solution of tincture of aconite. Eugene took advantage of the situation. First, he sought the advice of one of his underworld associates who knows something about poisons. Apparently, that individual did not know as much about the postmortem detection of aconite poisoning as you do.

"Convinced he could get away with the crime, Eugene entered Manuela's room when no one was looking and administered the poison."

Lefebvre recalled Legros's question about the method Bonnet used to poison his victim. He had not yet discussed the matter with Masson. "Do you know the name of the individual he consulted and the means of administering the poison?"

"No, Monsieur. He did not go into details, and I did not ask." She paused a moment before adding, "He broke his solemn promise to me. You see, M. Lefebvre, I haven't been fortunate in my relations with men."

"I understand, Madame. One more thing: Did you give the diamonds to Bonnet, or did he steal them? Before you answer, please know that my detectives observed you and Bonnet at a *guinguette* near Joinville-le-Pont. The acoustics on the almost-empty terrace enabled my men to hear most of your conversation."

Madame laughed softly and shook her head. "You are like King Louis XI, the ubiquitous spider. No one escapes your web. Yes, I gave my finest jewelry to him. I know I should have given him over to the police, but as I said, my feelings for him are complicated. I'm bound to Eugene by something I cannot understand. It's neither love nor hate. Perhaps it's just our mutual bad fortune. May I say something else about broken promises?"

"Yes, Madame."

"My husband promised me freedom and money, but all he left me was debt. Look around you, Monsieur. This mansion and all the exquisite things in it were purchased on credit." She turned toward the piano and stroked the keyboard affectionately. "My beloved Érard will be taken away. It's all mortgaged to the hilt. All I have left are the diamonds I gave to Bonnet. The baron took all the cash; he'll enjoy it with his Russian whore while I languish in prison."

"I'm sorry, Madame. I'm going to recommend leniency in your case. You'll need to appear before the magistrate and make a statement under oath. If you continue cooperating, you might avoid prosecution, but I can't promise anything."

"At least you're honest." She looked at Achille with an enigmatic smile that made him uncomfortable. After an awkward interval she said, "Do you like Chopin, M. Lefebvre?"

Her peculiar question worried him, but he decided to humor her. "Yes, Madame; I like his music very much."

"Good; I'll play for you. I promise it won't take long." Without waiting for an answer, she turned toward the keyboard and began the "Raindrop Prelude."

Achille watched and listened in uneasy silence. The piece began well enough, but as she continued, her false notes multiplied and the rhythm became uneven. *Could she be mad?* he wondered. If so, the credibility of her testimony would be seriously impaired. He would discuss the matter with Magistrate Leblanc.

⁜

The *juge* finished reading Achille's report on his interview with Mme de Livet. He filed it with the case dossier. M. Leblanc removed his glasses and rubbed his eyes. Then he leaned forward over his desk and asked, "Do you think she's incapable?"

"I don't know, Monsieur *le juge*," Achille replied. "I suppose we could take her to the Salpêtrière and have Dr. Charcot examine her."

"What a terrible thing for a woman like that. On the other hand, she could be shamming to gain sympathy."

"It's possible, Monsieur. When she first came to me to report her husband's disappearance, I thought she overplayed the role of distraught wife. Her emotional performance raised my suspicions. She reminded me of Mme Bernhardt. And I was correct in my assumption. She despises the baron, and for good reasons."

M. Leblanc smiled. "Ah yes, Mme Bernhardt. I saw her Ophelia; a most convincing stage lunatic. But when it comes to madness, I've seen nothing to compare to Mme Patti in the role of Lucia di Lammermoor. I saw her at the Opera several years ago. She raised hysteria to a high art."

"Without a doubt, Patti acts a superb madwoman. As for the baroness, I can't judge her mental state, but I do believe she finally told me the truth. I'd prefer not to see her prosecuted. She's suffered from her father's selfishness, her husband's cruelty, and her lover's mendacity; now she's ruined financially and socially; that's punishment enough, don't you think?"

"I agree, M. Lefebvre. 'Leave her to heaven,' as Shakespeare said. We want the baron and his fugitive accomplices. As for Bonnet, we have enough on him to get a confession and send the dossier on to the prosecutor for trial. If he confesses fully and shows remorse I'm willing to recommend transportation for life and spare him the guillotine."

"Very well, Monsieur *le juge*. I think we can persuade our canary to sing, and we could get more than Bonnet's confession to the Otero poisoning. He might have information that will help us locate the baron and his friends."

"Have you made any progress tracking them down?"

"No, Monsieur; not yet. Inspector Legros has sent out bulletins, and I expect the leads will start coming in. Of course, it's a job separating the wheat from the chaff, but we're concentrating on Le Havre as their most likely escape route. Perhaps we'll get lucky."

M. Leblanc frowned and tugged nervously at his long side-whiskers. "Let us hope so, M. Lefebvre."

14

THE MAN WHO WASN'T THERE

In the early-morning hours, on the outskirts of the old port of Harfleur, a barge bound for Le Havre chugged up the calm waters of the canal. The westward journey from the locks at Tancarville, where the canal joined the Seine, took about three hours. That morning's passage was routine, uneventful. The rural surroundings seemed peaceful and charming: tree-lined banks, ancient farmhouses, and inns at generous intervals, waterfowl circling above in a hazy sky.

The helmsman puffed on his clay pipe; his calloused hands gripped a weathered wheel that seemed like an extension of his sunburned, tattooed arms. His keen eyes scanned the channel before him, alert for obstacles lurking beneath the smooth, olive-colored surface. He was especially watchful in this relatively narrow and shallow stretch of the waterway.

Despite his watchfulness, with Harfleur in sight, the helmsman let his mind wander for an instant to thoughts of his pay packet and money to spend in his favorite tavern in Le Havre's Saint-François district. During this moment of distraction, he failed to notice a slight rippling near the stone embankment. The sound of creaking wood and scraping metal and the shock of a vibration that ran under the boat and up into the wheel roused the helmsman.

The captain came out from his cabin and shouted, "What the Devil was that?"

"I don't know, Captain. We must have scraped over something in the channel," the startled helmsman replied.

"There'll be hell to pay if the barge is damaged," the captain muttered.

After making a cursory inspection of the barge, he returned to his cabin and took out his chart and logbook. He circled the area in pencil on the chart and made an entry in his log: "Six thirty. One kilometer from Harfleur, encountered obstruction in channel right-of-way, not visible from above the water. Hazard to navigation." He would report the incident when they docked in Le Havre.

⚜

Achille sat at his desk, reviewing the de Livet dossier. He tried to concentrate on Bonnet's upcoming interrogation, which the magistrate had rescheduled for that afternoon. Achille scribbled notes on a pad, crossed things out, and interlineated. A recurring mental image interfered with his customary focus on the job at hand: the portrait of a woman on the verge of madness. Interfused with that disturbing vision of Madame de Livet at her piano, was the sound of a repetitious dirge, a Chopin prelude that began well and then went terribly wrong.

"Damnation," he muttered. He poured a cup of coffee from a lukewarm pot and lit a cigarette. *She ought to have left her husband and come to us with the truth*, he thought. *How difficult would that be for a woman in her position?* He pondered her conflicting obligations, to her husband, to her ancient family, to the law. *Is there a higher duty, a moral law that supersedes all others? That law should not conflict with the laws of France. I pity her, but she ought to have told us the truth from the start. If she had, Manuela Otero might still be alive.*

A knock on the door interrupted his thoughts. Legros entered. He seemed excited, as if he could not hold his news long enough to properly greet Achille.

"Pardon me, Chief. We've just received a wire from Le Havre. This could be the breakthrough we've been waiting for."

Achille smiled tolerantly. He had seen many such promising "break-throughs" peter out. "Calm down, Étienne. Take a seat. Would you care for some coffee? It's getting cold, I'm afraid."

"No, thank you, Chief." He sat and stared eagerly at Achille.

"All right, Étienne. What's the hot item that's burning up the wire?"

"It's actually two wires, Chief, and three separate but related incidents. An alert police commissary pieced them together."

"Very well. Can you please let me know what our friend in Le Havre alertly pieced together?"

"Of course, Chief. Last week, the police found a couple of very fine carriage horses wandering the streets of Harfleur. That's nothing much, by itself. Then, this morning a barge captain reported an obstruction in the channel near Harfleur—"

Achille's eyes widened. "Is it the coach?"

"It could be. But wait; there's more. The police commissary and harbor-master are friends. They often get together at a café near the docks. That is how the commissary learned about the obstacle in the channel. Now, the commissary had just come from the station where he had been questioning a vagabond named Brisbois. Brisbois is a familiar type. He scours the embankment searching for stuff he can sell in the local flea market.

"A few hours before dawn, the same day the stray horses were found wandering the streets of Harfleur, he was out with a lantern, scavenging along the canal about one kilometer east of the city. He was near a clearing that trailed down from the roadway when he spotted three individuals with a coach and horses. He covered his light and hunkered down behind a tree. According to the report, Brisbois saw two of the individuals unhitch the team of horses from the coach, and then all three pushed the vehicle down the embankment into the canal."

"Are the police still holding Brisbois?"

"Yes, Chief. They received my bulletin and thought we'd want to question the vagabond. They're also sending out a diver and equipment to clear the channel."

"I want to give that policeman a cigar. No, I'm going to give him two cigars and buy dinner for him and his friend, the harbormaster. Étienne, we're going to Le Havre."

"What about Bonnet?"

"Let him sweat. Another day in the cells will do him good."

Achille grabbed the telephone and called M. Leblanc to notify him of the change in plans. Then he dashed off two notes, one to his wife and the other to Gilles, his favorite crime scene photographer. Finally, he gave instructions to his clerk to get the train schedules for Le Havre and to wire the police, advising them of the chief's imminent arrival.

⤬

The interrogation room at the Commissariat de Police in Le Havre reeked of sweat, unwashed bodies, and tobacco, a familiar odor barely masked by a regular mopping with disinfectant. Brisbois sat at a wooden table in the center of the gray, windowless, gaslit chamber. He could have been thirty or fifty; it was hard to tell. Soiled, ragged clothes hung loosely on his lean frame; greasy locks streaked with gray straggled down to his bony shoulders; a matted beard covered most of his face. His gaping mouth displayed a few brown and yellow teeth; his dark eyes darted suspiciously.

The police commissary, M. Foucault, said, "Brisbois, these gentlemen have come all the way from Paris to speak to you. This is M. Lefebvre, the chief of the Paris Detective Police, and the other is Inspector Legros."

The vagabond seemed duly impressed by the importance of his visitors. He greeted Achille and Legros with a toothless grin and a fart.

Achille smiled. He grabbed a chair and sat across the table from Brisbois. "Now, my friend, would you like a smoke? I've brought some good cigars."

The vagabond's grin widened, and he nodded in the affirmative. After Achille produced the cigar and provided a light, Brisbois uttered his first words: "Thank you, Monsieur."

Achille let Brisbois enjoy his smoke for a minute before saying, "I'd like you to tell me exactly what you saw when you were scavenging down by the canal."

"Well, Monsieur, it's just like I told M. Foucault. Everyone knows I go picking down there around that time. I get my work done early, and I don't cause any trouble. You can't imagine the things people throw away. Good stuff; stuff you can sell. Anyway, that morning I saw something odd. There was a fine-looking coach and a pair of horses parked up on the road to Harfleur. There were three men on the road, next to the coach. I could hear talking, but I couldn't make out what they said.

"Two of them went to unhitch the horses. *Now why would they do that?* I thought. It seemed to me they might be up to no good. You've got to be careful when you're out alone in the early-morning hours. So I covered my light, got down, and hid behind a big tree. I figured I could see them, all right, but they couldn't see me.

"After they got the horses unhitched, they shooed them up the road. Then all three turned around the carriage and grunted, heaved, pulled, and shoved until it rolled down the embankment into the canal. You should have heard the great noise and splash it made. It floated for a while before going under, and I could see them watching it go down."

"Did you see what the men did after they sank the carriage?"

Brisbois frowned and shook his head. "No, Monsieur, I didn't. I was scared—very scared. In all my years scrounging around the canal, I never saw anything like that. When the carriage went down, I turned tail and ran off in the other direction."

"Well, that's understandable considering the circumstances. But why didn't you report it right away?"

"I did, Monsieur. I reported it to a gendarme. But the fellow laughed at me. He said I was drunk. Said I should go away and sleep it off. I'll admit I took a drop. I was scared. You'd be, too, if you were in my shoes."

"That's true, M. Lefebvre," Foucault said. "Brisbois does tell stories when he's had a few. But this time the gendarme should have listened to him."

"Thank you, Monsieur," Brisbois said to Foucault. Then to Lefebvre: "I'm an honest man. Everyone around here knows that. I did nothing wrong."

"That's right, my friend," Lefebvre replied. "You're an important witness. I'm sure M. Foucault will take good care of you. By the way, are you hungry?"

Brisbois glanced up at the commissary and then looked back at Achille. "Well, it is getting close to dinnertime, Monsieur."

Achille got up and turned to M. Foucault. "Please see to it that he gets a good meal and a bottle of wine, too."

"Very well, Monsieur Lefebvre. But we don't want him fuddled. He needs to take us back to the place where he said they dumped the coach."

Achille looked back at Brisbois. "Do you think you'll have any trouble finding the spot where the coach went into the canal?"

Brisbois laughed. "Monsieur, I could find the place blindfolded—drunk or sober."

"That's good enough for me," Achille said. Then, to Foucault and Legros: "Come on, gentlemen, I'm hungry, too. Let's discuss the case over a good meal. If the harbormaster's available, I'd like him to join us."

"I'm sure he'd be pleased, M. Lefebvre," Foucault replied.

Achille, Legros, and Foucault returned to the commissary's office. M. Foucault telephoned the harbormaster, and they agreed to meet at the café near the dockyard.

⌘

The dockland appeared like a waterfront forest overgrown with tall masts and towering cranes. The place echoed with the sound of steam whistles on vessels of various types, sizes, and national origins and from stationary engines powering the derricks that hoisted tons of freight, loading and emptying the vast cargo holds. The world's produce—raw materials, finished goods, and foodstuff—flowed into and out from the bustling entrepôt. An immense amount of human traffic also passed through the port, many bound for the Americas aboard the great French Line steamers.

The café occupied a convenient space amid the warehouses, trading posts, steamship offices, and ships' chandleries that serviced the port. A constant procession of wagons drawn by powerful draft horses rumbled up and down the quay. The place reverberated with the colorful patois of sailors, stevedores, traffic managers, and teamsters.

Achille, Legros, M. Foucault, the harbormaster, and Gilles, who had come out from Paris on a later train, sat around a table outside the café, savoring their wine and after-dinner cigars. Achille briefed the local authorities on the facts of the criminal investigation that they needed to know while avoiding any reference to international intrigue and espionage, which was information kept at the highest level of secrecy.

There was no lack of urgency as they discussed the case, but that was no reason to rush and spoil their meal. They could enjoy the food and drink in good company, the bracing sea air and the calling seabirds circling above in a clear, maritime sky, and still do their jobs. In that regard, they sometimes mocked their British and North American counterparts who always had to appear busy even when they were not, and seemed to view workplace conviviality as a moral failing.

"These cigars are excellent, M. Lefebvre," the harbormaster remarked. "And I hear you gave one to Brisbois?"

"Yes, I did, M. Picard," Achille replied. "It seems little enough, don't you think? The poor fellow has been very helpful."

"M. Lefebvre ordered up a bottle of wine for the old vagabond," M. Foucault interjected. "I believe he's made a friend for life."

They all laughed, but Achille said:

"I hope so, M. Foucault. In my job, I've enough enemies. I need all the friends I can get. By the way, I want to add how grateful I am to you and M. Picard. Connecting Brisbois's story to the barge captain's report and replying immediately to our bulletin was first-rate police work, and M. Picard's plans for retrieving the vehicle are a model of efficiency."

Foucault smiled and raised his glass in salute to the chief. "I had cordial relations with your predecessor, M. Féraud, and look forward to the same with you, M. Lefebvre." Then to his friend, the harbormaster: "We don't mind working with Paris, do we, Picard?"

"Not at all, my friend, as long as they send out gentlemen like Messrs. Féraud and Lefebvre," the harbormaster replied. Then to Achille: "The special barge is ready, Monsieur. It's fitted with a powerful steam crane, Rouquayrol-Denayrouze diving apparatus, and an electric searchlight. If the coach is in the canal, we'll haul it up for you, day or night."

"Thank you, M. Picard. We'll meet you on land. Once you get the carriage up, M. Foucault will provide the men and equipment to winch it back onto the embankment." He smiled at Gilles. "You may have to take your photographs in the dark, my friend. Any problem with that?"

"No, Monsieur; I've brought the right plates and lenses to work with the electric light."

"What about checking the ships' manifests and the inns, Chief?" Legros asked.

"Thank you for reminding me," Achille replied. Then, to Foucault and Picard: "We believe the suspects arrived by coach in the vicinity of Harfleur on the twenty-sixth, and remained there until the twenty-eighth, when Brisbois saw them ditch the coach in the canal. Some or all of them may have boarded a ship and already be out to sea. We need to check all the inns and the manifests of the outbound vessels. We have good descriptions and photographs of the suspects except for the one that goes by the name of Major Sims. Of course, we must consider the possibility that they are disguised and traveling on false passports."

"Of course, M. Lefebvre," the commissary replied. "I've already assigned men to investigate. We'll turn up something, I'm sure."

"Thank you, M. Foucault. Inspector Legros will remain here to coordinate the investigation with you and your men. I must return to Paris on the morning train to interrogate a suspect who might shed more light on this matter."

Foucault smiled and refilled his glass. "Very well, M. Lefebvre." He glanced up at the blue sky and inhaled the fresh salt air. "It's such a lovely day, gentlemen. How about another round of drinks before we go?"

"I concur with you wholeheartedly," Achille replied. He called to the waiter and ordered more wine.

⚬⚬⚬

At dusk, a barge-mounted carbon-arc search lamp swept a beam of intense white light around the canal embankment. An hour earlier, a diver had entered the turbid channel and located the coach resting upright on the muddy bottom. He fastened the block and tackle and returned to the surface. Once he was safely aboard the barge, the steam-powered crane lifted the landau above the waterline and Foucault's men winched it onto the embankment and blocked the wheels.

Achille and Legros recognized the coach from Aubert's description, and they noticed that the Russian eagles on the doors had been painted over. The police peered through the windows. A brigadier turned to the detectives with a grim expression on his face:

"There are two bodies inside, Messieurs."

An officer fetched a tarpaulin from a wagon; he spread it out on the grass near the carriage. Gilles set up his camera nearby. The police broke through a window and wrenched the door open; a stream of muddy water spilled over the doorframe. As soon as most of the water had drained out, two officers entered the carriage, removed the bodies, and laid them out on the tarpaulin. Then they returned to the coach to search for the cash-filled suitcases but found nothing.

"Do you recognize them, M. Lefebvre?" Foucault asked.

"This one matches our description of Lieutenant Denisov," Achille said after examining the corpse of a young man and comparing it to a description and photograph provided by Orlovsky. He then turned his attention to the older of the pair. Was it the baron? One week in the canal had had an effect; the flesh was bloated with the greenish tinge associated with decomposition. However, the individual's height, build, and dark hair seemed right; the expensive clothing, watch, and jewelry could be traced to determine if they belonged to M. de Livet.

Achille knelt by the body. He stared at the dead face for some time, scrutinizing each feature, the shape of the eyes, nose, mouth, and ears, the hairline and beard, comparing each detail to Mme de Livet's photograph of the baron. Everything matched. But the distinctive expression in the image taken from life, a sardonic smile, had died with the man. Finally, Achille said, "This *appears* to be the Baron de Livet."

"You are not certain?"

"No, M. Foucault. I'll reserve judgment until after they've been autopsied and returned to Paris for identification." Achille turned to the photographer. "Get some good photographs, Gilles."

"No problem, Chief," the photographer replied.

Achille and Foucault were discussing arrangements for the postmortem examinations and transportation of the bodies to the Paris Morgue, when a shout from a copse on the edge of the clearing interrupted the conversation:

"Over here, Messieurs! We've found another body." The cry came from a gendarme who was searching the area with Brisbois.

The detectives went immediately to the spot, where they found the officer shining his lantern on a corpse lying facedown, half-covered in a clump of weeds. Brisbois stood off to one side. He shook visibly, his eyes wide with terror.

"I . . . I didn't see this . . . this dead body before," the vagabond stammered. "I swear I didn't, Messieurs."

"Calm down, Brisbois," Achille replied. "No one has said that you did." He knelt by the corpse and turned it over carefully. The corpse on land was in a more advanced state of decomposition than those taken from the canal; its distended blue-green flesh was crawling with vermin, and the stench was overwhelming. Achille covered his mouth and nose and proceeded with a cursory examination.

The man appeared to be about forty, with sandy, close-cropped hair and a neatly trimmed moustache. He wore a three-piece brown suit; the fine fabric and expert tailoring betokened Savile Row. Achille made a mental note to check all the labels.

"What about this one, M. Lefebvre? Do you know who he was?" Foucault asked.

Achille looked up and shook his head. "No, Monsieur. He might be the one called Major Sims. At any rate, I have witnesses in Paris who could identify him, and I'm hoping for some additional information from Scotland Yard."

Foucault said, "I see. Can you tell how he died?"

"From the wounds on his neck and the bloodstains it's obvious his throat was slit. The killer might have cut both the jugular vein and the carotid artery, which suggests that he or she was an expert with a knife or razor as well as a practiced assassin. There's no sign of a struggle; I believe the attack was swift and took the victim by surprise. Moreover, I suspect he was killed *after* the coach and its two passengers were dumped into the canal." Achille got up and dusted off his trousers before adding, "Of course, we'll know more after the autopsies."

"You said 'she,' M. Lefebvre. Do you suspect Mme Behrs?"

"I certainly wouldn't rule her out," Achille replied.

"Do you think she could have acted alone?" Foucault asked.

"I doubt it, Monsieur, but then I never underestimate a woman's strength, cunning, and resolve. When it comes to murder, some women can be as ruthless and efficient as any man."

"Pardon me, Chief," Legros interjected. "Aubert saw three individuals leave the apartment on the Rue de Turenne: the baron, the bandaged man, and Mme Behrs. Denisov, the coachman, makes four altogether: three men and a woman. Now, we have three dead bodies, all of them male. We've tentatively identified Denisov and the baron. This one might be Sims, who we believe was the bandaged man. Brisbois says he saw three men push the coach into the canal. We cannot account for Mme Behrs. Was she disguised as a man? Was there a fourth man? Did she and the fourth man kill Sims after they got rid of the other two?"

Achille scratched his beard. "Good questions, Inspector. It appears two individuals killed three confederates and took off with suitcases filled with cash. I suspect Mme Behrs is one of the two remaining fugitives, and they may already be on a ship bound for who knows where. I'm afraid we have a few odd pieces left to our puzzle, and we'll have to adjust to changing circumstances to complete the picture."

Foucault turned to Achille. "This is certainly an interesting case, M. Lefebvre, and you may continue to count on me and my department. We're at your service."

"Thank you, Monsieur. I regret I must return to Paris in the morning, but I'm confident you and Inspector Legros will handle this end of the investigation admirably in my absence. And remember, we do have one great advantage over the remaining fugitives."

"What is that, Monsieur?"

Achille smiled. "The transoceanic cables can outrun the swiftest steamer."

15

A t eight A.M., Achille's train arrived at the Gare Saint-Lazare. He waited by the baggage car while porters unloaded three wooden boxes and placed them on a cart. They proceeded up the busy platform and out the main entrance to a black van waiting to transport the chief and the cadavers to the Morgue on the Île de la Cité.

Upon arrival at their destination, attendants placed the makeshift coffins on gurneys that they wheeled through a guarded back doorway and then up a dimly lit corridor to the dissection room. Achille followed. They entered the chamber and waited for the chief pathologist and his assistants.

Achille bantered with the attendants, one of whom he had known for several years. Jokes took the edge off this grim occupation carried out amid disagreeable surroundings: brickwork and plaster painted dingy institutional gray; the sharp odor of disinfectant and formaldehyde commingled with the stench of putrefaction; gruesome instruments displayed in glass cases; internal organs and body parts pickled in jars set on shelves.

The chief pathologist and his assistants arrived presently. The doctor greeted Achille with a familiar smile and a friendly handshake.

"Good morning, M. Lefebvre. I see you've made quite a bit of work for us."

"I'm afraid so, Dr. Cortot. They're all related to the de Livet case, and one of them might be the baron."

"You said *might* be? You are not sure?"

"I'm taking nothing for granted, Doctor. I want to bring in his dentist to make certain."

The pathologist nodded his approval. "That's good thinking, Chief Inspector. You can't disguise the teeth. By the way," he added, "those two fellows you put on display have been drawing quite a crowd, especially since *Le Petit Journal* featured your confrontation with the assassins."

Achille had read the article accompanied by a typically lurid illustration of the shootout, and his plan to put the bodies on public display had worked to perfection. A few of the assassins' friends had come out of the wood-work to nibble at the cheese. Achille's detectives stationed at the Morgue discovered the names and turned them over to Rousseau.

"I don't care much for sensationalism," Achille replied. "But I am grateful for anything that aids our investigations."

The doctor smiled shrewdly. "Of course, M. Lefebvre. Now I suppose we must get down to business and cut up the poor buggers."

The postmortem examination team worked efficiently. Achille lit a cigar and observed the grisly procedure with cool detachment, having witnessed many dissections. He did not mind seeing male cadavers eviscerated, but watching a female go through the same process was more difficult. On the other hand, looking on while the pathologists dissected a child was hard in the extreme, even for a seasoned veteran. He never forgot the innocent young faces, especially that of a little girl who reminded him of his daughter, Jeanne.

Once the postmortem team had completed their task, Achille consulted with the chief pathologist.

"What can you tell me about them, Doctor?"

"Let's begin with the throat-slitting case, M. Lefebvre." The pathologist led Achille to the table supporting the remains of the man tentatively identified as Major Sims. "Based on the state of decomposition, I estimate this individual has been dead for approximately one week." He pointed to the wounds. "There was a deep thrust and cut in this area that severed both the jugular vein and carotid artery. He would have lost consciousness almost immediately due to anoxia, the loss of blood flow and oxygen to the brain. Death would have ensued within minutes."

"I suppose it would take considerable skill and strength to inflict a wound like that?"

"Absolutely, Monsieur. A surgeon or butcher could have done it, or someone trained in hand-to-hand combat, a soldier or professional killer, perhaps. Do you have the weapon?"

"No, Doctor. We have men searching the area, but they've turned up nothing so far."

The pathologist nodded. "Years ago a friend of mine, a retired colonel now deceased, went to Japan to help train their new army. In the course of his duties, he witnessed a ritual suicide. The old samurai warriors initiated their self-immolation by slicing open their abdomen with a razor-sharp short sword called a *wakizashi*. That's excruciatingly painful, as you can imagine, and if left in that condition they could linger in agony for days. Therefore, in most cases they had an expert swordsman available to behead the suicide as a *coup de grâce*.

"In the act of *seppuku*, or *hara-kiri*, that my friend witnessed, the fellow performed his own *coup de grâce* with a swift, deep cut and thrust to the throat identical to what we see in this case."

"Are you suggesting I search for a Japanese warrior?"

The pathologist laughed. "Not necessarily, Monsieur. I was just telling the story to indicate the sort of skill and determination required to have done the deed. And the *wakizashi* would have been the ideal murder weapon."

"I imagine we can rule out suicide?"

"I believe so. In that case, you would have likely found the weapon still in his hand and the blade in his throat, although I suppose someone could have removed it. Besides, in my experience, those who attempt suicide in this manner bungle badly and make a mess of it. They lack the fortitude and skill to cut deeply and with precision."

"Do you think a woman, acting alone, could have killed in this manner? We found no defensive wounds on the victim's hands or arms, nor any cuts or tears on his clothing."

"I've never known a woman to kill like that, have you? I suppose a large, strong, cold-blooded woman with the speed and agility of a panther and the prowess of a samurai master swordsman *might* have done it alone."

Achille thought of Delphine in comparison to Mme Behrs. Delphine had the skill and the training, but he wondered if she had the requisite ruthlessness to kill so efficiently with a blade. He did not know Mme Behrs well enough to come to a definitive conclusion.

"I'm of the same opinion, Doctor," he replied. "Based on the information I've gathered thus far, I suspect he was killed by a man and a woman working together, one to grab the victim from behind while the other made the fatal thrust and cut."

The doctor nodded his agreement. "That seems plausible, M. Lefebvre. Now shall we have a look at the others?"

They turned their attention to the remaining corpses. Achille began the discussion with the following observation:

"Before we begin, you should know that neither of these individuals was bound, and we found no signs of a struggle in the coach. Moreover, on cursory examination we could detect no indicia of stab wounds, gunshot wounds, punctures, blunt force trauma, or other suspicious marks on the bodies."

"Our examination found no wounds, either. And what do you deduce from these facts, M. Lefebvre?"

"I believe these two were either dead or unconscious as a result of drugs or poison administered some time before they entered the water."

The doctor turned to Achille, lifted his glasses, and smiled. "You've simplified my job, Monsieur. It's difficult to determine the exact time or cause of death. The decomposition is not as advanced in comparison to the other individual. However, bodies submerged in a closed coach would not decompose as rapidly as one on land. Therefore, I estimate they've been dead for about the same period of time, approximately one week. And I concur with your deduction from the available evidence. We found some water in the lungs, and there are signs of asphyxia in both corpses. However, water can enter the lungs of a submerged body postmortem, and there are many causes of asphyxia. In addition, we noticed an inflammation of the lungs; certain poisons can have that effect.

"We've prepared specimens to send to Masson for analysis. If there's a detectable trace of drugs or poison in these fellows, Masson will surely find it. But regardless of his findings, given the totality of circumstances, I conclude that these three individuals were all victims of homicide."

"Thank you, Doctor. As always, I appreciate your professional courtesy and keen insight into each case. And I found your Japanese tale quite interesting. I'm hardly an expert, but I have devoted some time to the study of Oriental fighting techniques, strategy, and the warrior's code."

The doctor rubbed his chin and grinned. "I know that, M. Lefebvre. That's why I told you the story."

❦

"Madame, your breakfast is ready. Madame, please open the door. You haven't eaten in two days." Mme Renard carried a silver tray laden with a coffeepot, cup, and saucer and a basket filled with warm rolls, a slice of cheese, and a ripe pear from the garden. She knocked several times on Mme de Livet's boudoir door, a little louder and harder each time.

Two days earlier, after Achille had left the mansion, Madame closed the keyboard cover on the Érard, abandoned the music room, retired to her chambers, and locked the door. Mme Renard and Honoré had neither seen nor heard from her since.

The cook set the tray on the landing. She walked to the stairway, leaned over the banister, and called down to Honoré. "Will you please fetch the housekeeper's passkey? I'm worried about Madame."

The old gardener muttered, "All right, all right; I'm coming." A few minutes later, he came puffing up the stairs, key ring jingling in his hand. He handed the keys to the cook. "Do you think we should enter without permission?"

Mme Renard frowned. "This is an emergency. She's never locked herself up like this, and who knows what she might do under the circumstances. It's our duty to enter."

The old gardener shrugged and stood aside as Mme Renard unlocked the door and opened it slowly. She peered into the room. The curtains were drawn and the lights out. The electricity had stopped the previous day; there was no one left in the household to tend the generator.

Upon entering the room, Mme Renard could distinguish her mistress's fully clothed figure, sprawled facedown on the bedding. The cook ran to the bedside as fast as her legs could carry her. She reached down and felt the still-warm forehead with the back of her hand; her head lowered to Madame's lips, she detected the faint flow of air and the sound of slow but regular breathing.

"Is she alive, Mme Renard?"

"Yes, thank God." Mme Renard noticed a bottle of sleeping draught and an empty glass on the bedside table.

"Shall we call Dr. Levasseur?"

The cook frowned and shook her head. "No, we can't call him. Madame hasn't paid his bill, and after what happened to Manuela, I don't trust him. We'll telephone M. Lefebvre; he'll know what to do."

"The telephone? Does that contraption still work?"

"Let's pray it does, for Madame's sake."

The old man sighed. "The Hanged Man followed by Death. It was in the cards, wasn't it, Mme Renard?"

"Forget the cards, you old fool. We still might have time to save her. If the telephone doesn't work, I've just enough pin money left for a cab."

Mme Renard dashed out of the room. Honoré hobbled after her, shaking his head in dismay.

⚬⚭⚬

Inquiries led investigators to an auberge near the canal, not more than a kilometer from the crime scene. Legros and Foucault came out from Le Havre in a fiacre. On the way, Foucault remarked:

"I know the proprietor, M. Quevillon, quite well. I expect he'll be forthcoming. He runs a respectable establishment and wants no trouble with the police."

"I hope you're right, M. Foucault. This afternoon, M. Lefebvre and the *juge d'instruction* will interrogate the prime suspect in a murder related to the de Livet case. Any additional information I can wire to the chief prior to the interrogation should be helpful."

"Don't worry, Inspector. According to my detectives, Quevillon has been cooperating. And I heard you've made headway with the ships' manifests."

"Yes, Monsieur. We've narrowed the list down to a steamer that left port the morning of the twenty-eighth. It's headed for Las Palmas to take on coal. From there, it will cross the Atlantic to Montevideo and Buenos Aires."

"That's good news, Inspector. If the boat hasn't yet arrived in Las Palmas, you can cable the Spanish authorities to hold the fugitives long enough for you to get down there with a warrant. That is, if you can provide the Spaniards with sufficient information about the two suspects."

"The two are probably traveling on forged passports under assumed names. And we've had a bit of luck. It's a slow boat with stops in Lisbon and Tangier before it reaches Las Palmas. And even if we miss them in Las Palmas, we still have a good chance of getting them in South America."

The fiacre turned from the main road onto a tree-lined, gravel driveway that led to the inn. Legros looked out the window and saw a quaint, half-timbered Norman country inn with a slate roof and gabled windows, surrounded by well-tended flower beds and neatly trimmed hedges.

The driver parked the carriage near the entrance. The officers stepped down from the fiacre and entered the front door, with Foucault in the lead. As soon as they arrived in the foyer, M. Quevillon came out from behind the front desk to greet them. The proprietor was a short, paunchy, middle-aged man whose natural fussiness was exacerbated by the police presence.

Quevillon bowed curtly and wrung his moist hands. "Good day, gentlemen. Please come into my office." The proprietor gestured to a room hidden behind the desk. He obviously wanted to get the detectives out of sight as soon as possible, the case having already drawn unwanted attention to his establishment. The *auberge* had entertained fugitives, albeit unwittingly, and M. Quevillon worried that the incident would give his inn a bad name.

The detectives followed the proprietor into a sparsely furnished anteroom, secreted from the foyer by a *portière*. M. Quevillon led them to chairs set around a chintz-covered round table. Anxious as he was, the proprietor did not forget his manners.

"I hope you gentlemen are comfortable? Would you care for coffee or tea? Or, if you prefer, may I offer you something stronger?"

"No, thank you, M. Quevillon," Foucault answered. "We don't want to keep you any longer than is necessary."

Quevillon bowed. "Oh, thank you, M. Foucault. Thank you very much. You gentlemen have no idea how distressing this matter has been for me. My respectable inn has unknowingly extended its hospitality to a gang of criminals, three of whom have died under the most horrible circumstances. Can you imagine what my other guests will think, not to mention our prospective clientele?"

Foucault tried to calm the agitated innkeeper with reassuring words and a mollifying smile. "It's indeed a regrettable situation, M. Quevillon, but one in which you are completely blameless. You have a sterling reputation hereabouts, and I believe your cooperation in the investigation will enhance your good name. My colleague from Paris will bear that out. By the way, permit me to introduce Inspector Legros. He is assisting Chief Lefebvre in this case."

Quevillon bowed. "I'm honored, M. Legros. Do you *really* think my involvement in your investigation could add to the inn's cachet?" he added hopefully.

Legros followed Foucault's lead in emphasizing the positive public relations angle. "Yes, I do, Monsieur. I know of several instances where hotel managers and innkeepers received praise in the newspapers and the community for their cooperation with the authorities. Public commendation can attract law-abiding citizens to establishments such as yours, while at the same time deterring criminals from using your inn for their nefarious purposes."

Quevillon sighed with relief and mopped his brow with a handkerchief. "Thank you, gentlemen. Your kind words have eased my mind." He sat opposite the detectives. "Please tell me how I may be of assistance?"

Legros reached into his coat pocket and took out a packet containing Gilles's photographs of the coach and the deceased suspects. "I'm afraid these are unpleasant," he said as he handed the photographs to Quevillon. "The features have been somewhat altered by decomposition."

Legros also produced a photograph of Mme Behrs. Quevillon's examination of the pictures produced some surprises. He examined the postmortem photograph of the body tentatively identified as Baron de Livet for almost one minute before saying:

"This is either M. Czerny or his twin brother. Frankly, I can't tell one from the other."

The statement took Legros by surprise, but he tried not to show it. He calmly took out a studio portrait of the baron provided by Mme de Livet. "Please take a look at this picture, Monsieur. Can you identify the gentleman?"

Quevillon's eyes darted from the live portrait to the corpse on the tarpaulin and back. After another minute he said, "I'm sorry, Monsieur.

I can't distinguish between the two. They could both be photographs of M. Czerny—or his brother."

"When did the man you call Czerny first arrive at your inn?"

"The morning of the twenty-sixth, as I recall. Shall I fetch the register?"

"Please do."

As soon as the innkeeper left the room, Foucault turned to Legros and said, "What do you make of the name and the brother?"

"Schwarz, Le Noir, and Czerny—'Black' in three languages. The baron isn't very original in his choice of pseudonyms. As for this business about a twin brother, I don't know."

Quevillon returned with the register. He placed the leather-bound book on the table and opened to the page with the entry. "Here it is, gentlemen." He pointed to the signature, date, and time. "M. Czerny from Paris, arrived ten in the morning on the twenty-sixth."

Legros studied the signature. He turned to Foucault. "This will help in sorting things out. We have several samples of the baron's handwriting, including his signature." Then to Quevillon:

"How did Czerny arrive?"

"By fiacre, from the Le Havre terminus."

"Was he alone?"

"Yes, Inspector."

"Did you get a good look at his passport?"

"Yes, Monsieur; it seemed in order."

Legros turned to Foucault. "How's the trade in forged passports hereabouts?"

"Thriving, Inspector, as I assume it is in Paris?"

Legros nodded and returned to M. Quevillon. "Who issued the passport?"

"It was a Russian passport, Monsieur."

"He said he was a Russian citizen?'

"Yes, Monsieur."

"How much baggage was Czerny carrying?"

"Just one suitcase and a traveling bag."

"How many rooms did he take?"

"Two, M. Legros. He expected a party of four to arrive by coach from Paris later that afternoon and he paid for the other room in advance. You can see the entries on the following page."

Legros turned the page and made note of the following names: Messrs. Czerny, Denis, Simpson, and Bouleau. "You've already identified the two Czerny 'brothers.' Please look at the photographs. Can you identify Denis, Simpson, and Bouleau?"

M. Quevillon quickly identified Denis as Lieutenant Denisov. It took longer to identify Simpson as Sims, due to the more advanced state of decomposition. He also took a long look at Mme Behrs's photograph. Finally, he said, "If you cut this woman's hair and put her in male clothing, I'd say she could be M. Bouleau."

"Are you certain, Monsieur?"

"Yes, quite certain," Quevillon replied with conviction.

"Very well, Monsieur. We'll require these pages as evidence."

"I understand, Inspector."

"Thank you. Did Czerny pay in banknotes or gold?"

"Both, Monsieur."

"Do you still have the banknotes?"

"No, Monsieur. I deposited them."

"I see. Did you take a look at all the passports?"

"Of course, Monsieur. They were all carrying Russian passports, but the names are not what we think of as Russian. However, I've had other Russian guests with names that sounded German, French, or English. Going back to the days of Peter the Great, the Russians have employed Western Europeans to help modernize their country. And from my experience, all the upper-class Russians speak excellent French. Indeed, French is their second language."

"Did Czerny or the others say anything about their plans or what they were doing in the vicinity?"

"I only spoke to M. Czerny—that is, the *first* M. Czerny. He said he and his brother were business partners and the other gentlemen were their associates. They were concluding some transaction in Le Havre, after which they would all sail abroad."

"Did he say where they were going or reference the name of a particular ship?"

"No, Monsieur, he did not."

"I see." Legros pointed to the photograph of the coach. "Did you notice anything unusual about the landau?"

Quevillon thought for a moment before replying, "I saw fresh paint on the doors, as if someone had just covered over a family crest or some such thing."

"Did you think that odd?"

The innkeeper frowned and he started rubbing his hands together. "Perhaps, but I thought nothing of it at the time. Do you . . . do you think I ought to have reported it?"

Legros smiled. "No, Monsieur. It was a minor detail. Many people wouldn't have even noticed it."

Quevillon relaxed. "Thank you, Inspector. Is there anything else?"

"Yes, Monsieur. I need more information about their departure. There was an irregularity. You've already reported it to the police, but I'd like to go over it with you. I believe you know what I'm referring to?"

The innkeeper looked down at his hands. "Yes, Inspector Legros, I do."

"Please tell me what happened."

Quevillon turned the register page to the time of departure. "Around four in the morning of the twenty-eighth, I was awakened by a knock on my door. It was M. Czerny—the first M. Czerny, I *think*. He was very polite and apologetic. He said something urgent had come up in Le Havre and the party had to leave immediately to conclude a business deal, sign a contract and so forth, before they boarded their ship. He insisted on paying for both rooms for the remainder of the day to compensate for the inconvenience."

"I understand, Monsieur. Please continue."

"M. Czerny said that his brother and M. Denis had been drinking heavily and were in no condition to sign for their passports."

"And how did you deal with the situation?"

"I . . . I allowed M. Czerny to sign for them."

"Pardon me one moment." Legros compared the two "Czerny" signatures in the register. They seemed identical. He glanced at Foucault, who nodded his agreement.

Legros turned back to Quevillon and said, "Let's continue. Did you see Czerny's brother or Denis that morning?"

"No, Monsieur. M. Czerny said they were already in the coach, 'sleeping it off.'"

"I see. What about Bouleau and Simpson?"

"They signed, and I returned their passports. Then M. Simpson went to the stable to hitch up the team and drive the coach to the entrance."

"Did M. Simpson drive the coach upon departure?"

"Yes, he did. M. Denis was driving when they arrived, but he was drunk, so M. Simpson acted as coachman in his place."

"And that's the last time you saw or heard from them?"

"Yes, Monsieur. I heard nothing more about them until I was contacted by the police."

"Thank you, M. Quevillon. You've been very helpful. Now, if you don't mind, I'd like to have a look at the rooms."

"Of course, M. Legros, but you won't find anything. M. Foucault's men have already searched them thoroughly."

"What do you think, M. Foucault?" Legros asked.

"It's up to you, Inspector Legros. I sent two of my best men. According to their report, there was nothing of interest left in the rooms."

Legros concluded he had what he needed from Quevillon, and he was eager to follow up with the information and wire his findings to M. Lefebvre. "I'm satisfied, M. Foucault."

The detectives thanked M. Quevillon and ended the interview. Before they left, Legros said he would commend the innkeeper to his superiors in Paris, to which Quevillon replied:

"Thank you, Inspector Legros. If you, M. Lefebvre, or any of your colleagues are ever in the neighborhood, I would be delighted to have you as my guests."

❧

On the way back to the station Foucault said, "I told you he'd be informative. What did you make of all that?"

Legros smiled with satisfaction. "Our prime suspects are sailing to Las Palmas as Messieurs Czerny and Bouleau, carrying forged Russian passports and almost one million francs in cash."

"Where did they get the passports?"

"From Lieutenant Denisov, no doubt. He was the aide-de-camp to Colonel Mukhin, the military attaché, and could have easily gained access to the passports and the embassy stamp."

"What about the two brothers Czerny?"

"I don't know, but we do have samples of the baron's writing to compare to the signature on the register, and my chief will investigate the identity of the corpse we sent to the Morgue. As for Bouleau, I believe the 'gentleman' is the baron's mistress, Mme Behrs, disguised as a man. They must have induced the Englishman, Sims or Simpson—God knows his real name—to assist in the murder of the other two.

"The treacherous three probably drugged or poisoned Denisov and 'brother Czerny' before loading them into the coach, driving to the canal, unhitching the horses, and pushing the landau down the embankment into the water. Then our prime suspects took the Englishman unawares and slit his throat."

"There's no honor among thieves, M. Legros. An old saying, but true. I've seen it happen that way many times in my career."

Legros nodded his agreement. "The first thing I'm going to do is recheck the ship's manifest. I should find Czerny and Bouleau on the steamer we've already identified. Then I'll cable that information to the Spanish authorities and wire Paris for further instructions."

Foucault grinned and produced a flask from his coat pocket. "I think a celebration is in order."

"Thank you, my friend. I agree, but just a little one for now."

⚬

Orlovsky and Colonel Mukhin viewed the corpses on private display at the Morgue. Achille noted the Russians' reactions, especially those of Colonel Mukhin, who had been close to his aide-de-camp. Rousseau remained in a shadowy corner of the chamber, observing the scene with amused interest.

"Can you identify these three individuals?" Achille asked.

The colonel leaned toward Orlovsky and whispered to him in Russian.

"Yes, M. Lefebvre, we can." Orlovsky pointed toward the cadavers and identified them as follows: "This one is Lieutenant Denisov, the next is Major Sims, and that one is M. de Livet."

"You are correct as to the lieutenant," Achille said. "The man you identified as Sims is in fact a cashiered British officer, cardsharp, and confidence trickster named Rawls." Achille had just received this information from Scotland Yard. "As for the other, we're not yet sure who he is, but he's not the baron." The baron's dentist had confirmed Achille's suspicions.

Orlovsky stared at Achille with the bewildered expression of a stage farce cuckold who has just discovered that his heir is another man's son. The spymaster's face seemed so comically grotesque Achille had to cough and clear his throat to suppress laughter. Rousseau had a similar reaction; he turned his face to the wall and bit his lip.

Colonel Mukhin placed his hand on Orlovsky's shoulder to get his attention. Orlovsky turned around, and the two engaged in a heated conversation in Russian.

Achille let them go on for a minute before saying, "Gentlemen, if you please."

Orlovsky turned back to Achille. "Please forgive us, M. Lefebvre. We were so . . . surprised by this revelation. Do you know where the baron is?"

"We have good reason to believe that he and Mme Behrs are on a steamer bound for the Canary Islands. They are traveling under assumed names with forged Russian passports we suspect Lieutenant Denisov stole from your embassy. Inspector Legros has already cabled the Spanish authorities with a request to hold them until my men can get down there with a warrant."

"Do you think the Spanish will comply with your request?"

"We have good relations, Monsieur. I expect they will."

"Ah, I see. Thank you, Monsieur. Do you . . . do you know what happened to our money?"

"I can't say for sure, but if the fugitives still have the cash in their possession we'll recover it."

Orlovsky smiled. "Thank you very much, M. Lefebvre. Please excuse me one moment." He turned to the colonel and poured out a voluble stream of Russian in an optimistic, almost cheerful tone.

Achille watched Mukhin's hard features soften as a broad grin spread over his heavily bearded face. Orlovsky presently turned his attention back to the chief:

"My dear M. Lefebvre, we are profoundly grateful to you for your exemplary efforts in this matter, and we apologize for any inconvenience you have incurred due to—Lieutenant Denisov's malfeasance. The colonel and I pledge that in the future we will cooperate with you in a spirit of mutual respect and comradeship."

"Thank you, Monsieur. You may be certain I'll hold you to that pledge."

"Oh yes—yes, of course, M. Lefebvre."

Achille reached into his pocket and pulled out his watch. "Our business here is finished, M. Orlovsky. We will keep you informed as to the progress of the case. Unless you have any further questions or concerns, I'll bid you good day."

Orlovsky turned to Mukhin and mumbled a few words. The colonel came to attention, clicked his heels, and bowed. Orlovsky smiled unctuously, said *au revoir*, and left with his compatriot.

After the Russians were gone, Rousseau walked over to Achille. "Well, Professor," he said, "it looks like they're going to put the blame on Denisov."

"So it seems. The low man is always the scapegoat, and it helps when he's conveniently dead."

Rousseau grinned. "Do you have time for a drink? I'm buying."

Achille nodded. "As long as you're paying for it, I'll make time."

They left the Morgue and walked in the shadow of Notre Dame, up the Rue d'Arcole to the quayside, where they turned and continued on to the Rue de Harlay. The bright sky, crisp clean air, and autumn colors reflected on the water reminded Achille of the nearby flower market. "I keep forgetting to buy flowers," he muttered.

"What did you say?"

"I told Adele I'd stop at the market on my way home and buy flowers, but it always slips my mind."

"I suppose you have other things to think about."

"Yes, Rousseau, but flowers are important, too."

Rousseau smiled and shook his head but said nothing. They turned onto the Rue de Harlay, entered the brasserie, and found a secluded corner table. Rousseau ordered beer. When the waiter returned to the bar, Rousseau said:

"So, Scotland Yard came through after all?"

"Yes, they did. As soon as I wired my contact with a detailed description of 'Major Sims,' they replied with the report on Rawls. He was wanted in Britain on charges of fraud and forgery. Rawls was never a major. He served as a subaltern in the Second Anglo-Afghan War, so his 'intelligence,' such as it was, was more than a decade out of date. Shortly after the war, Rawls was drummed out of his regiment for theft and cheating at cards. He knocked about India for a while as a remittance man. Then, a few years ago, his family cut off his allowance. He returned to England and entered the London underworld. That's where he met the baron. The whole story smacks of Kipling."

"What's 'Kipling'?"

"Rudyard Kipling, a talented young Anglo-Indian writer. He's quite good, actually."

Rousseau shrugged. He muttered, "Oh, Kipling," and took a swig of beer. He wiped his lips on the back of his hand and added, "So you don't think the English will make trouble?"

"No, I don't. Rawls was an embarrassment to them. They're glad he's dead. He had no military secrets, and they are willing to disregard the Russians' role in the affair. However, I'm certain this incident has alerted the British to our secret ally's activities on French soil. But that's not our problem, is it?"

"No, it's not. I assume you've notified the Deuxième Bureau?"

"Yes, of course."

Rousseau swirled the beer in his glass before taking another drink. Then he asked, "The two stiffs you fished out of the canal; how were they killed?"

"Based on the autopsy results, Masson thinks they were poisoned with prussic acid. They were dead at least a couple of hours before they went into the water."

"Looks like you'll be able to close this case soon. Congratulations."

"Thank you. *Everyone* seems satisfied."

Rousseau looked up from his drink. "You aren't satisfied?"

Achille frowned. "No, I'm not. It's a disturbing case. The actions of a few greedy bastards might have provoked a war. What's more, none of the victims is blameless; not even poor Manuela Otero. After all, she learned the baron's scheme and used the knowledge in an attempt to extort money out of the baroness and Bonnet. She ought to have informed the police."

"It's a messed-up world. Always was; always will be. You know that well enough."

"I may *know* it, but I don't want to believe it."

Rousseau shook his head. "Is that a riddle? Remember, I'm a simple detective who learned his trade on the streets."

Achille swallowed some beer before attempting an explanation. "Our world is flawed—or 'messed up,' as you said—but we have a duty to improve it. Of course, we can't right all the wrongs in one generation, or even a hundred. But at least we ought to try. At any rate, I can't shrug things off, say the world's 'messed up,' and leave it at that."

Rousseau smirked. "You're ambitious, Achille. You've become the chief of detectives in record time, and there's talk you'll be the prefect someday, or even a cabinet minister. You'll have all the temptations of high office—honors, titles, *bribes*. As for your 'improvements,' see what people think of them when you try to change the world at their expense. You can make your own cross and climb your Calvary; in the end you'll die and the world will go on as messed up as it was before."

Achille looked down and stared silently at the diminishing head on his beer.

Rousseau gave his colleague a good-natured punch in the shoulder. "Drink up, Professor. Life is a bitch, but this beer's good, and I'm willing to buy another round."

Achille checked his watch. "Thanks, Rousseau. Just one more, if you please. I'll buy next time. And don't let me be late for Bonnet's interrogation."

"Don't worry, my friend. I'll watch the clock and nudge you if you forget." Rousseau raised his hand and signaled to the bar. After the waiter served them, Rousseau added, "And don't forget to stop at the flower market on your way home."

꩜

Achille and M. Leblanc reviewed the dossier in the magistrate's office. A cloth-draped table had been set in the center of the room along with extra chairs for the prisoner and a stenographer. The room was quiet except for the incessant ticking of the wall clock.

The stenographer knocked and entered. He bowed politely, greeted the *juge* and the chief inspector, sat, and began arranging his notepad, pens, and ink on a small escritoire. Moments later, the heavy tread of two guards and the prisoner echoed in the hallway. The small detail entered and stood at attention before the *juge*.

"The prisoner may be seated," M. Leblanc said.

The guards unbound Bonnet's hands, grabbed his shoulders, and pushed him down onto the plain wooden chair.

Bonnet had no advocate, not that a lawyer would have done him much good. He already knew his fate—a quick death in the Place de la Roquette or a slow one in *le bagne*.

Achille noticed the prisoner's unshaven face, unkempt hair, and blood-shot eyes. The cocky attitude was gone. A few days in a detention cell had had its effect. But then there was Bonnet's reputation as a tough guy, a street fighter. Such men typically showed defiance under interrogation; they did not crack easily. Something had profoundly affected Bonnet and changed him. Achille guessed that a dim spark of conscience, the helplessness of the situation, and Bonnet's feelings for Mme de Livet had caused this transformation; he would use all that to his advantage.

Bonnet's enigmatically passive expression reminded Achille of Moreau in the prison registry on the morning of his execution. The look seemed to pose a question: *Why am I here?* Was it a silent plea for understanding and mercy? The question seemed too metaphysical rather than specifically grounded in an empirical chain of cause and effect. M. Lefebvre was not a philosopher or a priest. He would provide an answer based on the facts in evidence as applied to the law. In that regard, he was like Rousseau, a detective doing his job.

Achille approached the covered table. He stared hard at the prisoner before saying, "The last time we met, under much different circumstances, you lied. Today, I expect you will tell us the truth." He lifted the cloth, revealing three exhibits: five thousand francs in banknotes, Mme de Livet's diamonds, and two brown medicine bottles. "Look at these items carefully; they are evidence of your crimes, including murder and fraud. In addition, we have witnesses who will testify against you." Achille pointed to each item and described them in the following order. "This is the five thousand francs we found hidden under the floorboards of your room. M. de Livet paid you this money to collaborate in his swindle and lie to the police; these bottles contained the poison you used to murder Manuela Otero after she threatened to inform on you and the baron; the diamonds were given to you by Mme de Livet to help you escape from justice."

Bonnet stared impassively at the evidence.

"Before you speak," Achille pursued, "there is something you must know about Mme de Livet. She's been committed to the Salpêtrière."

The news had its intended effect. Shocked by the revelation, Bonnet rose to his feet and cried, "You've put her in the madhouse? Why?"

The guards restrained him. M. Leblanc gave a stern warning:

"I caution you, Bonnet. Control yourself, or I'll have you bound to the chair."

Bonnet said, "Yes, Monsieur *le juge*." He sat obediently. The guards remained by his side with their hands on his shoulders.

Achille continued. "I'll answer your question. I didn't put her in the Salpêtrière. *You* and the baron are responsible. You used and abused her and entangled her in your crimes. She cared for you, Bonnet. She gave you her diamonds, her last valuable possessions. The baron took everything else. Admit it; you and the baron broke her in mind and spirit; you are the ones who drove her to madness and attempted suicide."

"No, M. Lefebvre. I loved her. I still do." Bonnet trembled; his face flushed, and tears filled his eyes.

The chief inspector paused a moment before saying, "Prove that you care for her. It's your last chance; your only hope of redemption. You can help Mme de Livet and yourself as well."

"What can I do, Monsieur?"

"Confess. Tell us how and why you poisoned Manuela Otero and everything you know about the baron's schemes. If you do, the *juge* will drop all charges against Mme de Livet. With that burden lifted from her mind, the doctors believe she can recover. Otherwise, she could spend the rest of her life in the asylum.

"As for you, M. Leblanc can recommend transportation instead of the guillotine. It's a hard life in Guiana, but you're strong. You'll survive. With time, if you work well and obey the rules, you could become a trustee. It's a chance to atone for your crimes and pay your debt to society. At any rate, it's better than ending your life on the scaffold before a howling mob."

Achille had correctly assessed the prisoner's state of mind. Bonnet looked down and nodded his head resignedly. "All right, M. Lefebvre. I'll confess."

M. Lefebvre smiled; his tone softened. "You made the right decision, Bonnet. Would you like a cigarette?"

Bonnet looked up at his interrogator. "Yes, thank you, Monsieur."

Achille walked around the table and gave Bonnet a cigarette and a light. The prisoner took a deep drag.

Achille remained next to the prisoner. "Are you ready?" he asked.

Bonnet took the cigarette from his mouth. "Yes, Monsieur. Where shall I begin?"

Achille glanced at the stenographer. "Make sure you get this all down." Then to Bonnet: "Begin with your introduction to the baron. Where did you meet? When did he hire you, and why?"

"We met at a bistro in Montmartre. That was shortly after Monsieur arrived in Paris."

"Is it the bistro where Pasquet tends bar?"

"You know the place, Monsieur? Boxers and gentlemen who follow the sport hang out there. But then, you're a boxer—you *would* know the place."

"Smugglers hang out there, too."

Bonnet smiled bitterly and nodded. "Yes, Monsieur."

"Was M. de Livet looking for a bodyguard?"

"That's right. He asked around for someone who was tough and reliable. Someone he could count on in a tight spot. He made me a fair offer. He was a good boss—treated me more like a pal than a servant."

"Did he have a particular need for your services?"

"Yes, Monsieur. Someone was after him for a swindle he'd pulled off in Cape Town."

"Whom did he defraud?"

"M. Rhodes."

Achille glanced back at the *juge*. M. Leblanc raised an eyebrow in response to the name. Achille continued:

"Do you mean Cecil Rhodes?"

"Yes, Monsieur."

"How much did the baron take him for?"

"A hundred thousand pounds, more or less."

"Did the baron deposit all that money in French banks?"

"Not all of it, Monsieur. He shipped most of it to a lawyer in Buenos Aires."

"Do you know the lawyer's name?"

"Maître Antonio Ricci."

"You said someone was 'after' the baron? I assume it was someone working for M. Rhodes. Do you have a name or a description of the individual?"

"No, Monsieur, but you can be sure he's a professional. The baron has guts, but he feared the assassin. Rhodes can afford the best, and he was out for more than the money. He wanted revenge and to make an example of the baron. Men like Rhodes don't forgive people who cheat them."

"Did the baron take any other precautions against the stalker?"

"Yes, Monsieur. The baron hired a double."

Achille thought of the body in the Morgue, but for the present, he kept that information from Bonnet. "Tell us about the double. Who is he, and how and where did the baron find him?"

"The baron put out discreet feelers and we located a man, a notary's clerk in Rouen named Rivière—Louis Rivière. The resemblance was remarkable; they looked like twin brothers. The baron made an attractive offer—good pay, a new wardrobe, a Paris apartment. Rivière was stuck in a low-paying job; he was bored. He jumped at the chance.

"The baron has a foreign accent and a deeper voice, but Rivière picked up on it fast. He's clever and a good mimic. And he copied the baron's signature like a master forger. To a casual acquaintance, the only noticeable difference is a scar on Rivière's chin, but that was covered when he grew a beard like the baron's."

"Did Rivière go to Aix-les-Bains in the baron's place?"

"Yes, Monsieur. The baron worked out the plan with his mistress, Mme Behrs, the Englishman Sims, and Lieutenant Denisov, a Russian officer who works at the embassy. They duped Denisov's superior, Colonel Mukhin, into buying fake military secrets. The swindle was set up at the spa and concluded in Paris. The baron was supposed to meet the others, including Rivière, at an inn in Harfleur, where they'd divvy the swag. Then they'd use forged passports provided by Denisov to get out of the country."

"And the baron paid you five thousand francs to lie to the police?"

"Yes, Monsieur."

"What role did Mme de Livet play?"

Bonnet finished his cigarette. He looked down at the floor and said, "She was to go to you with the same false story and act like a worried wife."

"Is that all?"

Bonnet sighed. "Yes, Monsieur."

"What was in it for her?"

"She'd be provided for, and rid of the baron."

"And free to go off with you?"

Bonnet looked up with a wistful smile. "That's what I hoped."

Achille stared at the prisoner for a moment before saying, "Sims, Denisov, and Rivière are dead. Are you surprised?"

Bonnet hesitated before saying, "The baron never told me . . . he never said—"

"Let me help you," Achille broke in. "You said the baron was being stalked by an assassin working for M. Rhodes. If Rivière's body was discovered and identified as M. de Livet, the stalker would give up the hunt."

"Yes, Monsieur. But what about the others?"

Achille smiled. "You know your former master. Is he the sort to share his loot and leave loose ends when there's a simpler alternative? He disposed of everyone involved in the swindle, everyone who could talk and betray him, except for Mme Behrs, you, and his wife. Of course, you and Madame would believe the baron was dead, and you'd be left behind to face justice while the baron and his mistress enjoyed their ill-gotten gains in Buenos Aires."

"That's not true, M. Lefebvre."

"What isn't true?"

"The baron told me . . . he said if things got too hot for me in Paris, I was to get out of the country and go to Buenos Aires. The lawyer Ricci would take care of me."

"What about Madame de Livet?"

"He said . . . he said he'd take care of her, too."

"Come on, Bonnet. This is your confession, your chance to come clean. You never really believed him, did you?"

Bonnet looked down, defeated. "No, Monsieur, I didn't. I . . . I wanted to take care of her myself. I thought if I could make it to Buenos Aires, I'd get the money from Ricci—one way or another. Then I'd send for her."

"A nice fantasy, but you never made it out of the alley behind the Avenue Montaigne."

"No, Monsieur."

"As for things getting hot for you in Paris, they certainly heated up after you poisoned Manuela Otero. She discovered the baron's scheme and tried to blackmail you, so you killed her. Didn't you promise Madame that you wouldn't harm the girl?"

Bonnet did not raise his eyes. "Yes, I promised."

"What made you break your promise?"

"You already know. She wanted money to keep her mouth shut."

"But didn't Madame agree to pay her?"

"I didn't want Madame to give in to blackmail, and things changed when Otero got sick and Madame called the doctor. He prescribed aconite for *la grippe*. I knew a large dose would kill her. A friend of mine knows all about poisons. She said aconite injected into the female . . . the private parts couldn't be traced. The doctor would say she died of natural causes."

"Who is your learned 'friend'?"

Bonnet hesitated a moment before answering. "Mme Raffin. She sells herbal remedies out of a shop in the Marais."

Achille glanced at M. Leblanc, who stared back in shocked disbelief, implying he was familiar with the herbalist.

Achille turned his attention to the prisoner. "Apparently, we know more about poisons than your friend."

"Yes, Monsieur," Bonnet replied.

"On the day Manuela was poisoned, you knew the prescribed interval between doses."

"Yes, I did."

"At that time, Inspector Legros was interrogating the household staff. You were no longer needed for questioning and were supposed to be out of the house running errands for Mme de Livet. No one was paying attention to Manuela. Is that correct?"

"Yes, Monsieur."

"You took advantage of the situation to come back to the mansion and sneak into Manuela's room."

"Yes."

"What did you do after you entered the room?"

Bonnet paused and took a deep breath before answering. "Manuela was dead to the world. She slept on her back with her legs spread. I went to the bedside, making as little noise as possible. I took the bottle of tincture of aconite and drew some out into a glass syringe. Then I lifted the bedclothes, pulled up her nightdress, inserted the syringe in her privates, and injected the poison. She woke up. I got on top of her and held her mouth shut. Her arm lashed out and knocked over one of the bottles."

"How long did she struggle?"

"A couple of minutes—no more. Then she lay still, staring at me. I can still see those eyes."

"Then what did you do?"

"I left the room, closed the door behind me, and went downstairs and out the front door. Then I walked around the block and dropped the syringe into a drain. I stayed out just long enough for the baroness to go up to Manuela's room to give her the next dose. When I returned, Madame and the servants were already gathered in the hallway. Inspector Legros came out from the kitchen and saw me standing with the rest of them, trying to get Madame to calm down and find out what happened to Manuela."

"Are you certain no one saw you leave or return after you poisoned Manuela?"

"I'm certain, Monsieur; I'm sure." Bonnet hung his head and covered his face with his hands.

Achille turned to M. Leblanc. "I have no more questions, Monsieur *le juge*."

M. Leblanc said to Bonnet, "Have you anything further to say before you return to the cells?"

Bonnet looked directly at the magistrate. "Yes, Monsieur *le juge*. Please don't hurt Mme de Livet. She's suffered enough."

"I'll drop the charges against Mme de Livet. On the other hand, your crime is diabolical and deserving of the severest punishment. Nevertheless, in light of your cooperation, I'm going to recommend transportation for life instead of the death penalty, but I make no promises. The final determination is up to the prosecutor, the trial court, and the jury."

"I understand, Monsieur *le juge*. Thank you."

The guards exited with the prisoner. Soon after, the stenographer gathered his paraphernalia, bowed to the magistrate, and left the chambers.

M. Leblanc frowned and shook his head. "I know Mme Raffin. She deals in homeopathic remedies and is in good repute—until now. I assume you'll bring her in for questioning?"

"Of course, Monsieur *le juge*."

"What a horrible crime. Did you have any idea beforehand of the method Bonnet used to poison Otero?"

"Yes, I did. I consulted with Masson. Otero had good reason to fear Bonnet. If she had been awake, she probably would have screamed when he entered the room. Legros and I thought it likely he gave her the poison while she was sleeping. According to Masson, in his *Historia Naturalis* Pliny the Elder wrote about the deadly effect of aconite when rubbed on the female genitalia. Pliny even mentioned an individual who used this method to murder his wives while they slept. However, Masson was unaware of any modern case where a woman was poisoned in this manner."

"How awful; and to think Mme Raffin might be involved in the murder. Why, my wife and I have taken her remedies with no ill effects."

"Perhaps she just gave information about aconite and its effects in response to Bonnet's questions. She may not have known he intended to use that knowledge to commit murder. At any rate, we'll know more after we've questioned her."

The magistrate frowned and shook his head. "A very sordid affair, M. Lefebvre. And I'm surprised a brute like Bonnet could show such gallantry toward Mme de Livet."

"I'm not; I rather counted on it. It's all he has left, his illusion of love."

"Is it just an illusion? Do you mean Mme de Livet didn't reciprocate his affection?"

"Certainly not, Monsieur *le juge*. What passed between them was, from her perspective, little more than a diversion. She also directed her affections toward one of my paid informers, a young prostitute. That information was vital to my cracking this case."

M. Leblanc's face twisted in disgust, as if a bad odor had entered his chambers. "At least that disposes of Bonnet. Thank goodness we needn't resort to fingerprint evidence."

"Thank goodness indeed, Monsieur *le juge*. The bottles are a mess; frankly, I can't distinguish one set of prints from another."

"But I thought you said we could use the fingerprints?"

"Only as a last resort in the interrogation, Monsieur; certainly not as evidence for the trial. I was prepared to trick Bonnet into believing the prints were proof positive of his guilt. Thankfully, I didn't need that ruse; he sang like a canary."

The magistrate narrowed his eyes and leaned forward over his desk. "You didn't tell me the prints were utterly worthless, Chief Inspector."

"Pardon me, Monsieur *le juge*; I didn't think you'd want to know."

"You're a lucky man, M. Lefebvre."

"Perhaps I am, Monsieur *le juge*. At any rate, I hope my good fortune continues. We still need to catch the baron and Mme Behrs."

"I've already issued the warrants for their arrest. Who's going after them?"

"I'm sending Legros and Adam. They've already booked passage to Las Palmas. We know the name of the ship the fugitives are on, and the Spanish authorities have agreed to hold them for us."

"Well then, I wish Adam and Legros good hunting and a bon voyage." M. Leblanc looked up at the clock. "Where does the time go? Are you working late, M. Lefebvre?"

"No, Monsieur *le juge*. I'm dining with my family this evening. And I have an errand to run before I go home."

"Oh, and what sort of errand is that, if I may ask?"

"I'm going to stop at the market to buy some flowers."

"Ah yes; I'm certain the women will be pleased."

Achille smiled. "I sincerely hope so, Monsieur *le juge*."

16

Paul Féraud had retired to a country house on the outskirts of Pontoise, about thirty minutes by train from central Paris. The place retained its rural character, for the most part, despite the smoke-belching factories lining the Oise, and the concomitant riverine railway and barge traffic.

One Sunday afternoon following the conclusion of the de Livet case, Achille, Adele, and Jeanne visited the old chief. Little Olivier remained at the Paris apartment with his grandmother and Suzanne.

Adele admired the two-story, slate-roofed house, set back from a narrow road and surrounded by a stone wall. The visitors passed through a creaking iron gate and proceeded up a gravel pathway to the residence, which sat on a plot of land that sustained several old apple and pear trees. Jeanne immediately made the enclosure her playground, especially an apple-tree swing. The child charmed her "Uncle Paul" into swinging her and kept him at it almost to the point of exhaustion before Adele prudently intervened.

In the late afternoon, M. Féraud's housekeeper, Victorine, a middle-aged widow from a nearby hamlet, began preparing supper. Jeanne asked if she could help. Adele said, "If you're a good girl and Victorine doesn't mind."

Victorine smiled at Jeanne. "I don't mind, Madame, as long as the little one behaves."

"Oh yes, I'll be good," Jeanne promised.

Achille and Féraud overheard the kitchen conversation. Féraud poked his head into the doorway and announced, "We have a couple of hours until supper. If you ladies will excuse us, the chief and I are going for a walk."

"Very well, Monsieur," Victorine replied, "but please don't be late."

"Don't worry, Victorine; there's plenty of time." The old chief turned around, grabbed Achille by the arm, and urged him toward the front door. As soon as they were outside, Féraud said, "There's a tavern just up the road, and I'm buying."

They passed through the gate and turned onto the winding lane. Pale autumn light filtered down through treetops, highlighting leaves shaded gold, scarlet, yellow, and green. The air was pleasantly crisp and filled with the sharp, smoky scent of burning foliage. The contiguous metropolis seemed in another world. Away from the tall buildings, bustling crowds, and familiar street noise, they heard birdsong, chirring insects, the monotonous rasping of a saw cutting firewood, the intermittent barking of a dog in a neighboring house, and the distant cry of the whistle on a Paris-bound express.

The old chief paused to light a cigar. He took a few satisfying puffs before saying, "Fill me in on the de Livet case. All I know is what I've read in the newspapers."

Achille shrugged. "Well then, you know about as much as I do. Bonnet is on his way to Saint-Laurent, Mme de Livet is recovering in the

Salpêtrière, Mme Behrs is in custody, the baron is missing at sea, and the Russians got most of their money back."

Féraud cocked an inquisitive eyebrow. "That's for public consumption, Achille. This is strictly between you and me."

Achille smiled; he had assumed Féraud would want the full story. "All right, Chief. The Russians are asking for more than the money. They want Mme Behrs. She's a Russian national, you know."

"Will they get her?"

"That's up to the government. My job is done; M. Leblanc and the prefect are pleased. Behrs or Berezina is charged with several serious crimes, including murder. She duped the Russians and our intelligence service, and she might have killed the baron. For all we know, she could be an assassin hired by Cecil Rhodes."

"An assassin working for Rhodes? There's nothing about that in the newspapers, either."

Achille shook his head and laughed. "I should certainly hope not! I got the information about Rhodes and the assassin from Bonnet, but he never suspected Mme Behrs.

"The baron disappeared in the early-morning hours before the ship docked in Las Palmas. The Spanish authorities arrested Mme Behrs, who was traveling on a forged passport, disguised as a man. When they questioned her about de Livet, she said he had been drinking heavily the previous night. He woke up before dawn with a terrible hangover and went out on deck to get some air. He hasn't been seen or heard from since. She told the same story to Legros and Adam, and she's sticking to it.

"If we hadn't arrested the woman in Las Palmas, she might have gone on to South America with the loot from the baron's swindle. There's a lawyer in Buenos Aires named Ricci who could know more. He may also have a hundred thousand pounds belonging to Rhodes. I've wired an inquiry to the Argentinean authorities, but so far it's a dead end."

"Sounds like a closed case."

"As far as I'm concerned, it is. Frankly, I don't care what happens to Mme Behrs, as long as she's not on the loose in France. As for Rhodes's money, that's his problem."

The old chief shrugged. "From what I've heard, a hundred thousand is pocket change to M. Rhodes. By the way, what happened to Mme Raffin? I heard you let her go for lack of evidence."

"I'm afraid that's right. She claimed she answered a hypothetical question about poisoning a sleeping woman and that Bonnet put it to her as a joke. She said she had no idea Bonnet was actually going to kill someone. And he corroborated her statement."

"Do you believe that story?"

Achille shrugged. "I don't know. At any rate, we couldn't connect her to any other crime, so we hadn't enough to keep her in custody or charge her. However, we'll certainly be keeping an eye on her from now on. And I don't think M. Leblanc and his wife will continue purchasing their herbal remedies from Mme Raffin."

They continued their walk. After a moment, Achille stopped suddenly, as though he had forgotten something. He turned to Féraud and said, "Oh, there's one thing I do need to take care of."

"What's that?"

"There's a young woman staying with us, Mignonette Hubert. She was a witness, one of the de Livet's servants. I need to find her a position. She's a nice girl. You wouldn't happen to know of anyone looking for a maid?"

"As a matter of fact, I do. Victorine is leaving at the end of the month. She's going to live with her sister's family in Rouen. I'll miss her. Anyway, you can send the girl on to me."

"Thanks, Chief. I'm certain you'll like her. But I must warn you. Legros is sweet on her, so you might find him hanging around Pontoise. He may even take her off your hands someday."

"Well, I expect you'll help me out by keeping the young man busy."

They continued toward the town. When they came to the tavern, Achille stopped and looked around. "You know, Pissarro lived and painted hereabouts."

"Pissarro, you say. Is he an Impressionist?"

"Yes, Chief. One of the best."

"Do you think so? I wouldn't know. It's all the same daubery to me. I'm afraid I don't share your interest in modern art. Now, before we go in I have a little confession. I said the drinks were on me. I lied."

"I see. Do you expect me to pay?"

Féraud shook his head. "No, the drinks are on the house. The proprietor knows who we are. You see, there *are* some advantages to being the chief of detectives."

Achille laughed loudly, and the old chief joined him. The lowering sun brushed the treetops. The detectives' shadows lengthened as, arm in arm, they entered the tavern.

ACKNOWLEDGMENTS

I am grateful to Donald P. Webb and Bill Bowler for reading and commenting on my early drafts of this novel. Many thanks to my great agent, Philip Spitzer, and his associate, Lukas Ortiz, for their outstanding representation, and thanks also to their associate, Kim Lombardini, for her kind assistance and sense of humor. Thanks also to Claiborne Hancock and his staff at Pegasus, most particularly my excellent editor Bowen Dunnan.